··

Wet Places at Noon

UNIVERSITY OF IOWA PRESS   Iowa City

Lee K. Abbott

Wet Places at Noon

University of Iowa Press,
Iowa City 52242
Copyright © 1997 by Lee Abbott
All rights reserved
Printed in the
United States of America

Design by Richard Hendel

http://www.uiowa.edu/~uipress

Printed on acid-free paper

Library of Congress
Cataloging-in-Publication Data
Abbott, Lee K.
    Wet places at noon / Lee K. Abbott.
        p.   cm.
    ISBN 0-87745-605-4
    I. Title.
PS3551.B262W48   1997
813'.54—dc21   97-20595

02   01   00   99   98   97   C   5   4   3   2   1

Examine your conscience.
Think. Meditate. Shilly-shally.
—Flannery O'Connor

This book is for Mark;
for Paula and Nancy; and for
Roger, Siri, and Cassie Glenn.

. . . .
Contents

Acknowledgments

The author is happy to acknowledge the timely support of the Ohio Arts Council, through its Major Artist's Fellowship Program, and the Department of English at the Ohio State University.

These stories, some in significantly different form, first appeared in the following publications: "A Man Bearing Snow," *Epoch*; "On Tuesday Nothing, on Wednesday Walls," *New England Review*; "The Way Sin Is Said in Wonderland," *Story*; "The Human Use of Inhuman Beings" as "One More Lie I Learned," *Southwest Review*; "How One Becomes the Other," Fiction Syndicate Project (National Public Radio) and *Gulfcoast*; "As Fate Would Have It," *Boulevard*; "A Creature out of Palestine," *Ploughshares*; "The Talk Talked between Worms," *Georgia Review*.

Wet Places at Noon

The Way Sin Is Said in Wonderland

ONE

The first time they met, Eddie pulled out the pistol. A Soviet Makarov 9-millimeter automatic with rust spots on the barrel and a faded red star on the black plastic handgrip. This was '72, the summer before the bailout from Saigon, the occasion a welcome-home barbeque for Bobby, her husband, and his buddy from MR II up near Con Tien.

"This is I-Beam," Bobby said. "Short for IBM, he's smart."

Turned out he almost had a degree in physics from the University of Houston, but Carol Ann didn't know that yet; she only knew that he was a wiry so-and-so, slope-shouldered and skinny as a file but surprisingly soft-spoken, as if all Uncle Sam had asked him to do during his hitch was to sit atop a jungle roost drinking skim milk and nodding hunky-dory to the dignitaries making merry on the promenade below.

"A pleasure," he said, and then nothing: just the two of

them, the afternoon August sun a huge orange behind his head, while Bobby hurried away to say howdy to the new people coming through the gate into the backyard. "Eddie," he said, "L-for-Lonnie Heber."

She got her name out then, Carol Ann Spears, surprised by the mealy mouthful it was, and what she did, a teacher at Zia Elementary near Pecan Acres south of town, and then she realized that her hand was still locked in his — a cold thing big as a paddle — and it crossed her mind when she again engaged his dark eyes that here was a fellow with secrets you might need a whole lot more than *open sesame* to find out.

Throughout the afternoon, she watched him. He took a chair near Bobby, and didn't say much. Let Bobby do the bullshitting. "Should I tell 'em about the S-2?" Bobby said once, and Carol Ann discovered Eddie Heber staring at her, grinning this time as if the two of them — he and she — had made a connection the grits and white-bread folk between them wouldn't comprehend if you wrote it down and drew pictures of the sort her second graders whooped over.

"Sure, help yourself," Eddie said, and Bobby was off, his an escapade that seemed to take as long to tell about as it did to live through.

She picked up a little — the LT, the boonie rats, the LURPs, Sam the Sham — before she went back to her conversation with Rhonda Whitaker and Ellen Dowling. Rhonda's boy, Jerry, was deficient in history, plus being a cut-up in class. Still, a minute later, she could feel him again, Eddie Heber. A smile with too much tooth in it. A face so alive it required concentration to watch. Spooky. He looked like a fugitive that had raced all night through prickers and brambles to get here.

That's the way it went until dusk. A volleyball game started, girls against guys, and every time she jumped or chased the ball when it rolled over to the Hoovers' fence, he was watching, this funny little fucker from Albuquerque. She felt naked, like a specimen, like the hamsters in the cage in the science corner of her classroom — just a piece of business for his amusement — so after the third time she had to bend over in front of him, her shorts squeezing up her thighs, she thought she'd just march right up to him, get in his face, tell him she didn't appreciate his — what? — his leering, and he could just smack his lips somewhere else, she didn't care what had happened in Vietnam. But when she spun around, he was gone. His chair had a half-dozen empties beside it.

"C'mon," Bobby was saying, wanting the ball. "Let's go, Carol Ann. Everybody's waiting."

Then she saw him talking to Ellen Dowling by the keg, and he seemed bigger, more muscular, less bowed and clutched-up, a whole other order of human being — like something born in midair and half an idea that wouldn't make sense until you were eighty or eight thousand.

The Millers, Hank and that airhead of his, Carla, went home first. About nine. After that, folks started drifting out in twos and threes — the Krafts, Mr. Preston who owned the hardware store where Bobby, having flunked out of State, had worked after his reclassification to 1-A. "Welcome home, short stuff," they said. "Glad you're back." Then the Fosters took Rhonda home — she'd squabbled with George, her creepy husband, and he'd left with a couple of Bobby's old Bulldog teammates from Las Cruces High. About eleven, Margie and Louis Delgado said adios. Carol Ann was tired. Bobby had been home two days, and all he wanted to do was screw. Wanted her to take it from behind, wanted to do it with the lights on, like they were on a stage. And all he'd talked about was this Eddie Heber. This primo buddy of his. Coming down from the Duke City for the cookout. "Me and Eddie," Bobby had said, "we were tight." *Tight* — a word Bobby had wound up his whole face to say.

She'd taken three personal days, gotten the sub herself — Mrs. Feldman — done the lesson plans, made the slaw and the potato salad, called all the guests, and now, watching Bobby scuttle back and forth like a dog between bones, she was beat, hollow as an echo. It wouldn't make any difference to Bobby: he'd want her any way. He was feeling good — loosey-goosey, he called it. Wouldn't be spit to him that his buddy, Eddie L-for-Lonnie Heber, would be snoring on the couch in the living room. You could hear through the walls in this place — that's what the builder was famous for, ticky-tack and walls you could poke your pinkie through — but Bobby wouldn't care. He'd want to party. To shake his tail feathers. His phrase. Then, like the blackest of black magic, her thoughts flying whichaway, Eddie was beside her, light-footed enough to be a ghost, his lips almost against her ear, his whisper a knot she couldn't find the beginning to.

"What?" she asked. Outside, Bobby was bear-hugging Sammy Vaughn and then playing grab-ass with Sammy's ex-wife Alice. Somewhere a car door slammed and somebody — Harry Hartger, another of Bobby's old bosses — was singing a Joe Cocker tune he didn't have the recklessness for, and here came Eddie Heber again — at the other ear this time — smelling of beer and charcoal and English Leather, his the voice the devil might have if it popped up in your living room near midnight to watch you tidy up. "What?" she said.

"I said you're probably a heartbreaker, right?"

The pistol came out then. He reached under his shirt, a Hawaiian eyesore he later said he'd bought as a joke.

"I know you," he said, half his face closed, the other half open like a closet door. "I know your hair, the size of your shoe."

For a moment, Carol Ann thought it was a squirt gun or maybe a cap pistol — a toy remarkable and cunning as theories about lived life on Mars — and then, clearly, it wasn't, and when he pulled back the slide and it seemed entirely possible that a round had been chambered, she could see that whatever was in him had turned around at least three whole times.

"You were a Zeta girl," he said. "Pledge chairman."

His jaw was slowly working, a sheen of sweat at his temples, his eyes beer-glazed and starting to go red at the corners, his breathing quick and labored as if he were thinking about sex or had done the impossible — like carry the ocean to her in his arms all the way from California without spilling a drop.

"Over there," he was saying, "I saw your picture a million times. Made Bobby get me a copy."

Later — after she and Bobby had divorced, after Eddie had reentered her life — she remembered this moment for what didn't happen. She did not panic. She remembered turning toward him, not increasing by much the arm's length between them, just swiveling as if on a pivot. A man, marvelous as a maniac from a movie, was standing in front of her. He seemed shiny and slick, more a figure sprung from a dream than from any crossroads on earth. He had something in his hand — a gift, possibly — but her own hand was coming up to decline it. She remembered being clear-minded, her thoughts as shaped and ordered as pearls on a string, and after she gently pushed the gun aside she advanced on him, feeling his heat as she got closer, stopping at the point where, if her breasts were to brush his shirtfront, he might vanish like a soap bubble.

"I made up stories," he was saying. "You were wearing a dress, a white one. The boys at LZ Thelma loved that story."

Outside Bobby was still messing around. Tonight, he would want her, sloppy and rough and over in a wink. After that, she would sleep, scrunched over to the edge of the bed, the ex-PFC sprawled beside her about as easy to rouse as a log. It would be morning after that, and him starved for her anew.

"Where'd you get the gun?" she asked.

Firebase Maggie, he said. Belonged to a dink.

She was almost his height and close enough now to see he had excellent teeth, white and straight, not yellow and fang-like as she'd feared. A tunnel, it seemed, had opened onto a distant and severe light.

"You kill him?" she wondered.

"Found it," he said. "A dozer dug it up when some concertina wire was being strung at the perimeter."

She was nowhere now, she thought. She had stepped through a gap — a seam, a tear — and had tumbled into a world as deformed as dreamland itself. She had slipped through in an instant, quick as a wish, but she was not alone.

"You trying to scare me?" she said. "Or just piss me off?"

He seemed to ruminate then, something in his face gone to tilt, and it occurred to her that he might be suffering a fever. What was it they could get over there? Dengue or beri-beri or malaria.

"I'm drunk," he said, but unslurred in a manner that gave her to understand he was sober as a surgeon.

"You sneaked up on me," she said. "That's not very sporting, Mr. Heber."

The other half of his face had come open now, as if a strong wind were blowing from his insides out.

"You get in the habit," he said. "It's like smoking."

Here it was then — for reasons she understood she would need no less than a lifetime to comprehend — that she kissed him, tenderly at first and with her eyes open, him staring at her too, but little in his expression to say that he hadn't expected their love affair to begin this way, not even when, before she let go, she bit his lip. Hard.

"I bet you're a son-of-a-bitch too," she said.

In 1986 they met again. It would turn out that he had been married as well, had three kids, all boys, who now lived in Redondo Beach with their mother. He had been sliding, he would say. Drifting, coming undone — pick a word. Worked in aerospace for a while. LTV in Dallas. A computer company in San Antonio. Then — boom — a layoff. Squabbles. Fights. Tears like a river. Two days in jail in Houston. Worked the offshore rigs for a time. Next a breakdown. Total. Bugs on the walls, the night sweats. Visions. Voices from the TV. It was the booze. It was want and venery.

She hadn't heard him come in. At her desk, school over for an hour, she was marking a spelling test. A-l-l-i-g-a-t-o-r. R-e-p-t-i-l-e. The cold-blooded family you were wise to step over or avoid altogether. She was thinking about her boyfriend after Bobby Spears, a slim-hipped rancher up the valley who raised polled Herefords. He liked to race motocross in the hills near Picacho Peak. Did impressions — Nixon, Porky Pig,

Johnny Carson. Then, as if he'd materialized with a poof from a flashpot and a blast of horns from the biggest of the big bands, Eddie Heber was in the back of her room, sitting at Tiffany Garcia's desk, a cigarette going, his eyes flat again and dispassionate as math, and part of her seemed to have gone from wet to dry without any heat in between.

"If you're looking —" she began, but he was already shaking his head. He'd found what he was looking for.

When he said her name, something caught in her chest — a bone, a clot of tissue — and the air sucked out of the room. She would have known him anywhere: a light, weird and cold as a glacier, seemed to come off his skin. He was too pale, too much of everything lonely and still and sad. His hair was long now, past his shoulders, as sleek and beautiful as a matinee Apache, longer than her own; and except for that, he seemed not to have been gone long at all, only minutes, as if he'd just stepped out to use the toilet. But when he rose, she could see that maybe his face had come off and had been put back in pieces, the features loose on his skull, parts from different puzzles of the same scene.

"You can't smoke in here," she said. "Mr. Probert has a cow if anyone smokes in the building."

She was apologizing, she realized, and suddenly felt too big for her clothes, her life too small for anything unrelated to Eddie Heber.

"You want to go for a ride?" he said.

But when he sat near her, another desk scooted up close, she understood they wouldn't be leaving for a few minutes yet. He seemed to be composing himself, pulling himself into a shape she wouldn't be frightened by. She was stunned by his size. He was bigger now — weights, she would learn; he'd done sixteen months in Parchman, in Arkansas, a 4th degree assault — and she thought about him without his shirt, without any clothes whatsoever, between them only light and air and time.

He'd gone off the deep end, he said. It wasn't a Vietnam issue. It was human. The wires too tight. The wheels spinning too hard. The twentieth century — all loop-de-loop and greed and the low road of scoundrels. Now he had a lawn and yard service. *Greensweep*. Been in town for over a year. Rented a house on Espina, up near the Armory.

He had shoved the words in her head. That's what she thought later, that he had not spoken at all — not using the old-fashioned organs of speech, at least — and that somehow it had become time for her own short story.

"Bobby Spears," she began.

He nodded, gravely. "A girlfriend. You got fucked over."

Carol Ann caught herself looking at his cigarette, its smoke like a cloud with curls and a beard. Eddie Heber knew. Everything.

"Me and Bobby had drinks about ten months ago," he was saying. "At the El Patio bar in old Mesilla. Bobby Spears is a rock. He never changes."

"That was a long time ago," she said. "I'm better now."

In the silence, she could hear him breathing again, like that night over a decade before. His breath was language itself, she thought. It told you *who* and *why*, gave you information about the way you could behave, what you could expect. It wasn't complicated, just queer as reflections in a funhouse. Talk to be talked in the afterlife.

"Where's the gun?" she asked. She had to get that settled.

He stubbed out his smoke on the bottom of his boot. His hands were coarse, the fingers long and thick as hot dogs, the nails oddly well-manicured. Plus, he had a tattoo now, a dragon on his forearm — "Jailhouse art," he would say eventually.

"Threw it away," he told her. He'd stepped out on the chopper platform — this was at Texaco 31 — and pitched the weapon into the Gulf of Mexico.

She had stood, the flutter of her heart the only thing about this encounter that didn't surprise her.

"I want that ride now," she said.

Before they went to his place, he drove south on I-10, almost down to Anthony, then turned back north on old 85, the two-lane nearer the mostly muddy Rio Grande. Time seemed to have stopped, the air thick with heat, sunlight scattered everywhere in splinters and spikes.

He'd been crazed, he said. An affliction. Once he hadn't been able to use his hands. They'd been hooves. Mallets. Whole days had passed when he couldn't talk. He'd seen a doctor. Another. He was angry, he told them. Genuinely and profoundly teed off. The world had failed him. He tried vitamins, yelling in the woods — the works. The world got fuzzy at the edges. Cynthia split. She hadn't needed a lawyer because he'd given her everything — the Ford, the house, even the Oreos in his lunchbucket.

It was late now, the sky west of her, toward Deming, rich with blood and wispy clouds with yellow undersides, everything too high and too filmy, and she thought she'd just awakened from a hard, terrible sleep — a sleep with too many people in it, too much jibber-jabber and too much peril to be alone in — and the first person who'd appeared to her upon waking was this man next to her, the one saying that he hadn't made love to a woman in three years, maybe a little more. The pinching under her heart had started again, but Carol Ann found she had a place in her head where she could arrange herself against him.

In his driveway he hurried around to her door and held out his hand — a gentleman. Touching him was like touching a circuit only God could flick the switch for — God, or another entity said to be lavish with lightning and brimstone. And while he guided her up the sidewalk, she wondered how she would explain this peculiar turn of events to her colleagues, particularly Ruthie Evans, her best friend, or to her students when Eddie began picking her up in the parking lot, or even to Bobby Spears himself should she bump into him in the Food Mart.

She was once Carol Ann Mobley, she told herself. Her mother was Rilla, to honor an ancient relative in Texas; her daddy was Bill but called Cuddy by the cowboys who worked the ranch. She had other thoughts, all impossible to collect:

The Way Sin Is Said in Wonderland 9

a wind, vicious as an argument, had come up to spread them willy-nilly. She believed she had asked him a question — "That night, what were you talking to Ellen Dowling about?" — and she believed he had answered — "You," he was thought to have said, "you and me" — but he was fumbling with his keys and all she could do was wait for the ground to quit shaking.

She seemed to recognize his house, the marvelous clutter inside. Afterward, she felt she'd suffered a vision, the present undone year by year by year until she was a child, a girl who was yet to grow up and go to college and meet a boy named Bobby who would bring into her life a man named Eddie who would unlock a door to a future she could barely walk through.

She was counting now — the world's snowflakes, the Sahara's grains of sand — putting between herself and whatever was coming next numbers she hoped one day to get to the end of. Eddie Heber had sat her down, swept several magazines off the sofa, *People, The Statesman,* a much-thumbed paperback Webster's, and he put a club soda in her hand; he was talking to her, one word — love — coming at her again and again, his voice the last ton of a twenty-ton day. It was a replay, she believed. She had already done it: she'd already peeled off her clothes and urged him down on top of her. She'd already felt him, fretful and needy and clumsy but cool as wax, move her this way and that, her hips rising, her fingers on the knobs of his spine and on his shoulders and on his knees, the strangled noise he made trying to hold himself back, her hands not strong enough for his head, her legs hooked behind his heels, the carpet scratching her back, boxes and crates and motor parts the only items to look at except for a face empty as a hoop.

Then it was over, the replay, and she was still dressed, out of numbers to count and soda to drink, and she had asked him if he was going to be bad for her.

He hoped not, he said. But one never knew.

"One?"

"A turn of phrase," he said. "Nothing personal."

She was studying his living room, a corner of the kitchen,

the hall. Back there was the bedroom, she guessed. One would have to rise, one would have to walk. A path led through the books, the unbalanced-looking piles of them, the titles as much about rocks and trees as they were about stuff you had to know to survive what daylight revealed. Somehow, one would have to put oneself on that path, past the laundry in a heap, past the speaker cabinets and the snapshots that had spilled out of a grocery sack.

Robert Spears, she thought. That was a man she had known, as were Karen Needham's brother and Tim Whitmire. J. T. Something-Something, a mechanic with a scar across his nose. Another who'd imagined himself Conway Twitty, a date as dull as water was wet. A decision had been reached, she realized. Later, these were the rooms she remembered when she wondered where she had abandoned herself. There: by the cushions. There: by the wobbly-looking table in a corner. There: near the end of a path to another door to pass through.

Now she was moving, her joints loose and oily, and Eddie had fallen in behind her, saying please excuse the mess. He was sorry. He'd intended to do more.

"That's all right," Carol Ann told him.

She had given pieces of herself away — a piece to every man she'd ever loved — and now, like coins and like words and like threads, they were all coming back.

TWO

He took her dreams first, little by little, the weight of them and their meaning. She dreamed of her daddy's ranch outside Clovis, the land wind-whitened and parched, and he took that. Eddie Heber. In junior high she had been a cheerleader, the Falcons, green-and-white pleated skirts with an appliqué megaphone stitched on the sweater. He took that, asking her to cheer for him, and applauded vigorously when she returned to bed. She'd broken her arm — her left — in a fall from a borrowed bike in front of her church. He grabbed that, and St. Andrew's itself, as well as the summer camp she went to in the mountains near Ruidoso. Her first snowman, her crush on Davy Crockett, the Ed Sullivan Show when she listened to the Beatles ask to hold her hand — he took those, and many times that first week she awakened with a start, her ears ringing, the sweat cold on her forehead, the sheets a tangle around her legs, and feared to see everything he'd taken suspended near the ceiling like stars to be wished upon.

Other times she found him staring at her. Or a part of her. Her ankle. The mole on her shoulder. A shaving nick on her knee. It was like being watched by a plant. Once she found him with a penlight, bent to her chest in wicked concentration. "Don't move," he said. Nothing else in the room was visible, as if beyond the light was only blackness void as space. The sheet around his shoulders, he smelled like well-water and Marlboros, rusty and stale. "Ssshhh," he said. He held her lipstick, a red so blue in this light that it looked like ink. "You're beautiful," he said, the word as much made from iron and silver as from air and tongue and teeth.

He drew on her then, around her nipple, his mouth set hard as a knob, as if this were work that required precision and monk-like patience, a version of top-secret science practiced underground. A moment later, he kissed her there, his lips soft as hair. A jolt surged through her, static sizzling up her spine. She wanted to say *no* as much as she wanted to say *yes*. She was in her skin. And out. Close and far. He would ruin her, she thought. He would take her apart hook by hasp by hinge and put her back together haphazardly and jury-rigged, the outside in, the private public as her face. Morning was coming, hazy and already squawky with birds in the tree outside their window, and she knew she'd soon find him on his back, his lips smeared and swollen and red.

For days — when she wasn't at school and when he wasn't mowing lawns or hauling yard trash — they talked. It developed that he could cook. "Baked fruit curry," he said once, showing her with a flourish the cherries and the pineapples and the peach halves. "Dilly bread," he said another time. "Eggplant casserole." They were announcements, these dishes. Declarations as formal as those that bigwigs got when they entered a ballroom to a fanfare. In return, she told him about her wedding to Bobby Spears, the Justice of the Peace who'd performed the ceremony in the living room of her daddy's house, Bobby's haircut a whitewall like the one he would get a year later from Uncle Sam. Her sorority sister, Sandi Harrison, had played the piano, "Cherish" by the Association. Her dress had come from Juárez, her own design of lace and satin and pearl buttons up the back. She had a lot to say, she felt, and exactly the right person to hear the whole of it. He drank — Bacardi, George Dickel, Buckhorn beer — and she talked. He cooked — Chocolate Cream Roll, Tamale Ring — and she told about her cousins, Julie and Becky Sims, and how her mother danced the Hully Gully and the first time seeing her father without his dentures, until the string of her had unwound and gone slack and she understood, less with her mind than with the worn muscle of her heart, that Eddie Heber was crazy.

"My boys," he said one evening. Petey and Willie and Eddie Junior. They were like him — agile as waterbugs and pesky, in and out of everything. They could cook, too. He'd learned it in the service — that's what he'd been, a chef, his MOS. An E-4 with a soup spoon. Cooked for the brass in Hotel Company with the 1/26. Petit Fours, Salmon Mousse, Lemon Meringue Pie — as at home in a pantry as was Picasso in a garret in gay Paree. Working for Uncle Sugar was like working at the Hilton Inn. The ruling class billeted in Airstream trailers, played golf on a three-hole course the Seabees had hacked out of the bush.

"Could've been Mexico," he said. "Puerta goddamn Vallarta."

Still in his workshirt, the sleeves rolled to the elbow, he was making almond macaroons. After school, she'd spent the afternoon searching for rosewater, three teaspoons of it, and now he was putting the recipe together — the egg whites, the superfine sugar, the flour, the blanched nuts — moving between the baking sheet and his bottle of Black Jack on the counter. He'd become handsome, she thought. His hair was still long, tied back in a ponytail, his face now brown as a Mexican's, and she remembered that night, years and years before, when he was skinnier, drawn and wasted like a castaway, a man with a pistol and the hooded, melancholy eyes of a vagrant. He had not been trying to scare her, she thought. Not really. Even then, he had been in love. Love could make you do anything, maybe howl or drive in a circle. Love might even involve guns.

Vietnam, he was saying. Best time of his life. Fucking aces high. Like Bandstand without the dress code. All the brutal business in the highlands or the delta never got anywhere near him. Steppenwolf on the 8-track, Budweiser in the fridge. Direct phone link with the World. Tried to ring up Bob Dylan one night, tell the guy he was full of it. No answers were blowing in the freaking wind. Hell, nothing blew over there. By comparison, R & R was a major disappointment. Couldn't wait to get back in the bush and rustle up some Knickerbocker fritters for X-mas.

"That's not what Bobby said," she told him.

"Bobby," he said. He could've been referring to a tree he'd trimmed. "Bobby was a clerk. During the day, he typed COM / SIT reports, hustled the commissary files."

For a minute, she refused to believe it, a Polaroid of Bobby in camouflage coming to mind.

"He bought the outfit in Hong Kong," Eddie told her. "On Nathan Street. I got a suit, looked like the lost member of the Temptations."

In the next hour — Humbug Pie, with raisins and molasses — he showed her more of himself. He'd been a liar, he confessed. In high school. At Houston. Sophomore year, for example, he'd told a girlfriend that his parents were dead. Marge and Gene. In a car wreck near Portales. They were alive, he said. Retired. They liked to ski — Sandia, Angel Fire over near Taos, up in Utah. His dad had worked for the Air Force, an engineer. His mom —

A question was coming, she realized. When he was finished, however long the current monologue took, however roundabout the getting there, he would ask her something —

about them, certainly, but also about the vegetation and the land and the humans that they were upon it — and she would have to get an answer out without stuttering like an idiot who'd only learned English the week before.

"Fix me a drink?" she asked.

He made her a Cuba Libre — too sweet, she would recall — and he told her about Cynthia.

"Maiden name Lanier," he said. "From Galveston, a bona fide heiress. Oil. A million cousins and uncles, mostly in Louisiana. A gruesome people. All named Tippy or Foot or Beebum."

"You hit her," she said.

The next second, she would remember, was the longest she ever lived through.

"Once," he said. "During a spell."

Another second came, it too filled with pins and points.

Afterward, he said, Cynthia had sicked a mob of close relations on him. Spent a week in Baylor Medical.

The sun had gone down a while ago and the kitchen, except for the light glaring over the stove, had become gloomy and choked with cigarette smoke. He was almost to the end of himself, she decided. All the bounce had left his voice, the ends of his sentences coming in whispers. Only dribs and drabs were reaching her: Fort Smith, Arkansas. A Starvin' Marvin. Light that turned the skin yellow as mustard. The walls wobbling. Behind the register, a female redneck, sullen as a snake. A quarrel about change. About the magazine rack. About the swirl the universe made going down the drain at his feet. Glass shattering, Pepsi bottles rolling like bowling pins. An arm, his own, sweeping along the service counter. *The Globe.* Castro playing voodoo with Kennedy's brain. Finally, a fist, his own. No more redneck Betty Boop standing up. Just, when the cops arrived, Edward L-for-Lonnie Heber sitting splay-legged in an aisle gobbling brown sugar from the bag.

"Eddie," she said.

She had his attention now, like being looked at by every peasant in China.

"Don't be crazy anymore, okay?"

"It's my temperament," he said. "I take offense."

He had put food in front of her — a wedge of pie and a macaroon, both cool — and she tried to eat a little. The light was in her eyes, still harsh as a screech, so she made him turn it off. She was thinking about her job — the numbers and shapes and science she was employed to pass on to the children that the neighborhood sent her. They liked geography, these kids. Tanika had chosen Zanzibar; Ellen Foley, Egypt. Cotton came from one place, copper from another. Everyone had a country to be responsible for — the tribes that rampaged the hinterlands, the chiefs who rose up to lead them, what they ate in their own huts and hovels, and what they loved first in a fight. That was the world, she thought. Ice at one corner, hot sand at another. That was the world, a patchwork you memorized for a test. That was the world — a spin of fire and smoke and wind and sweets to eat in the dark.

"Carol Ann," Eddie was saying.

He'd found her hand, and she, her heart a racket in her ears, could tell that his question was coming now — would she move in with him? — but she had her answer ready, the words of it as simple as those the lucky say in war.

After Valentine's Day, two weeks of living with him, she thought of the gun — Eddie's Makarov, scraped up from a field the LT had ordered cleared for horseshoes. She'd had a cold — the sniffles, chills occasionally — so she stayed home, faked a seal-like cough for Mr. Probert, then lay in bed all morning being serious with Donahue and Sally. At eleven, Jerry Springer came on — "Centerfold Sisters," the girls blonde and top-heavy and humorless as nuns — so at the commercial she shuffled into the kitchen for a cup of red zinger. She was at the cupboard when she realized it was still here: the pistol.

Eddie hoarded, nothing decrepit enough or useless enough or sufficiently broken to throw away. Everything, she realized, had come with him: clothes, notes he'd scribbled to himself, a stack of *Times Heralds* from Dallas, shoes he'd scuffed the heels from, books he'd quit, letters and bills and cards from the kids. He'd made his way to her, she thought, gathering scraps and scraps of paper along the way — another trail — and, if she wanted, she could track backwards through his life, the piles and mounds of it, until she came upon him at, say, fifteen — or five, or twenty — and could see him there, crumpled in his hand the first thing that marked the path he was to travel through time.

In what had become his reading room — the third bedroom, already tiny and now cramped as an attic with cassettes and periodicals and accordion files — she sat in his chair, the footstool in front of it laden with catalogues and maps of places he'd, so far as she knew, never been to, places like France and mountainous Tibet, as remote and strange as lands you found in pop-up books about fairies and gypsies and high-hatted wizards.

For a time, she toyed with the switch to the floor lamp. On and off. A cone of light over her shoulder, then a wash of morning as gray as the paint on warehouses. He'd stuck foil on all the windows. A bulletin board dominated one wall, his customers scheduled in a grid that went till the new century. She was pleased to see that he'd planned to be busy through 1999 — the year, according to Mr. Probert, that Jesus, willful and heedless as a spendthrift, was returning to boil the mess man was. She imagined Eddie then, over fifty, still lean as pricey meat, that figure beside him maybe her own aged self in a dress too fussy with snaps and buckles to be anything but science fiction.

Eddie was an optimist, she decided. Every morning, he made lists — prune Mrs. Grissom's firebush, take down the shed at the Samples' house, get insecticide from the Mesilla Valley Garden Center — and he drove away in his pickup knowing what led to what and it to another until, at sundown, he could come back to this room to draw another X in his calendar. An X for then, an X for now. X's enough for the future — maybe for jealous Jesus Himself — and whatever sob-filled hours came after that.

She sighed when she looked at the metal file cabinet underneath the grid. That's where it was, she thought. The gun. For a moment, laughter from the TV reaching her even here, she wondered what he would say if he knew that she had opened a drawer, the top one, all squeaky and warped, and found it there, the barrel rust-flecked as she remembered, a web of cracks running up the grip on one side. She was curious about how his face would work, the chewing movements at his temples, if he knew that she'd held the pistol, absently rubbing the faded red star, studying the peculiar markings near the trigger guard, before she put it back — that squeak again — and went to see, as she was doing now, what opinions the bosomy Miss Septembers had regarding certain monkeyshines between girls and boys.

Once upon a time, she thought, Eddie had had a secret. Now she had one.

The end of February. March out like a lamb. Easter. He was fine for those months. May flowers. Then June and he arrived for the class party on the last day straight from work — a new home he was landscaping in Telshor Hills, another big shot with a wallet like a loaf of bread. He ate a square of the spice sheetcake he'd baked the night before, drank Kool-Aid, even wore a party hat when Alicia Lynn Pinney — the Miss Priss in the third row — pointed out the rules. Parties and hats went together like salt and pepper. Afterward, when she was cleaning up, he told her she could relax.

"It doesn't happen the way you think," he announced. "It's gradual."

He was sitting at her desk, smoking with deliberation, flicking ashes onto a paper plate.

Other rules, she guessed. Out the window, she could see some older kids — sixth graders, maybe Ruthie Evans's kids — gathered around the tether-ball pole. It seemed probable that a fight would start out there. Or a powwow.

"It builds," he told her. "Something goes haywire. The waters rise."

In the hall, a bell was dinging: three-fifteen. School had ended, officially.

"You're warning me," she said, a question. The first of many. Like rules.

His shirt stained with sweat, a line of grit on his brow from his headband, he looked like a warrior who'd scrambled out of the hills for food.

"I fill up," he was saying. "It spills."

Outside the sixth-graders were wandering off in pairs or alone. Mr. Probert was out there, she assumed, persnickety and loud as a drum. He looked like a man who'd removed his own sense of humor with a chain saw.

"You'll tell me when?" she asked.

Reaching for a fallen column of Dixie cups, he had stood, not hurriedly.

"I'll clean up," he said. "I'll tell you when."

For the Fourth of July, he took three days for them to visit her folks in Clovis. Since she'd left for college, her father had put in a pool, so he and Eddie sat under the awning on the cool deck drinking Pearl Light while she floated on a rubber raft near the diving board. Every now and then, she could hear them chuckling softly, then her daddy teasing her mother who wouldn't leave the porch for the sun. "That water's cold as scissors," she said once. The light here was different — thinner somehow, less wrathful than in the desert — the landscape grassier, not so hardpan but without tooth-like mountains at the horizon to show you how far you had to go.

On the Fourth itself, they watched the fireworks from the city twelve miles south, miniature bursts of gold and green, like showers of foil, the sounds of the explosions arriving well after she'd seen the glitter against a sky black as the cape a witch wears.

"Incoming," Eddie remarked once, before taking her hand to let her know he was fooling. It had been like this in Vietnam, he told her father. A swimming pool, a Porterhouse steak for each trooper, and an Air Force light show far, far away.

That night, after her parents had gone to bed, Carol Ann

wished Eddie sweet dreams at the door to the guest bedroom where he was to sleep.

"They don't know," he said. "About us, I mean."

She couldn't see much of his face, just eerie glints from his cheek and nose. She hoped he was smiling.

"They're old-fashioned," she said. "Mother would be upset."

His hand came up then, out of the darkness, and reached into the cup of her swimsuit to hold her breast. He was dry, nothing in his touch to suggest that she was more to him that wood and nails and strings to pull.

"You didn't tell me you had a nickname," he said. "Squeaky."

Laryngitis, she said. In grade school. It was, well, embarrassing. Sounded more like a frog than a mouse.

"You had a horse, too," he said. "Skeeter. It threw you out by the corral."

His hand was still there, unmoving. He could have been wearing a leather glove, and for a second she thought to go in the room with him, that she would shrug off her top and lie beside him until whatever was kicking at his heart ran out of anger.

"I like your parents," he told her. "They're stand-up people. You don't get much of that nowadays."

He had stopped smiling, she supposed. You could hear the earnestness in his voice, the sour note it was. She guessed he was thinking about the heroes he rooted for in the books he bought — books whose covers were all about doom and distress and deeds wrought by righteousness. In those books, standing up was a virtue. So far as she understood, the vices included hypocrisy and back-stabbing. In Eddie's books, the characters suffered no fools. They rose up, indignant as children, and let fly with arrows and poleaxes and lances.

"Eddie?" she said.

His hand had moved, like a claw. Down the hall, her father was coughing, a wheeze without any charm to it. She had been Squeaky once, she thought. She had been a Mobley, then a Spears. Now what? What were you in the dark? *One.* That had been Eddie's word months and months ago. What were you when the gears slipped or ground or disengaged completely?

"It's happening," he said.

She nodded.

"Forewarned is forearmed."

THREE

In early August, he stopped cooking. For several days he ate only peanut butter from the jar, then macaroni and cheese. He stared at the TV, yelled abuse at the gussied-up newsfolk NBC had hired to educate him.

"You could see a doctor," she told him one evening.

Only as a last resort, he said. It was like breathing through a soaked washcloth. They wrenched open your skull, dropped a torch in there, wriggled their fingers in the slop.

His hand was shaking in a fashion she suspected he was unaware of. It got better as you got older, he'd told her on the drive back from Clovis. He was getting older all the time.

"You're proud, aren't you?"

He smiled at her then, the whole of his face engaged in the effort.

"I am the King of Pride," he said. "The absolute fucking monarch."

On Thursday, the day his letter to the editor appeared in the *Sun-News*, he was working for Judge Sanders, putting in a rock and cactus garden, so she drove over to park at the corner, far enough away to be inconspicuous. She'd seen the list — ocotillo, monkey flower, brittlebush, gravel from an arroyo behind A Mountain — his handwriting square and tight, as if written with a chisel.

They'd made love the night before — he only to her, she believed, but she to eight or nine of him. One of him had been feverish, another chilled enough to get goosebumps. One laughed, another whistled from the foot of the bed and lunged at her like a tiger, his head wagging heavily, his eyes wide as nickels. The one in the refuge of the corner, knees to his chest, was not the one who rose from it, slow and shaggy-seeming. She hadn't been horrified, she thought now, recalling the steady thump of her heart. The love-making itself had been tedious: a matter of tabs and slots and deliberate movement. Eddie had been dry weight, all bone and ash — flesh that rocked back and forth regularly as clockwork. Once he sang along with his boombox — Patsy Cline, she remembered — but his voice had run out long before the music did, and when she lifted his face to look at him, she discovered that he was gone, the shell of him slick and unfeeling as glass.

"It's like a landslide," he said. "Imagine a mountain crashing down on your head."

He was a shade, she'd thought. Insubstantial as a ghost. And for a time, astride him, trying to make him hard, she believed he was trying, in a way twisted with love, to protect her from the knowledge that life was not glorious and purposeful and prodigious with reward. They were a kind, he and she, dragged upright by time but too stupid to follow the generally forward direction thought best to go.

"Help me, Eddie," she said. "Please, help me."

He was trying, he said.

Again, she asked, but this time he said nothing, so she leaned into him, his smell at once tangy and greasy, salt and lemon and soap, her face against his neck, her lips to his ear, saying the word *love* with as much bite as she imagined a dictator might say the word *kill*.

Much later — after she'd gone away, after he'd come back to himself — she realized that this was the first time she'd told him she loved him, but it was a sentence she remembered cleaving to, like a monotonous beat, for one minute, then two, as pure and aggrieved the last time said as it was the first. The covers in a heap at the foot of the bed, she grew cold as she spoke, the *I* of her pressed into the *you* of him, not knowing what she hoped to prove, then knowing — from his witless moans, from his hand stroking the small of her back — that she had everything to prove: he would be worse before he was better — yes, she understood that — but he had to know, even in the worst of it, that she loved him.

So she kept saying it, a speech delivered into his neck and shoulder, to his cheeks and his forehead as she kissed him, into his chin after he smoothed back her hair, to his lips until he'd stopped trembling and she was quiet and it seemed that nothing — least of all sentiments having to do with the soul of her — had been said at all, until they reached a point in the night when he drew her to his chest to tell her to listen closely to the clatter and bang in him that were his various demons.

"I'm scared, Eddie," she said.

So was he, he told her. He was helpless.

On one wall several shadows were at play from the flickering candlelight, none of them meaningful or part of love.

"Tell me about the picture," she said. "The one Bobby made for you."

It was her spring formal, he said. She looked like ice cream to him. The only cool thing in the world. The LT, a West Point grad, had said Eddie's affection for it bordered on the inordinate.

"That was wrong," Eddie said. "My affection was as ordinate as the day is long."

Scarcely an inch apart, they lay side by side. Like an old couple, she thought. A modern schoolmarm and the King of Pride. She thought of her parents — Rilla and Cuddy — lying, probably like this, as distant from her as she seemed to be from Eddie. Once, when she was seven, she'd watched them nap, and she had tried, standing at the door to their bedroom, to imagine their dreams, wondering at last if, where in them it was dark and breezy and broad as heaven, they dreamed themselves lying each by each, inert and almost breathless, no one but Carol Ann to beckon them back to the wakeful world.

"Let's go to sleep, Eddie," she'd said.

Yes, he said, an answer with too much hiss in it.

"I love you," she'd said.

And he'd said it too, the terrible simplicity of it all she could remember between then and now, between Eddie looking as if his arms would fly off in agony and Eddie now bustling back and forth in the sun at Judge Sanders's house.

In her lap, she had the *Sun-News* open to the letters page. It was mid-August, school to start in three weeks, and already some lamebrains were writing to complain about a teachers' strike Carol Ann didn't think would actually happen. At home, reading his letter had frightened her, but here, only a half-block from him, she tried again, saying aloud the first paragraph — it seemed as long as her forearm — until her eyes came free of the page and she could see that Eddie was stock-still at the door to his pickup, his head tipped back, the sky blank and almost white behind him. Edward L. Heber, the letter-writer, was not lunatic. Edward L. Heber was angry. *Things are out of whack,* he'd written. *Collapsed and ruined. There is hunger. And ignorance. And false piety. And* — but she'd stopped again, Eddie with a broom now, leaning on it and again gazing upward.

He was a moralist, she decided. Maybe that was good. A hopey thing with wings.

For another twenty minutes she watched him work, the yardage between them filled only with heat shimmering up from the asphalt. Load after load, he was shoveling out gravel, carrying it to a pile near the walk leading to the Judge's front door. Clearly, this was how he managed — one simple under-taking at a time, scoop, walk, dump — his manner calculated and efficient, as if he could do this, happily and well, until he found himself at the bottom of a pit, alone at last with the one stone that had made him furious. She tried to conceive of the inside of his head — the fountain of sparks in there, the rattle — but a second later she realized he had stopped, in mid-stride almost, as fixed as a scarecrow.

"What're you doing here?" he said.

Still carrying the shovel, he had taken only a half minute to reach her — she'd timed it. Amazingly, he had not dropped even one pebble.

"I don't know," she said. "I should be over at school, but —"

She shrugged. What with the union yakking about the strike, she didn't see any profit in fixing up her classroom if in a week she was going to be walking a picket line and generally making a spectacle of herself. "I thought we could go out to dinner tonight," she said. "Maybe a movie after."

It was blabber. What she really wanted to do was grab his sleeve, make him leave the shovel here, the truck there, and get in the car with her. They would sit for a while, another lovelorn couple in paradise. She would hold his hand — or he hers — the afternoon would wear on, dusk would arrive, then twilight, then night itself full of random twinkles or a moon on the wane.

"I made a call," he said. "This morning."

Before she understood completely what he'd done, she sought to rewind time, yank the cord of it back so that he was not here, beside her window. She yearned to be young again, the ideas of love and loyalty as alien to her as were orchids to Eskimos.

"Bobby Spears," she said, a statement of fact, like the number of bushels in a peck.

The shovel jerked now, a handful of gravel spilling.

"He's got an extra room," Eddie said. "You'll be safe there."

Her lungs filled then — a gasp, nearly — and she feared Eddie would be turning now, going away, back to his work, back to the truck, back to the thirty-two steps between it and the mountain he had contrived to erect in the front yard of a retired Federal Court judge. He was trying to protect her again. Maybe that was good too.

"Don't be mad, Carol Ann," he said. "I don't know anybody else."

"What about the girlfriend?" she asked.

They were married, Eddie told her. The girl — Sally or Sarah, he wasn't sure — was pregnant. Bobby was different now.

"This seemed like a smart idea, Eddie?"

He looked beleaguered, a beast run to ground by hounds and horses.

"I only had one card left," he said. "I played it."

On the seat next to her, the paper was still open, the rage and sorrow of this man not anything any citizen would remember tomorrow, or the days to follow. Elsewhere were articles about mayhem and conniving and the snapped-off ends of hope. *We are craven*, Eddie had declared to his neighbors, and to his neighbors' neighbors, and to anyone else who could read left to right. *We must mend. Now.*

"How long?" Carol Ann wondered.

He didn't know, he said. Six weeks maybe, more or less. It'd been quite a while since the last episode.

She thought about the night before, watching him sleep, the peace it had seemed to bring him, then her own sleep, nothing but wire in her dreams — fists of it, huge coils sprung and flyaway and mangled — then awake and seeing him frozen in the hall, the light a streak in front of him, his face shriven and collapsed, a scary amount of time going by before he shivered to life again and stumbled toward her.

"I'll give you a month," she said. "I couldn't last any longer."

Okay, he said, little in the word to indicate it had any meaning for him.

"I gotta go back to work, Carol Ann."

"Okay," she said, her turn not to mean too much.

He moved then, the shovel a counterweight to keep him from falling over in a heap. His tattoo had come into view, crude and obviously unfinished, the handiwork of a B & E offender named Pease. Sometimes, Eddie wore a bandage to cover it. He was ashamed, he'd told her long ago. A dragon, he'd sneered. How fucking pathetic.

"Eddie," she called.

More gravel fell.

"What'd you see last night?" she asked. "In the hall."

He told her then, but she believed she hadn't heard correctly, so she asked him to repeat himself — "Fire," he said, the way "sin" is said in wonderland. And while he walked away, she thought she could see it too, the yellow and red of it roaring up and up, and the terrifying wind of it overtaking everything in front of her — the trees, these houses, the telephone poles, shrubs, Eddie's truck, at last Eddie himself — until all that remained was rubble scorched black as a nightmare.

FOUR

She guessed that he cracked — caved in completely — her second week on the picket line in front of her school. She had not gone to Bobby's house — "It would be too complicated," she'd told Sally, Bobby's pretty wife; instead, she rented a furnished efficiency in a four-plex Mr. Probert owned up the valley toward Hot Springs, a place where she learned, the instant the door shut behind her, that a day could have too many hours in it, an hour too many minutes, time as mixed and fluid and dreadful as heartsickness itself. She woke too early, she discovered. Stayed up too late, darkness a thing that seemed to have texture and depth.

The first few days, she didn't eat much, once almost fainting on the line, so each morning thereafter before her shift, she made breakfast — a bowl of Cheerios, wheat toast and jelly, a glass of grapefruit juice — and sat in front of it with the promise to herself that she would do this — and the next chore, plus whatever ought to follow — and then, for one creaky revolution of the planet at least, she would not have to do it again. Often as she ate, she wondered what Eddie was doing, the idea of him so urgent and so virile that sometimes he seemed to appear across from her, his hair gleaming, his face soaking up most of the light she needed to see by.

Several times she called, his machine clicking on to say he was not in. He'd bought a gag tape — the voices of Daffy Duck and Bogart and Ronald Reagan — and twice, aiming to be cheerful, she left messages in the style of Marilyn Monroe and Yosemite Sam. The last time she told him the gossip she was hearing — Rae Nell Tipton was divorcing Archie, the slime; Mavis Rugely had a goiter — but she quickly ran out of silly news and, the tape whirring like a breeze, she suspected he was squatting near the phone, his own cigarette going, a comforter over his shoulders to keep him from a coldness no one else in Dona Ana County could feel.

"Go to bed, Eddie," she said softly. "Put the beer down, honey. You need rest."

She imagined him shuffling back to the bedroom, all the lights on so he could see the winged creatures in the night that had swooped down to scold him.

"Lie down," she told him, and when she assumed he was settled, the covers bunched to his neck, she began to talk to him again, hers the voice she used at school when it was time for nap and dreams fine as mist. They would go places, she promised him. Canada. Niagara Falls. Florida. If he wanted, he could invite his kids. They'd rent a van, maybe a Winnebago, and in the summers they'd drive all over America. She'd camped a lot, she reminded him. She knew the forest. Plus, she liked to climb, the steeper the better, get to the peak of a mountain and shout into the valley you'd left. "I'm a good sport," she said, listening closely. He wasn't asleep, she thought. He remained alert there, still suspicious, his gaze as watchful as a stray dog ready to run.

"It's okay, sweetheart," she said and took enough breath to start again on the list of vistas to visit and adventures to share.

The next day, she thought she saw his truck a ways down the block from the sidewalk she marched up and down on, but she couldn't be sure: Kirby Holmes, the loudmouth from the classroom next to hers, was telling another of his Cajun jokes — a sing-songy anecdote with too many wishy-washy characters in it and about nothing life-or-death that could actually happen between men and women. She became distracted — Kirby was jumping around and making her look here and there — and suddenly what might have been Eddie Heber, maybe standing beside his pickup, his wave constant and spiritless, was only emptiness, just a street that went up and up and finally over a hill, a curve going on and on into the sterile and wild desert.

He had cracked — she knew it — so that night she drove over to his house. "Oh, Eddie," she sighed, as much exasperated as frightened. All the lights were on — inside and out, as far as she could tell — the place had a glow she figured the cops might worry over. After she used her key to get in, she suppressed the impulse to turn around, to close up the house again, and disappear.

"Eddie," she called.

A tornado had torn through here, it seemed, and she wondered where in the litter of tipped-over furniture and strewn paper and crumpled clothes she would find him.

"It's me, baby," she said, then again and again until she tired of the echo.

Cautiously, she picked her way through the living room, magazines like stepping stones laid out by a child. He'd been drinking Coors, she noticed, at least a case of empty cans stacked in a lopsided pyramid beside his chair, and for a moment she presumed to smell him, the sand he brought home in his jeans, oil and gasoline from his mowers, the sticky goop that trees left on his shirt. In the next moment, she made a lot of noise — coughing, slamming the door — the hopeful half of her certain that he would rush out of the bedroom now, or the bathroom, and lead her somewhere by the hand as he had the first time she'd come here; but she could see the holes in the plasterboard, the hammer plunged in a gash near the kitchen entry — dozens and dozens of holes, precise and in a pattern that she suspected would remain awful even from over a mile away — and she knew that Edward Lonnie Heber had lost his ability, miraculous as love itself, to appear in her life out of thin air.

In the kitchen, she found the knife on the counter, its blade crusty with dried blood. Next to it was a smeared handprint — three fingers and the heel of his palm. Another smudge. And a third, droplets spattered against the backsplash and on the floor tile leading to the hall. Her heart in her throat like a squirrel, all claws and climbing, she told herself to calm down

— "An accident," she insisted and, after another moment to believe it, insisted again — and followed the splatters to the bathroom where the sink was splotched with prints and speckles of blood, the medicine-cabinet door hanging open. He'd had an accident, she thought. He'd gotten out iodine, mercurochrome, and Curad bandages, the box of adhesive tape ripped apart as if he'd attacked it with his teeth. From the tub she picked up a towel matted with more blood. He had been crazy. And bleeding. And bending over here to — what?

Sitting on the edge of the tub, she was thinking hard about not thinking even one little bit. "Be calm," she told herself.

Later, when he came home and she could see that he'd tried to slice out the tattoo on his arm, she told him that she'd run throughout the house then, out of thoughts to think, at once furious and miserable. Numb and trembling, she opened every door, even the closets, a part of her convinced that he'd fled into one and that she'd find him curled on the floor, unconscious in a nest of shoes and workboots, only the body of him left to holler at or pound on.

She went into the backyard, she told him, into the utility room at the back of the carport, that she'd looked behind the stockade fence he'd built to hide the garbage cans from the street. She told him what her heart was doing, the ragged riot it was, and how quickly she'd run out of breath and that she'd stubbed her toe in his study when she'd seen that his X's had stopped, all of them; and that she'd only sat when she played back his messages, hearing voice after metallic voice, men and women alike — some fretful, a few downright offensive — asking where the hell he was or would he come on Wednesday; and then came her own voice, whispery and strained, at the instant she spotted his note to her on his wall calendar, a little girl's voice almost that asked him to call her, to say he was all right, that she missed him, even as she read his note once, then twice, then a third time before the sentences, clearly too ordinary to be only about him and her, made sense: "It's bad," he'd written. "I'm checking myself in. Don't know how long. I knew you'd come."

Somewhere a car horn was blasting. It seemed endless, noisy as news from hell.

I can wait, she told herself.

In the morning, she called Ruthie. She had not slept, she thought, though she did remember bolting up rigid and saucer-eyed three or four times from a dense and muddled state akin to sleep. She had been dropping down a hole, the bottom hurtling up silently to catch her.

"I'm going to have to skip my shift," she said.

"No problem," Ruthie said. "You'll miss Rae Nell's celebration, though. The ice-cream man's supposed to come by, union treat."

Ruthie went on — harmless chitchat about Rae Nell's separation, plus Mr. Probert's scowling at the pickets from his office window — but Carol Ann could not listen.

Dawn had come up sparkling and sharp, the destruction around her plain to even the most innocent eye. She was being evaluated, she felt, and the image of a big book — an old-timey ledger of a book, sizable enough for the paws of Goliath of Gath himself — had come into view. A hand seemed poised over a newly-turned page, ready to begin the burdensome process of recording about her what had been true and not.

"It could be a while," she said. "You shouldn't count on me."

"You sick, Carol Ann?" Ruthie asked. "You sound pukey."

She considered what Eddie had left her, a whole year to keep her occupied. She had been drunk, she felt, all life's elements — the mineral included — beautifully sensible now that the fog had cleared between her ears. She would clean, she had decided.

"Personal business," she said. "Eddie says howdy."

After the first room, she developed a rhythm, trying to empty her mind to keep from crawling into bed and tugging the spread over her head for a year. Still, there were times — too many times, she would remember — when she found herself stopped, her eyes fixed on a wall or a doorway, the next thing to patch or to polish too much like the last. In the bathroom, she kept finding blood everywhere, as if he'd stood in the center of the room spinning, his arm outstretched, drops flying in a spray. She imagined him under the light fixture, weeping and turning and beating his arm against the sink, his head full of squawks and howls and cries and groans, blood in streaks and splatters.

While she worked, she played his boombox — the Rascals, Simon and Garfunkel — keeping the music low so she would hear the phone when it rang. In the evening, she exercised with the barbell she'd uncovered in the storeroom by the Weber grill, and toward midnight, after her shower, she wrote letters on the portable Olivetti Eddie used for his monthly statements. "Dear Bobby," she typed, congratulating him on his marriage, on what a lively wife Sally seemed to be, and wishing him good fortune with his new baby. In too many pages, she explained their life together. They had been young, she wrote him. Babies themselves. They couldn't know what might make them joyful. Then she stopped, nothing between her brain and the keyboard but hands that seemed strange as boots on cows. In the background, the Everly Brothers were warning a bird dog to stay away from their quail; that bird dog was to leave their lovey-dove alone. "You were once a good man," she wrote. "You can be so again."

The next letter went to Eddie's kids, in care of their mother. "I am Carol Ann Mobley," she began. "I used to be a teacher." They were children, she remembered, the oldest — Petey, the towhead — no more than a seventh-grader, so she put down only those features of her character that they wouldn't be disappointed to discover on their own. "I am a Democrat," she wrote. "Except squash, I like most vegetables. I love your father very much. I oppose disloyalty and cheating. Maybe next summer we can meet, go to Yellowstone." She saw them in the wilderness, like pioneers, self-sufficient and content to feast upon the bounty nature provided. They had a house hewn from timbers Eddie had harvested. They bathed in streams, walked the hills and dales they owned. In the evening, after dinner, they stood in a circle, holding hands and looking upward to whatever eye was looking down.

That evening the last letter went to Milton E. Probert, Principal: "I quit," she wrote, adding the word *respectfully* above her signature before crossing it out. Respect had become irrelevant. As had duty and worklife and civility, all the notions which made the past the past.

"Don't give the children to Kirby Holmes," she printed on the envelope after she sealed it. "He's a jerk and a show-off."

His call came later in September while she was wishing for rain, a sooty sky of it, a grade of weather from the meaner verses of the Bible.

"It's you," she said. The letter the night before — "The last of the last," she'd told herself — had been to her parents. *I am getting married,* she'd written. *The man you met last summer. He's sick now, but he'll be well soon. Expect us for Christmas.* "Where are you?"

The VA unit, he said. William Beaumont Hospital at Ft. Bliss.

"That's in El Paso," she said. "I know that."

His reply had been toneless, impersonal as a suit, as if he'd been taught to talk by spacemen.

"I could drive down," she said. "A visit."

She didn't know how, but she could tell he was shaking his head, and after a few seconds it came, his *no.* He was in tough shape, he admitted. They'd given him stuff, the medics. Drugs. His face had puffed up. "I looked like a pumpkin," he said. A moment passed — time like a maze dark and big enough to lose your way in — before she realized he'd made a joke.

"I called your customers," she told him. "You're in California, they think, a family emergency. Most of them understood."

She had more to say — that, in fact, she'd mown several lawns herself, that she'd learned how to run the weedwhacker, that she'd even cut down an upright willow with black leaf disease. Many, many days had passed, she wanted him to know, and she was a quick study, but he was talking again, words coming to her as if they'd come to him down a wire from heaven, punctuation a courtesy only necessary to the crawling ugly order of beasts, little to suggest she wasn't listening to an angel, infernal as a machine, that could only chatter at top speed.

"Slow down, baby," she said.

Here it was then that he told her he'd cut his hair.

"It's a butch," he said. "I look in the mirror, there's a tennis ball with ears."

She remembered him as he'd been when they met — years and years ago. An eon, it seemed. There had been people — ghouls themselves no doubt. Games had been played. She could remember laughter, throaty and barking. Arms and legs and hips and corners to round, shouts that became hoots, the music of horns, all brassy and clanging like sheets of metal, and always his eyes fixed on her, no matter where she was. It was like thinking about the age of dinosaurs and bogs, the world too wet and smoky and hot to support any animals except those pea-brained and ponderous, a time of bruise-like skies and churning, molten seas when humankind was not yet even mud.

"I'm forty-one," he said. "Christ, I'm supposed to live another thirty years."

Something had ended, she realized. Something new had begun.

"Eddie," she said, "what were you doing? Before you came to school that day — all those months before you took me home?"

His answer had no consequence, she thought. They had it, the pistol. It was Russian, she recalled. Mar-something. Or Mak-. In that drawer, the screechy battered drawer. She'd held it earlier that day, light as a book you could read in an hour. It had once been Eddie's, now it seemed to be hers. Whatever. It was there — useful or not.

"I was following you," he was saying. "There are probably laws against that now, right?"

"I-Beam was mustering his courage," she suggested, his nickname from that other era.

By the same instinct of heart and happenstance that earlier she had known he was shaking his head *no*, she believed now that he was nodding *yes*, and for a second she imagined following herself as he had. Carol Ann in pursuit of Carol Ann. Seeing how crummy and humdrum her life had been. Pointing to the ruts she'd worn in the world, the lines she would not cross. But Eddie had mustered his courage, he'd caught up with her. Courage. That was all it had taken.

"When I was little," she told him, "I wanted to be someone else."

He knew the feeling, he said. Another joke without much ha-ha in it.

"A girl you read about in a magazine," she said. "With red hair. A ballerina. I could make her up and be her, Eddie. My voice changed. I had green eyes and could speak the most fluent French. Her name was Sabrina."

He liked it, he said. Sounded exotic.

Sitting at the kitchen table, the phone like a weight against her ear, she understood she had only a fixed amount of conversation left. Only a dozen words — possibly fewer — none of them less precious than gold or rare jewels from the vault of Ali Baba himself. In the background she heard hospital noises, goblins and wraiths and specters on the loose, and Eddie's breathing in the foreground like waves washing rocks. Only a few more words, she thought, then she could lie in the tub, the water to her chin, perhaps a glass of wine handy, and not know how the next minute would turn out.

"Come home, baby," she said. "Sabrina says come home."

On Tuesday Nothing, on Wednesday Walls

First among firsts here is that I am typing to you from my new apartment, a two-bedroom townhouse-like up-and-down that, according to the jumbo billboard outside my window, is part of something called the Shadow Lakes. Like many names in this New Mexico desert, it's meant to be jokey, mainly because, owing to sun and shine and sand, the property has no lakes and you'd need to stack two or three of our trees root to crown in order to hang your doomed self. Still, I am in residence, close enough to be useful to my ex-wife, Grace Hartger, if the washing machine explodes, but far enough away that my former dog, Raleigh, won't accidentally sniff me up and drop by for a no-animals-allowed visit.

It wasn't always this way. In fact, in the days before the days that are now, it — which is me and Grace Ellen and this apartment and even Brownie Woodward — *it* was downright bizarre, and too sad to have need of jokes or any other smart-mouth vocabulary meant to take the oooommmppphhh out of the unpleasant lessons we are now and then obliged to learn about ourselves. I am referring, in particular, to that month when, though divorced and as out of place in my house as is a convict at a cotillion, I was absolutely unable to move out.

"I can't do it," I told Grace Ellen one night.

We were in the TV room, me in a chair I still miss the stuffings of, Grace Ellen on the sofa a giant step away and clicking through the channels that Viacom had sold us as wee-hour entertainment.

"You can't do what?" she said.

With my shoulders I made a gesture intended to be mostly good-humored.

"Move out," I said. I was paralyzed, I told her, or too tired. Or too whatever, a blank she could fill in herself. I couldn't explain.

"You're telling me," she said, finding something she could chuckle at on the Shopping Network.

We'd been divorced for at least two weeks already, agreements made, papers signed, lawyers paid — everything done that is done when a man and a woman have long before run out of love, not to mention the words that become the stand-in for it afterward when what has kept you huffing and puffing together are only the bills you have to pay and the children you are putting through college. And so here they were, him as good as her, neither one angry or bent up, just folks in their forties seeing what could be seen now that the growing up was over and the going onward would be alone.

"Did you find an apartment?" she asked.

I had looked, I told her. The *Sun News* had an entire page for looking.

"What about renting?" she said. "Renting might impress me."

She had taken aim on me, her expression sidelong with curiosity, and it occurred to me that I ought to excuse myself, use the bathroom as my get-away, and so end up in my son Eric's room, his bunk beds having been mine for over a year.

"Grace Ellen," I said, "what would you say if I sort of paid you rent for a while?"

We were both watching the TV now, an episode of *Lucy* in which all the world's inhabitants — the neighbors, the handymen, the visitors from business and pleasure — seemed foreign and frenzied, their hands waving wildly and their faces stricken with madness.

"Harry Hartger," she began, "you are an insane man, you know that?"

I shrugged again, nearly the only thing to do when the obvious is pointed out to you so kindly.

"The deal is," she said, "I got to get on with my life."

She'd been saying that for weeks now, the "get" and "on" and "life" about as sensible to me as Turkish is to tumbleweeds.

"And you too," she told me.

For a time those words hung in the air, the savvy of them plain as paint, then she came over, made room for herself on the ottoman my feet were only partly on, and spoke to me as I imagine she speaks to the infirm she nurses when she occasionally has bad but necessary news.

"I let you stay here," she said, "and what happens? Me in one room, you in the next. That's no good, Harry Hartger. I'd get a boyfriend, and you'd be ranting and raving."

I said *Yes, ma'am*, and meant entirely the respect of it. She was being her wise self — that self of numbers and order and A+ penmanship that I, at nineteen, couldn't wait to slobber over when, as a sophomore at NMSU, she was dropped into my life courtesy of Chemistry 210 and a seating chart that had put the H's one behind the other.

"I'll tell you what," she began.

I said *Yes, ma'am* again and waited to hear the plans she'd planned for me.

"I'll help you," she said, cheerfully. "Tomorrow, after clinic. You pick me up, we'll find you a place."

She was right, of course, and I told her so — though I kept to myself the other truths that might have been told, those having to do with how frazzled I felt and how my insides were threatening to run away with my out-. In me at least, the difference between saying and doing seemed as great as the difference between being and not.

"You're a good man, Harry," she said. "We're done here, is all. Kaput."

I nodded again, being brave. And good.

"You got two sons you can be proud of," she was saying, "a business that makes you more money than you know what to do with, you don't smoke, you don't drink overmuch, you got most of your hair — Mister Hartger, you just need a place of your own, that's all. You'll see."

So I tried to.

We said good-night, stood for a moment in the hall when maybe a friendly kiss seemed possible, and then went our separate ways, her to her bedroom, me to Eric's where I lay with my hands behind my head and considered the stuff that boys leave behind when they race off to be men somewhere — the soccer trophies and the beer-bottle collection and the books about being strong or handsome or able to right the wrongs that afflict us.

Outside the wind was up, my windows rattling and the branches from our cottonwood scraping up and down on the roof like claws. Lying there, I was a knot it would take an Ahab, or an axe, to undo. Like a kid in the dark, I was reciting to myself that song about the foot bone and the ankle bone, the connections they make each to each and to all the bones of the world; and then it was morning, light and noise pouring in, and I hadn't yet come to the boniest bone of them all, that one atop your shoulders, that one you use to ram into walls that won't tumble down on their own.

You're wondering, I bet, about the *why* of our *what*. It was more than the running down of love; it was the breaking of it. I was a philanderer — a word old-school enough to be about the sort of sin my father once encouraged me to flee in fear of. I am not proud to admit this, nor would I be proud to admit that I had violated any of the other rules sent down to keep the peace among the backward and condemned kind we are. Still, for half a year, on account of the crooked thing I am, I did have a girlfriend. She was herself married and didn't seem to mind what could be done on my desk or on my office couch when work wasn't nearly as interesting as an hour spent going "Oooohhh" and "Aaahhh" or seeing new flesh sashay your way with a smile as naughty as its underwear. Yes, I was discovered; and, yes, Grace Ellen Hartger, angry as she ought to have been, directed me to stop; and, yes, I tried, but with only having my character to fall back upon and it weak as a whisper, I failed. Stories were told, me telling most of them, lies as fine and fussy as needlepoint. And promises made, me most of those too. And finally time, which seemed utterly and completely to have stopped, started jerking forward again by clanks and clinks and screeches until — inevitably, I guess — we could look at each other, Grace Ellen and her husband Harry, and see the truth of what was true long before a part of me ever touched a part of Misty C. Crumley, salesperson.

Well, the next day, as instructed, I picked Grace Ellen up; and, as I might have been instructed, I said, "Goody" to the news that she'd spent her free time — the noon hour, roughly — making calls and taking directions to the dozen places where, as it is written by Mother Goose, I might live happily ever after.

"Harry," she said, "I feel girlish again, you know?"

I hadn't felt kid-like for years.

"We got all day, honeybunch," she said. "I'll even let you take me out to dinner later."

The first few were no-no's from the get-go: too small, too dismal, too near I-10, too noisy, too dark, too flimsy — all the too's that have to do with living high and right and long. Yet hers were the gay spirits of song and dance. Her eyes twinkled, and I heard more "gee whiz's" from her in two hours than I'd heard in about twenty years, not to mention vivid and sailor-like exclamations in reference to how the dirty and shiftless and deadbeat among us leave the places in which they've been rude and otherwise ragged-minded.

By rush hour we arrived at the Shadow Lakes.

"Lordy," she said, "isn't this a sight?"

We were parked outside the manager's unit, my Caprice's air-conditioner useless against the heat God had chosen to punish us with, but I could tell that Grace Ellen was as delighted to see this place as Coronado had been his own city of gold.

"It says swimming pool," she began, reading from the ad she'd circled. "Utilities paid, including water. No kids, lease-purchase option, furnished or un-. What do you say?"

Only a year before, on my way to and from the office, I'd watched these places going up — you know the kind: on Tuesday nothing, on Wednesday walls — and now I was imagining the industry-acceptable sad sacks who lived there. It had lumps for landscape and concrete patios a Hibachi grill would look big on. Still, sad to admit, I could see myself therein, one of those peckerwoods who stroll the Mesilla Valley Mall for company and take too much pleasure in the "howdy" of the mailman.

"Grace Ellen," I said, "you could reconsider, you know."

She began refolding that paper in a manner that was both painful and astounding to watch. A minute later, it had become the size of a *While You Were Out* sticker.

"Harry Hartger," she began, "what're you afraid of now?"

I was afraid of many things — of disasters big and small, of the elements gone whichaway, of craters which might open beneath us, friend and foe alike, and swallow us hellward. Most of all, however, I was afraid of being alone and anonymous, a shuffling thing with only time and memory on its hands.

"Well?" she said.

I wouldn't be crazy, I told her. Not at all.

"Don't be a crybaby," she said. "Come on."

And so it was that we went round that layout in the company of Alicia Pinney, an Assistant Manager with hair remarkable and complicated enough to be a pretty interesting essay about what it is ex-cheerleaders graduate to after college.

"Furnished or not?" that woman wondered.

She wasn't addressing me — evidently, I was no more to this than are chickens to cheese — so I shut up.

"Not," Grace Ellen told her. "We'll get that stuff tomorrow."

For a minute, Assistant Manager Pinney went "Hmmmm," tapped her chin with her pencil, and studied most painstakingly a map of what she called "the complex."

"I have just the one," she announced.

I rather liked Ms. Pinney at that moment, in particular her toothy, rah-rah smile, and the way she hooked us by the elbows, Grace Ellen and me, to show us what was showable about the match she was making — a domicile, she assured us, that was nearly ninety percent mover and shaker. Forget for an instant that I was slow-footed as a mule and had to be turned left and right to see what was important about this. Remember only that it was something to watch how Ms. Pinney and Grace Ellen marched through that place, ooohhhing and aaahhhing about this and that, and how at the end of our tour — at the end of squealing, "Oh, boy" to disposal and trash compactor and security system and manadatory smoke alarms — they seemed to be less agent and client than sisters long and lost.

"He'll take it," Grace Ellen said.

Alicia Pinney gave a squeal an Aggie might enjoy after chugging twenty yards for a touchdown, and turned to me.

"Mr. Hartger?" she said.

I had my head cocked, like a dog. A whine had come up — in the distance, I thought, or possibly close at hand — and I feared it would not cease.

"Harry," Grace Ellen said, "get out your ballpoint."

I've thought a lot about this moment — the leading up and the falling away from it — and I have to confess to you now that somewhere between the signing of the lease and the writing of the check, I had turned dry inside. I had thoughts too, I suspect, but they were like lightning we have at the horizon out here — startling and spidery and happening to the other guy. My hand shook, I can tell you. And I believe the walls may have tilted, the way they will in dreamland. But then Grace Ellen poked me, and I came back to myself — piece by piece by broken piece — my brain pushing my hand across the page.

Shopping for furniture was similarly a matter of rolling in the direction Grace Ellen shoved. At Dunlap's department store, we picked up items useful for sleeping and eating and sitting on, plus those accessories, according to Grace Ellen, that make a house a home. She bought linens and flatware and fancy Swedish china I could show off to the people who would visit me. She got me an encyclopedia to refer to and a genuine, oil-painted picture of a snow-capped mountain alleged to be the tip-top of paradise, plus a clock radio with enough buttons and toggles to satisfy the vast and wanton intelligence of Albert Einstein himself. Somewhere along in here, I begged off. "You can do this without me," I said. And so, while she was going up and down Main Street, hunting for conveniences to keep me company, I hid out in my office, saying "yes" to those citizens who came into my showroom for the Chevies and Geos and Toyotas I sell.

Thereafter, this is how my time went: thump, thump, thump, as much between minutes as there is land between sea and shining sea. In the morning, having sneaked out of my wife's house — I couldn't bear any more carefree conversation about can openers and carving knives — I would appear at work nearly at sunrise and stay there through the evening, my only distractions those messages that my secretary Adele Fayard brought in to say that, golly, I now owned hand-blown wine goblets from Mexico or that I had napkin rings made out of real sterling silver. Mainly, I concentrated on my paperwork, the black ink of which has made me rich and a member of two country clubs. For lunch, I ordered out or picked at what I hadn't eaten the day before. I felt old, I tell you. And decrepit, with too much of myself to know but too little time to know it. Songs came to mind, silly lyrics I could not find the beat to, and every now and then I'd come awake to myself with a shudder and see that, independent of mind or method, I'd made a chain of paperclips you'd need both hands to lift.

And, alas, this too: I called Misty C. Crumley.

Clearly, I wasn't thinking. Or, if I was, I was thinking like a bird or a bug or a plant. In any event, as I would tell Brownie Woodward, there came a time — the Thursday, in fact, before I found my key taped to my bedroom door and Grace Ellen's note — when my hand grabbed the phone and the connections were made and there came Misty's voice, a decade younger than my own, saying that she knew it was me and, as she had reclaimed her former life, that I had but five-four-three-two seconds to hang up. Obviously, Harry Hartger was no more to her now than a mistake her husband Howard, and her pastor Dr. Weems, had had the generous heart to forgive her for.

"Don't bother me," she said. "Or I'm gonna call Sheriff Gribble."

She could do that, I thought. She was a woman given to direct and significant action.

"Oh, Mr. Hartger," she said, "I just want to be good, you know?"

That evening, had you looked, you would've spotted me at the El Corral Lounge, where I sat by myself and heard Uncle Roy and the Red Creek Wranglers sing the singable relative to heartache and what cowboys knew about it. I was one of several in there, but not the one with his toe tapping or unafraid to sing along, so eventually I hauled myself up to go for a drive, the hither and yon of which might look from above like the tortured trail a drunk makes falling down.

This was my low point, I thought. Only lower was the floor you could collapse on or the ground to embrace. News was coming at me from KOBE-FM, new examples of age-old double-dealing and outright tragedy, but I felt as distant from them as I did from Grace Ellen.

"Move," I said to myself, and waited for the middle of me to do what had been begged of it. "Come on," I said.

The El Corral lot was virtually empty of cars — just pickups and motorcyles and one camper you might expect a legion of gypsies to clamber out of — and I considered what it would be like to own one of those vehicles, and where on planet Earth I could venture at the wheel of it.

"Okay," I said and came near bending over in relief when my hand, as if on strings, grasped the gear shift.

An hour later, I found myself stopped outside my mother's house, that spread in Telshor Hills she moved into after my father's heart had seized up and killed him. The lights were on, and I supposed I would be welcome, but Marv Papen's truck was parked in the drive, and a part of me groaned to see it. They were lovebirds, still in the wooing and cooing stage, and I was sharp enough to recognize how awkward it would be to ring the doorbell. One of them would come to the door — Marv, probably — and then where would we be? One smitten, the other smote.

So, the inside of me slumped in the center, I turned myself about and aimed downhill.

I invite you now to watch me pull into my — actually my ex-'s — garage. That's me, suitcoat dragging behind, letting myself in through the laundry room. That's me on tiptoe, aware of the late hour and the frights that rise up in it. That's me at the sink, guzzling a glass of water. And that over by the stove? That's Raleigh, my mutt, head hardly raised, me a biped he's so bored with he doesn't have to wag anymore. And that's me too, shuffling down the hall, a light left on to show me the way. And that? Well, that's a key made by Schlage. And that — the Post-it your hero has plucked off the door to read? That, folks, is the note, typed as if for business, in which the former Mrs. tells the squinty-eyed Mister that his bags are packed and that, come tomorrow, she'll call to see how he likes the decor she's picked and whether there's enough to eat in the refrigerator.

Stay with me now. This is another ridiculous part.

I feigned being in good sprits when she called. She said how was I, and I said fine as wine, an answer I did well not to leave entirely in my throat. Then she mentioned how proud she was of me, and did I need anything anywhere, to which, after eye-balling everything which had already been done on my behalf — the pewter-topped canisters, the mahogany desk organizer, the deer-antler bookends, the thunderbird wall sconce — I said, "No, thanks."

"Harry," she said, "this'll be an adventure, trust me," a remark it took a newsworthy effort to agree with.

Aside from two dealers' conventions and several gents-only poker parties in Guy Millsap's cabin near Ruidoso, this was the first time in twenty-two years that I knew I would not be sleeping next to, or nearabouts, Grace Ellen Hartger, and for a time that evening after she called, I endeavored to find joy in that. She was right, I told myself. This was indeed an adventure — Footloose Harry Hartger and the Rest of His Lived Life — which I undertook to see myself at the center of: the clothes I might own, the pals I was yet to meet, the femme fatales who would sweep into my arms. I saw myself at the Picacho Hills Country Club, in the men's locker, telling jokes that theretofore I could get neither the gist nor the timing of. I saw myself at the Vic Tanny's on the bypass, pumping up and sweating out the half-dozen poisons that make you stupid and tired and slumpy. For an hour, folks, this was a lovely life to live, my world composed and tight and smooth at the corners, the me in it as hale as any twice-life-size hero found in Hollywood. Then the sun went down — Ker-plunk — and I was obliged to put aside the lies I was telling myself and take up again whatever it is you take up when you have been ordered out of one place and into another.

By 8:30, the time out here that "Cheers" is over, I was in pajamas and standing in front of the mirror to see how new I looked. "Well, well," I said, not in delight. Grace Ellen had picked them out, nightwear roomy enough for a circus fat man and so decorated with words — "sylvan," "verbatim," "salubrious" — that I felt like a six-foot dictionary you could read from across the street.

By nine o'clock, I had sat or stood wherever it is possible indoors to sit or stand. I had tried out my sofa, my La-Z-Boy in its every position, my dinette set, my toilet seat, the ends of my two beds. I looked out each window, raised and lowered the shades, and tried, like an assassin, to see what had wandered into my field of fire. I saw stars blinking in heaven, the Dippers and other hot hunks of gases the Martians are hiding behind. In the east, the Organ Mountains looked like dark humps, camels and buffalo and Ferdinand the Bull. Outside, my nerves ragged and spitting sparks, I rang my own doorbell and rushed in to get the full effect of its dong-dong-dong. I tried my lights, which were in fine working order, and ran the dishwasher to have more mechanicals to nod over.

"A new leaf," my ex-wife had said to me, and so, as the hours crawled away, I turned over a few. "I will read," I told the four walls looking out for my welfare, and took in hand one of the ten thousand magazines Grace Ellen seemed to have bought me. Sitting up straight, I aimed to lose myself in whatever came after the "once upon a time" it could have started with; but soon I had reached the end of a paragraph, and deep knee bends seemed like less wear and tear on the mind. After that, I thought to practice the trombone I'd put away after high school, a thought which gave way to another about where we might be in the next life, which itself gave way to a letter I could write; and then, heart kicking in my neck, I was slumped here, at this typewriter, and gazing at a page of x's and y's and number signs, that speech which is a cartoon character's when he has toppled headlong into peril or fury or common heartache.

My loneliness had shape that night. And density. And hue. In bed, I took an inventory of myself — one little piggie gone to market, another off in mischief elsewhere — and waited to count the sheep that are supposed to vault over you when it is after midnight and morning is rumored to be coming your way like a freight train. I did not toss. Neither did I turn. Rather, before I got up to sleep in the car, I lay still, arms at my side, and followed my thoughts, struggling to reconstruct — nail by board by screw — the juke joint they'd clearly come from. I mumbled the names of my children, Eric and Samuel, plus where it was I was born and what my favorite subjects had been in junior high.

"Biology," I said. "Algebra II. Edgar A. Poe."

And then, if the brain is a box, I had run out of thoughts to sort through, those remaining to me only brittle or chipped or too short to hope with.

I was at the bottom of me, clearly, amazed I had fingers to flutter or feet to stand upon. Were this situation a book, I think, I would have been at the end, that chapter wherein it is revealed who is who and what what, after which (where there should only be words about fortunes found and deeds dared) there is nothing except a note about the mean-minded pissant who'd been stingy enough in his heart to create such a brutish hoax.

So I got up — not moaning, not sighing — and threw on my overcoat to go out to my car to wait for daylight where, as it turned out, a compassionate Assistant Manager named Alicia Pinney woke me up and sent me forward again.

The letter from Brownie Woodward arrived after nearly a month of this unbecoming behavior — a month of sleeping in the car or, more often, on my creaky office couch; a month of finding myself unable to stay in my apartment much after dark, a month of saying I was in when I was so clearly out; a month of saying *yes, terrific* to Grace Ellen's questions regarding my life on the loose; a month, I have to tell you, that seemed to have taken ten to pass.

He'd been thinking, he wrote. His own life had gone round and round, and he'd been ruminating about it — the in and out it had been and how, as crock to crow about, it wasn't much more than your standard one-page résumé, a piece of history he wouldn't know at all but for the fact that, Jumping Jesus, he was actually living it.

"This is the thing," Brownie had scrawled. "I saw a movie the other night. On cable. *Stand by Me* — maybe you know it?"

Sure. It was your familiar buddy movie, with your basic fat kid, your misunderstood hood kid, your kid from Loserville, and a sober Richard Dreyfuss as your humble narrator.

"Anyways," Brownie wrote, "it had a line in there about the friends you make at twelve being the friends you make for life. Something like that."

I didn't know that at all; guess I'd fallen asleep before they'd gotten to the moral parts. Still, I'm a sucker for plain talk like that, a statement without the *but*s and *if*s and *maybe*s that get between you and knowing one perfect thing between the ears.

"The other thing is," Brownie had said, "I've got a layover in El Paso next week. Thought you could drive down and we'd meet at the airport. Or the Hilton across the street. We'll get together. Be twelve again. Ha-ha."

He had more to say, of course — that he was doing fine ("still stroking and poking," he said), and that he hoped the same for me — but, as we used to put it, the meat of the meat of it was this: he missed me, missed as well the youth we'd had, and was at a point now where he could, courtesy of Delta Airlines and his job, reintroduce himself to the fellow with whom he'd swum the flumes and drunk beer and learned the wa-watusi.

So what did I say, he wondered. Was I game for a trip down memory lane? Or was he, Brownfield Woodward the second, just a pear-assed sentimentalist with lousy taste in movies?

I was out of my chair at this point and looking west from my window. Beyond, but far enough away to make you dizzy, was the mesa leading up out of the valley; and beyond that, the desert, sixty miles of which separated me and the next town with any daydreamers in it, Deming; and beyond that, more miles and more hardy scrub that thrives on dirt and wind and heat. Desert everywhere. A clean but inhospitable plain of prickle and thorn and spike, with bare and vicious-looking mountains thrust up to remind us that, without scales or wings or wriggly feelers, we were as wrong and useless as tits on a teacup.

"Call me," Brownie had scribbled, and I seemed about to.

Before circumstance had separated us — him to the United States Army, me to the rigors of frat life (Phi Delt) and Business Administration — we'd been pals in that desert, ours a two-member club that read *Battle Cry* by Leon Uris and climbed C Mountain, the flattened mound our high school whitewashed every fall. When Kennedy was shot, we'd had Mrs. Sutherland for American History, hers the shapeliest legs teenagers in the eleventh grade could gaze upon. We'd been to Juarez, lost our cherries to the same whore in a dive called White Lace. Our first drunk was together, a bottle of Frangelica my mother had forgotten about. We'd even bought a car together, a '61 VW bug, painted it optic orange and used it, on alternate evenings, to court the same sweetie, Miss Michelle Parker (now of, so I hear, Columbus, Ohio).

And then, as Grace often said when I began to worry over the past, the future came and it was time to fish or cut the goddamn bait.

"Brownie," I announced when he snatched up the phone, "you get to be the fat kid, all right?"

That night I got drunk. Not sloppy or all at once, but as I imagine my accountant, Archie Meents, might: one drink upon another upon another until the sum of you — eyeball, arm, and ear — is sodden and about as appealing as nose hair.

After work, I drove to Grace Ellen's. She'd gone to her sister's in Albuquerque for a visit, and it had fallen to me to take in her mail and let Raleigh dig in the backyard for an hour or so. I felt good, tucked in at the edge of myself, able to move from A to B without washing up elsewhere in the alphabet.

I talked to my mother briefly, heard two or three jokes

that had come to her via her bald boyfriend. Marv Papen, I learned, had the gift of gab.

"How's your place?" she asked. "I've been meaning to get by."

It was okay, I told her, at a loss for other lingo.

"You seeing anybody, Harry?" she wondered. "You got to get out some."

She'd been talking with Grace Ellen, I guessed.

"That's no secret," she said. "I like that girl, son. Always have."

I had a beer in hand — maybe one several months old — and I was watching Raleigh whirl around in search of a tail that seemed to have betrayed him.

"What about that woman?" my mother asked.

A piece of me cracked loose then and went rattling downward. The last time I'd seen Misty C. Crumley, she'd told me how much, in the climbing on and off of love-making, I reminded her of her husband Howard. "Plus you got a cute fanny," she'd said. "I like 'em spongy."

"I don't know who you're talking about," I said.

"That Pinney person," my mother said. "Alicia Pinney. Marv knows her father. Hell, Marv Papen knows everybody. Says he's gonna run for Congress."

I thought about Assistant Manager Pinney. She'd made a habit out of catching me sleeping in my car. The other day, she'd wagged her finger at me, made me sit with her over coffee and *my-my*ed her way through the middle plot developments of this misadventure. "Knew a guy like you one time," she'd said. "Married a sixteen-year-old and went to Fiji."

"I got to go, Mother," I said. "Something's burning."

I was making my way toward a second beer now, and considering what should best come after.

"Your poppa would've known what to do," she said. "That man had an answer for everything."

She was right: my father had had more ideas than Bayer has aspirin. He'd had the idea to teach his dog, Mooch, to sneeze, and did so. He'd had ideas about the Tri-Lateral Commission, plus about who was diddled when Reagan sat down with Nancy to make high crimes and misdemeanors. He'd had ideas about what was good for you (exercise and sunlight and regular napping) and what was not (sugar from Cuba and dancing on Sunday); and it had become my private belief that ideas — the awful weight of them, the massive pile they made — were as hard on the heart as they were on the head.

"One more thing," my mother was saying.

Outside, Raleigh had contrived to get my attention by doing a backflip.

"Was that you outside the house the other night?" she asked. "Marv peeked out the windows. Said a prowler was picking his nose in a Caprice."

I remembered — her house ablaze with light and loud music, her only child weeping in his car.

"Next time, come on in," she said. "He was teaching me rope tricks. We needed an unbiased observer."

After that, I had me a Scotch, three cubes and four fingers — enough, so my daddy once declared, to take the pitter out of your patter. It was dark now, and my erstwhile neighbors were returning home from the things they do (which, I was inclined to think, were as much about mischief as they were about money). I had known these people for years — many of them, the Hubbards and the Prescotts and old Ace Perkins, for over a decade — but I found myself unable to guess what made them go when going was called for, or stop when the signal came for that. They were not crass-minded or likewise wretched. They were not he-men or heroines, not fancy-pants or much given to the lah-di-dah in personal comportment. In a movie, they'd be much as I was — one of the thousands who get to walk on and gasp when a mystery tumbles from the sky.

Another Scotch. Same fingers, fewer cubes.

Outside, I threw a stick for Raleigh, shook my head over his version of meaningful activity. I had the lights on, our backyard lit up like Yankee Stadium, and, feeling foolhardy and reckless, I undertook to practice my pitching motion. I was Nolan Ryan and Goose Gossage and Fernando Valenzuela, and then, when the booze bushwhacked me, I was the Wild Man of Borneo, and Raleigh and I had settled in to watch his stick whirl over the cinder block wall into the darkness.

"Damn," I said.

Raleigh trotted back to sit at my feet, his expression unmistakably pitiful, as if he were appealing to whatever God dogs have for the power of speech. The phone had started ringing — Grace Ellen, it would turn out to be — but Raleigh had commenced a lecture about what a sorry so-and-so I was; and I, in a world cracked down the center, was impressed enough to let him finish.

"My apologies," I said, stumbling over a dozen newly necessary s's.

"Ruff-ruff," he said, which is canine for *spare me.*

Indoors, I switched to bourbon and stood guard over the phone in the kitchen.

"Ring," I commanded, and, when I was thirsty again, it did.

"Harry Hartger," she said, "is that you?"

Que pasa, I had muttered, and almost immediately discovered I was sputtering Spanish.

"Harry?" Alarm had crept into her voice.

No, caramba, I said, then squawked some gobbledygook that might have sounded sensible coming from a mouth-breather like Pancho Villa. I wasn't supposed to be here. I was supposed to be in Apt. 4F, Shadow Lakes, being a being on its own, and the recognition of that had driven me into babble and fear.

"*No se,*" I said, before hanging up. "*Naranjo, la boca, el diablo.*"

Here it was that I made the choice to drink from the bottle.

She would call again, I knew. Right now she was probably ringing my apartment — double-checking — or gabbing to her sister Marge about the dingaling she'd once married in St. Timothy's on Alameda Street. Me? I was having a debate with the cabinet and countertops I leaned against. I imagined the picture I was: tie loosened, shirtsleeves rolled up, head wobbling atop the stick of me, ideas spilling out like water through a sieve. In the living room, the clock had begun to chime the hour — ten o'clock — and I obliged myself to scramble in there to tell it to pipe down. I had once wanted to be a race-car driver, so I sped around that room in high gear, my mouth a motor, me a contraption in danger of losing traction on the turn.

The phone rang again when I was in the hall exchanging pleasantries with a wall I seemed enamoured of. I had turned on her answering machine and knew I had a few seconds to wait before she'd be scolding me again.

"Harry Hartger," she said presently. "I know you're there."

Words had come to me, but not any I could move from mind to mouth: *help* and *sorry* and *please*.

"You pick up the phone right now," she ordered, but I was heading elsewhere, trying to keep the right side right side.

"Oh, Harry," she said, exasperated, "this is not funny."

From the doorway of my former bedroom, I agreed. I could find nothing amusing about the lurching I was doing, nor about the limbs of me I was shocked to find.

She really upbraided me then, several sentences that gave me to understand that she knew where I had actually been sleeping at night, and how I was, this evidence to the contrary, a big damn boy and that my behavior was no more flattering to me than was stealing from the collection plate; seconds later Marge grabbed the line to second that emotion. "This is shameful," she said. "You know better than this, Harry. You have a better nature, now live up to it."

With a click like a boom, they hung up, and I was rolled up against the bed, regarding the underside of my world. I was speaking to myself as well, saying, "Head, do this" or "Arm, do that," but the two of them, and all they were attached to, were ignoring me. I didn't feel ruined, I think, just disconnected and widespread, like parts for a thingamabob you've lost the instructions for. I missed Grace Ellen, was all. She had a nightie I missed the touch of, and a way of sleeping sprawled that was a full-time challenge to avoid. I missed her haircut and that gum she could pop like a backfire. It was grief I think I had — grief which is ache and throb and pinched breath and you only able to meet yourself with a "Huh?" or other syllable that can mean eight things at once.

Then I was sober.

I was sober, and I was in her walk-in closet, the door closed behind me.

She was on the machine again, surely saying what she'd said before — "Harry, go home; you go home now" — and I, in the jungle of her wardrobe, the smells of her everywhere, was saying that, Lordy, I was home. I touched a sweater whose stripes made her look taller, and a dress that disguised the belly she fretted about. A blouse came to hand, and another that felt like skin to my face.

You may not understand this twist of the story, how the up had become down, the left right or under over, but I do. I see me smiling and breathing deeply. I hear again the music in my head, that tinkly-jingly produced by xylophone or accordion or kazoo — instruments it is not possible to frown in the company of. Best of all, I see me lay me down to sleep, my pillows her shoes and boots and slippers, my blankets a dozen outfits I know the price and occasion and mood of — things to wear when you're glad or serious or ready for the world to call you by name.

A week later, Brownfield Woodward strode off his plane like a man used to being first in line. He found me, and, until he came to a halt within hugging distance and started laughing, he bore down on me like a guy late for his own parade.

"What's so funny?" I said, confused.

I'd been to the men's room and thought my zipper was down or maybe I had toilet paper hanging from my pants. I felt about as picturesque as a car wreck.

"Look at us," he said.

After a week of sleeping behind my desk, plus the taking up again of cigarettes that I'd found you could smoke two or three of at a time, I was in no condition to look. I'd spent last night on a line road in the desert behind the university golf course, watching the twilight thicken, talking to a telephone pole and trying to make contact with the wildlife hooting and shrieking around me.

"What do you mean?" I wondered.

He pointed. Me, then him.

"Twins," he said. "Alphonse and Gaston. Tweedledum and Tweedledee."

I followed his finger back and forth. I took note of his suit — blue — and my own. Blue, too.

"Red ties," he said.

His had teeny sailboats on it, mine a sprinkling of something like rice.

"Let's see the shoes," I told him. A picture of Grace Ellen had come to mind, vivid as fist-fighting, and I was trying to keep myself from toppling over in a heap.

"Tassels," he said.

I indicated my own. "Lace ups."

He looked good — maybe too good, I want to tell you; maybe his features had been lifted and polished, the left-over skin gathered up under his hair and held in place by staples and wires and thread. Still, he was more or less the slope-shouldered middleweight he'd been.

"Let's get a drink," he said. "I hate riding with the poor."

I'd last seen him over twenty-five years before when we'd driven (yes, in our VW bug) to the Post Office on Water Street one morning at dawn so he could catch the U.S. Army bus to the induction center in Ft. Bliss. That August had been unexpectedly cold, frost on everything, and we'd stood around with about twenty other kids, mostly wisecracking and listening to one wall-eyed pachuco suffer through a teary adios from his mother (and about five minutes from his father concerning what a stupido he was). The bus had arrived after that, and everybody shut up when the sergeant, having identified himself as the meanest mother in the valley, called roll. We'd shaken hands then, Brownie and I. "Take care," he told me, and I assured him I would. Care was my middle name. "Let me know how it goes with Michelle Parker," he said. And that was the end of it: he'd climbed aboard, the bus tooted twice, and now here we were, brought together by crapola from a movie and the crosswise proofs that are time and the U.S. Post Office.

"Brownie," I said. "I got something to tell you."

We'd taken a table in the concourse lounge by the window, and down below us on the tarmac were a handful of ramp guys chewing the fat on those miniature trucks they have.

"My wife and I," I said, "we're divorced."

Here it was, I think, that I should have realized that we weren't twins at all, just fellows with a common root in the past, him as much a stranger now as he had been a friend then. But I didn't. I had my mouth open, my brain was go for liftoff, and there was little to do but get out of the way of myself: so I told him.

Everything. Misty C. Crumley. Howard Crumley, her husband. Crawford Prouty, my attorney. The Shadow Lakes. What sleep is like in the backseat of a car. Brushing my teeth at work. Grace Ellen's closet. Telling my boys what a bum their old man was. My mother. Her bunkbuddy, Marv Papen. How my dreams seemed broken down the center, or warped and crumbly. The cold that runs in the joints and freezes you up cell by cell. And then I was finished, and the guys on the tarmac below had all gone wherever it is they go when it gets dark.

"Misty?" Brownie said.

For the first time I took a sip of what had become mostly water in front of me.

"It was lust," I told him. "Pure and simple."

He nodded, obviously acquainted with the phenomenon.

"Assistant Manager Pinney?"

"She's watching out for me," I said. "Like a sister. Comes over at all hours to make sure I'm not passed out in the flower beds. She's a firecracker. Likes to play Twister."

He shook his head a little at that, sighed in a way that sounded like *Jesus H. Christ*, and for a moment I felt I'd shot through a door to a kingdom where what you are is as clear to you as is the difference between a kitchen match and a flamethrower.

"You'll get over it," he said. "Easy come, easy go — you know how it is."

Overhead Muzak was pouring down — Otis Redding without the hardship and the spit — and I, telling myself I could leave now, took note of what was outside and up.

"Had a guy threaten to shoot me once," Brownie was saying.

Be polite, my mother had always told me, and I was. Brownfield Woodward, loud and indifferent, had become company to pass an evening with. Pass and move on, I told myself.

"Vietnam?" I asked.

Germany, he said. The Army had turned him into a disc jockey, given him a zillion watts of power and let him blast Beatles records at the communists. "No," he said, "this was later. After discharge. My first wife's father."

"First wife?"

He held his arms out wide, the whole room included.

"Busted dreams," he said, and a minute later he was into the part of his story that came after the parts about Uncle Sam and going to college in Georgia and, several years down the line, finding himself working for Ted Turner's TBS and learning how to root for the Atlanta Braves.

I wasn't listening very hard, I have to tell you. Sure, his life was full of hoopla — a wife Alice, kids, a cat that messed on the rugs — and I made sounds to say that I was hearing some of it, but mainly I was shaking my head over the pair of us. And then, happily, I wasn't hearing anything at all. In fact, I seemed to be across the room, unrelated to the look-alikes by the window, me merely a guy with a hundred bucks in his pocket, a place to go afterwards, and a handful of notions about how to get there.

"I got no complaints," Brownie said at last.

The bar was empty now, and Brownie excused himself to go to the gents', stopping by the register to pay the bill. I was thinking again about Grace Ellen. Before taking to the desert last night, I'd stopped by to pick up the birthday present Eric had sent me from college. It was a belt, silver-tipped and braided, just the fashionable thing for my leisure hours. The whole time I was there, Grace Ellen didn't say a word to me. She just stood in the doorway, arms crossed, hers the expression she reserves for Raleigh when his behavior has been way out of bounds. Her hair was up, the flyaway parts almost tendril-like, and on her cheek was a smudge that only twenty months before I might have asked to taste the grit of. From the doorway behind her music was pounding out — Eric's kind, all about the humps and hollows you think you can avoid by being careful and smart — and she had on the jeans that pulled her butt up high and tight. It came to me then — probably the way insight comes to scientists, or the devil's voice from the TV to the nutty — that I loved her. I had been wrong: love was not gone; it had been there, on two legs in front of me, and I, breathless and tongue-tied as an idiot, then stumbled backwards from the door, the sidewalk rolling under my feet, trying to say goodbye.

"I'm taking a few days off next month," Brownie said when he got back to the table. "Why don't I come up for a visit. Be your houseguest."

"What about Alice?" I said. "The kids?"

They could fend for themselves, he said. This was modern times, people fended like there was no tomorrow.

We were almost back to the gate. In a half-hour he'd be five miles overhead, and I'd be halfway up I-10, fending for my own self and trying not to wander the map till sunup. It was almost laughable.

"We'll raise some hell," Brownie said. "I want to see how the old town is."

We'd shaken hands again, and he'd tightened the knot of his tie, and then, while we waited on either side of his briefcase, I told him about Michelle Parker. I felt sixty percent good. This was fact, like his what-me-worry remark about his gun-toting father-in-law, and I was going to take considerable comfort in giving it.

"Dumped her," I told him. "Right after the Fourth of July picnic. Started dating a Zeta Tau named Carol Mobley."

He seemed to take that in, chew the ends of it.

"Never liked Parker's laugh," he said. "Horsiest laugh in America."

For a minute we watched the stampede toward the door and the Delta guy who'd organized it. Brownfield Woodward, I was saying to myself. A name alien as any from Zulu.

"What about the VW?" Brownie said at last. "I really liked that car."

Destroyed it, I told him. Drove off an overpass the next summer. Lost control. While he was in Germany yapping at the Reds, I was flying through the air trying to get to Grace Ellen's house.

The reason we don't have eyes in the back of our heads, my father used to say, is that if we were to part our hair — or lift high our hats — all we'd see is the wreckage we've run from. Sure. And maybe that's just one more idea added to those others that killed him. I don't know. All I know is that when I pulled into my parking space in front of my apartment — Alicia Pinney walking away from my doorstep — I felt empty, the husk of me filled with light and wind and dust.

"What's that?" I asked, pointing to the dish Alicia had set on my porch.

"Tuna casserole," she said. "I had extra."

I told her thanks and made to unlock my door. It was dark, the sky like velvet, the breezes cool and steady out of the west, and I was having three thoughts, then thirty — all of them simple and similar, like buttons in a bucket.

"You going somewhere?" I said. Hers was an outfit yellow as sunset and short as what girls wear when school is out.

"Grace Ellen's," she said. "We're playing Yahtzee."

That was fine, I thought, and said so with the Vegas smile you'd expect from a car salesman. The Shadow Lakes. Home. I was as new and clean inside as the apartment I'd opened. I had a second question, one for which I had the words, and soon enough, nothing about me trembling, I had summoned the courage to ask it.

"There'll be gentlemen, I guess," I said.

Alicia Pinney gulped, a bit embarrassed, and allowed as how, yes, there would be gentlemen. One for each of them.

I could see what awaited me inside — knick-knacks and geegaws and furniture — and I was trying to attend to both the indoors and the news coming from Assistant Manager Pinney.

"That's fine," I told her.

I was thinking about water — from the sky and the sea, from the hose and springs that gushed out from underground. Water upon water upon water. A torrent of it rising here and elsewhere. And after a time the water stopped, its surface like foil all the way to the horizon, light spinning off it in splinters and spears, and Alicia Pinney's mouth was open and I could hear her calling to me from the last dry acre in America.

"You okay, Harry?"

The air-conditioning had kicked on, a blast of it frigid on my face.

"Just sleepy," I told her.

She had placed the casserole dish on the coffee table and stood at the door again, ready to go.

"I'll check on you tomorrow," she said.

And then she had left, and the water, denser and warmer and clearer than you'd think, was rising again, good in the way that water is to those without it.

A Man Bearing Snow

When the bombing started, Jonathan realized he stood in danger of using again. It was a feeling both frightful and exciting, having to do once more with going as far and as fast as physics and laws respecting human durability allowed, and for an hour, before he called Willie and while he listened to the blizzard beat at his house, he imagined himself as he had been twenty-two months before — unspeakably happy, albeit strung out and bloated, as attractive as spoiled meat.

"It's a weird time for addicts," he said.

"It's a weird time for everybody," Willie said. "Just ask the camel jockeys."

Theirs was a foul connection, the distance from Cleveland to North Hollywood filled, it seemed, with squeaks and bristling noises somehow reminiscent of gristle on bone.

"Speak up," Willie was saying, "I got world-class distraction here."

"That's what you always say." Willie had dozens of distractions in his life, among them a wife, Nikki, a monster house in Palos Verdes, and a daughter, Alexandra, at Stanford.

Jonathan stole another look, his zillionth, at the TV. No change. As much outgoing as incoming.

Maybe, he thought, it had been a mistake to call. Maybe Willie would be something less than sympathetic.

"I should've been a priest," Willie was saying. "A one-day work week. Jesus, I got more comings and goings than LAX. I got a guy wants his fiddlehead ferns on his fois gras — go figure."

Willie went away once, twice — hand cupping the mouthpiece, muffled chatter in the background, the whole bit — before returning with a rush that Jonathan thought unique to the busy world of eating and appetite.

"Hold on, amigo," Willie said, "I'm getting a fax from the ICM poohbah. He's got a yen for tuna nachos and cornpone."

They had known each other over twenty-five years, dating back to Lovett College at Rice University. Many times as undergraduates, like fish heaved onto the muddy banks of a river, they had found themselves flopping about on land when the sun came up — drunk or stoned, often both, giggling but still able to address issues of mutual importance. They, smart-aleck cowboys, had a history together. Now, earnest as an undertaker, Willie was waxing eloquent about mango sorbet, lobster medallions, and rosettes of chestnut puree, and Jonathan feared they had no history at all. Only a past.

"We're bidding the Oscars this year," Willie was saying. "It's like Iraq but without the gunplay. In my trade you must be fast and accurate. You must be sneaky, too. Sneaky is the mogul's analogue for good luck."

Jonathan watched his hand, which was trembling again, and then looked ceilingward toward a noise somewhere in heaven to deal with. They had returned. The heebie-jeebies.

"I was up in the Hills last night, a Halloween party, very posh — misrule and such, ladies in lamé. We frapped till the cows came home."

"So there were movie stars," Jonathan said. "Sounds like fun."

"I hobnobbed, my friend. Elbows, shall we say, were rubbed. They were eating, almost literally, from my hand."

Jonathan tried to conceive of it, movie stars at their feed. He liked telling his Ohio acquaintances that his best friend, William Clark Perry, was a caterer; from him, Jonathan had learned that Cher, like royalty and tyrants, employed a full-time food-taster. There were worse ways, Willie had said, of earning thirty K a year.

"Say, do you think I could come out there?"

"You don't want to do that," Willie said.

Jonathan considered the disorganized personality of his surroundings, in particular his cluttered desk. A lot of collateral damage there too.

"Oh, but I do," he said. "How 'bout a little hospitality, my friend?"

"Trust me," Willie said. "The timing is all wrong. I'm up to my ass in asparagus and almond paste."

Jonathan closed the volume nearest him, *Decedents' Estates and Trusts*. Months ago, a client had died, suddenly and remarkably intestate, whereupon it had fallen to Jonathan, as legal-eagle and master of the mumbo-jumbo, to figure out how to divvy up the DuPont-like assets, among them a vicious half-breed dog named, unaccountably, Blue Boy. Of the heirs — all Episcopal bigots sharing, besides the name Clifford, greed of Homeric proportions — none wanted the beast, so several minutes had passed in one senior partner's office yesterday when Jonathan feared he would be asked to board the unruly animal at his place. Worse yet, owing not only to his junior status but also to some unbecoming feature in his character, he knew he would have replied, without hesitation, "Yes."

Now he struggled to remember where, in fact, the dog was.

"I saw a sign yesterday," Willie was saying. "From the freeway. This was in Santa Monica. Actually read, *Oral, Anal and Kink Here*. This is just too much for the Texas boy in me."

"This is your idea of a joke?"

Right, Willie said. His idea. Jonathan was better off in Cleveland. Cleveland was a very serious city.

Jonathan heard himself breathing, ragged and shallow, an individual in incipient distress. He checked himself for other symptoms — cold sweats, ear-ringing, retinal flashing. It was time to speak straight.

"I'm out here — what? — twenty-some years," Willie was saying. "I still feel like a tourist. Just got a more expensive wardrobe."

"I'm getting ready to go off the wagon," Jonathan began, stunned by the quaintness of his speech. "Big time, Willie. I got the heebie-jeebies bad."

Static rose up on the line, like fires crackling.

"Speak slow, Jon-boy, you're mumbling."

He said it again — the cravings, the rise and fall inside, the memory fades, the way time had hills and ridges and ruts, the palpitations, the voices that gargoyles have.

"Damn," Willie said, very nearly a word with no meaning, a sound like a sneeze, then Jonathan was told to hold for a jiffy: more distractions, not the least being the Porsche man. "When was the last time you bought a car?" it seemed Willie had been saying a minute earlier. "They come to your house, your place of business. You are quizzed, a history is taken. Talk about the frigging heebie-jeebies."

On the portable TV could be seen war footage, Baghdad lit up and exceedingly spooky. Like a Christmas tree, the pilots had been saying for the last hour. Fourth of July. Years and years before, Jonathan had seen the same phenomenon outside Long Binh up near the Laotian border. It remained as noteworthy to him now as it had then to the E-3 typist-personnelman he'd been. He could remember the radio chatter, the showers of sparks, the bombs bursting in air, the muted whomp-de-whomp left behind when the flyboys turned toward Guam. Fourth of July indeed.

"Sorry," Willie was saying, "you can't believe the headache this is. Dietary needs, colors, textures — it's food, for Christ's sake. The junk is to be eaten, not worshipped."

"Look," Jonathan said, "I shouldn't have called — "

" — Wait a second, buddy. You're not fooling, are you?"

Jonathan allowed as how he was definitely not fooling. Since detox, fooling — Willie should forgive the lame but appropriate figure of speech — was a province entered only in full battle gear, night-fighter cosmetics included.

"Shit," Willie said, worry in his voice at last. "What've you done?"

Jonathan thought about his recent activities, specifically several calls to players and pashas in what he assumed could only be termed the narcotics industry.

"Just say yes, okay?" he asked. "I may not come, but I'd like to have the option just the same."

"Crapola," Willie said, and immediately, Jonathan recognized how much more than miles stood between them. *Crapola* was a word with a lot of meaning, none of it appropriate in this desperate a context.

"I'm gonna hang up," he said, feeling woebegone and contemptible. "Think of this as a bad dream. Really, I'm ashamed of myself. I'm doing some bonehead stuff lately."

"Man," Willie was saying, evidently more for his own benefit than for anyone else within earshot. "Man, man, man."

"Pretty strange, huh?"

"Plain exasperating, my friend," Willie said. "I thought you were doing AA, Al-Anon. You made promises."

For an instant, Jonathan thought to deny it.

"I tried, honest. The flesh is weak, Willie. The flesh is certifiably feeble."

"Don't tell that to Nikki. She'll kick your butt from here to Hialeah."

Jonathan studied a face on TV: ashen, a little goggle-eyed, semi-grotesque. A long night, he reasoned, lay ahead. Perhaps, given the gruesomeness and horrors now in residence between his own ears, many long and terrible nights.

"Listen, Willie," he said, "I feel better already, really. I didn't mean to frighten you."

"What's Donna say? What's her point of view on this?"

Something important inside gave an ugly lurch upward beneath his breastbone, and a vision of her arose before him — shimmering and, like a cubist painting, composed of hair attached to eyes attached to toes attached to knees — but he sought to keep to himself the knowledge that as of a month ago he had no girlfriend named Donna. Some details Willie just did not need to know. Not yet.

"I'm gonna get off, Willie. I got someplace to go, an appointment. Say howdy to Nikki for me, okay?"

"I'm scared for you, compadre."

Jonathan reflected upon it — Willie, in his offices on La Cienega Boulevard, big as Humpty Dumpty, his Brussels sprouts on the boil, waiting for the Porsche man, afraid. The cows had definitely come home.

"Me, too," he said. "I'm scared for me too."

Again, Jonathan confronted the image of himself in Long Binh, a Bachelor of Arts in History at ease in a lawn chair, Thai stick in hand, Jimi Hendrix on the 8-track, watching ordnance of epochal fury falling at the horizon. That's how it had been over twenty years ago. Now it was different — all video games, and Starfleet versus Klingons, microchips and lasers, witchery from the next century of science. Then, before Willie could be heard saying "Yes," Jonathan found himself wondering about the dog, the ill-tempered Blue Boy, and the many Cliffords who might own him, not to mention a comely dental assistant named Donna.

"Sure," Willie was saying, "c'mon out. We'll do Disneyland again, I'll take you for a spin."

That was great, Jonathan said. Better than great.

"But no dope, my friend. Alex says dope is loserville. Booze is done now. We'll go up to Palo Alto, get plastered with my daughter."

"I could help cook," he suggested. "You could send me on errands, give me one of those hats to wear. I look snappy in headgear."

Willie laughed heartily. He was, Jonathan could tell, relieved to have found humor in this phone call.

"No market here for Ball Park franks," he was saying. "In the hills, pal, we don't melt cheese, we flay it."

And then Jonathan had hung up: it was just him alone, plus various voices from CNN saying what it was like where the wickedness was.

He took a bath, as hot as he could stand. He had gone around the house, switching off lights, tidying up, pretending that his mind hadn't entirely left him, but while the water filled the tub and he sat idly in it, he fell victim anew to logic that delivered him at length to the conclusion he dreaded most about himself: it was time, ladies and germs, to bump up again.

"Huh-oh," he said wearily. As if on a tether, he had been dragged to the brink of himself, and he had no problem seeing Jonathan Wayne Gordon, Esq., the flake having come again so easily to hand, putting it up his nose, rubbing it against his gums, even — and here he chuckled a little at his own kookiness — peeling back his skull to sprinkle it, like powdered sugar, atop the glistening, tender wrinkles of his brain.

It was insight which raised him out of the tub and back to the phone. He would call Merri Jane, he thought, and then whatever was happening with him would happen in a different way. Merri Jane was hard-nosed, not above demanding he stand on his head and cluck, and what he understood was that he needed someone to tell him what to do and to provide the conscientious instruction by which the doing would be most effectively done.

"A month or two, then *shazam*, it's Little Lord Fauntleroy

ringing my bell," she said at first. "This sure is a peculiar turn of events, isn't it?"

"What can I say?" he began. "I'm in the wilderness, I need a lover."

"You need a collar and leash, Jon-boy. You've been very ugly to me."

He imagined her at the other end of the line. She was a marvel, truly. Romance with her required the same intelligence and attention to the fine print as did filling out a robber baron's tax return. He didn't know what he'd do if she said no.

"Morally speaking," she was saying, "I have the high ground here, correct? A virtual vista. I mean, as far as tawdry affairs go, right?"

"Of the high grounds," he assured her, "you have the loftimost."

"Goody gumdrop," she said. "I like being able to see the so-called rubble strewn across the barren plain."

Jonathan was thinking about her husband, an engineer with city planning. He liked Ray Riley. They'd met at the firm's Christmas party, and Jonathan had been tickled to discover, courtesy of conversation on the topic of poontang, that the spouse of the woman he'd been cheating with was himself not unfamiliar with deceit and irony.

"This is positively karmic," Merri Jane was saying. "I tried your office this afternoon. Your secretary didn't have a clue."

Jonathan remembered little about himself at lunch. He recollected the hour and the place but nothing afterward save anxiety and unseemly self-absorption.

"Is he there?" he asked. "The Ray-man."

Negative, she said. The Ray-man, poor guy, had a meeting at the mayor's office, a train trestle in politically urgent need of repair. The Ray-man would not be home till late. Real late.

"So you could come over?" Jonathan said. "Or we could meet halfway."

"I'm a Gemini," she said. "We're headstrong, heedless. We, sweetie pie, do not dillydally. We get hungry, we eat. We get horny, we honk."

"Very sexy," he said. "What about Libras?"

She seemed to snicker. She loved this part too, the pre-coital badinage.

"Libras, dear heart, can't find their heinies with both hands and a road map. I brook no folderol from such as they."

He imagined himself as he was after every encounter with her, exhausted and moderately sore in the joints. The first time, Merri Jane had finessed him into the third-floor conference room, hiked her skirt to show him underclothes that would turn out to be as interesting to her as they were appealing to him — garter belt and black thong panty, he remembered. "It's the Frederick's look," she'd explained. "On the outside, I'm Supergirl. Underneath, it's one hundred percent Madame Whoopee." In the clinch, she'd advised him that hers was a ferocious carnal appetite that more readily led to rough stuff than it did to love. She also had an intriguing argot, archaic expressions like "perforce" and "betimes," and it was often disconcerting, on the downside of orgasm, to hear, in place of the customary small talk, an exclamation like "alas" or "hark" or "forsooth." It was like waking up in the sixteenth century.

"You've been avoiding me," she was saying now. "That's not nice, Jon-boy. I see you ducking around corners, very childish."

"I've been busy," he said, thinking that if need be, he'd tell her about the Cliffords and Blue Boy, even about his plans to split his head open and let the light come shooting out.

"And now you want me?"

That was the idea, he said, but said so in too many words.

"Maybe there's someone else now," she began. "Mayhap I am elsewhere spoken for."

He could believe that. Merri Jane was a very special girl.

"What about your sweetie?" she asked. "Isn't that what co-habitation is all about?"

He had a choice, he saw. He could tell the story. Or not. He thought about the snow outside. Snow and more snow. Piling up in feet. So he told her — that his girlfriend, sigh, had left him — and afterwards he was happy he had done so without any panic creeping into his voice.

"So you're randy and bereft, how sad."

Sad-schmad, he said. He was trying to be brave. In many ways, he was trying to be more like a Boy Scout. Mature, responsible, all the etceteras.

Something was banging around inside the walls of his head like a bag of marbles, and when it stopped Merri Jane was her old self again, wired and full of whoop-de-do.

"Say it," she was telling him. "You're needy."

"I could weep," he offered.

"You could beg forgiveness," she said. "You could abase yourself."

"What if I whistled 'Dixie'?" he said, which made it her turn to be delighted.

"I like you, Jon-boy, you have panache, flair. Besides, so far you're the only one to keep pace with me."

He hemmed for a minute. Hawed. In and out of bed, she had two speeds — rest and overdrive — and he imagined himself as he was after she had ridden over him like an eighteen-wheeler careening down Pike's Peak.

"I want the palaver, Jon-boy. What can I tell you, I'm a slattern, a tart. That's why you dig me."

"Absolutely," he said, and went forward deliberately, his judgement now in complete free fall, about how vital she was to him, how much he missed her, how completely she accepted him, all his vices, how inadvertently neglectful he could be. It was a confession so forthright he shuddered.

"You're groveling," she said.

That was true as well, he thought. It was not the first time.

"I'm making up my mind," she said into the silence.

She had been a paralegal with the firm for over two years, as efficient as a Nazi, as much a freak with her work as he was with his. Except between the sheets, or during dialogue kindred to the sheets, she treated him with respect, even deference, though what he knew about her away from the office and the bedroom could have been scribbled on a bookmark. She was a Case Reserve graduate in psychology, as humdrum as oatmeal — her phrase — and at one time very good at intramural volleyball. All they had in common, Jonathan realized, was infidelity — in addition to the single-mindedness of barnyard fowl.

"I could, I suppose, make up a story," she said at last. "Give me a couple of hours."

"No sooner?" he said. "I'm kind of frenzied here, Merri Jane. The walls are moving, I hear things."

"Duplicity takes planning, honeybunch. I must be inventive, cunning."

"Terrific," he sighed.

"Somehow," she began, "I expected more enthusiasm, more whatever. A fanfare would be nice, a marching band."

Jonathan conducted an inventory of himself. No matter how pathetic, it was time again for more truth.

"My hands are shaking," he said. "I feel flush."

Deary-me, she said, more a tsk-tsk as anything heartfelt. *Gadzooks*, she said. *Gollywhillikers.*

"The key's under the mat," he said by way of good-bye. "Just let yourself in."

But, as if he'd skidded through two turns in the conversation, she was talking about her outfit, the latest treat for him, va-va-voom. It was leather, she said, with snaps and buckles, the panties made from, so help her God, Touch-me Panné, very silky. Sent away for it, Adam and Eve, a place in North Carolina — Carrboro, to be exact, which was probably not a real store, more like a mailbox for people such as herself. It was fantasy, Jon-boy. Just like he liked, play-acting, making stuff up and then seeing where it went, right?

"And the shoes," she said just before hanging up. "Pumps aren't the word for them, big fella."

He felt the weight of his years, all forty-six of them like building blocks stacked one atop another and balanced on a string. In Vietnam, he'd led a life as described by the Beach Boys and Pabst Blue Ribbon beer. Back in the world, he'd renewed his friendship with Willie, played at public school–

teaching for a while. That had brought him to the mid-seventies. From there, he supposed himself a victim of time travel possible only in science fiction, many years compressed into few: he'd picked up his J.D. at Texas and, sheepskin in hand, he'd plunged into the future, wide-eyed. That was 1980.

He was tired, he thought. It was modern times now, and what he had to show for his eleven years at the grindstone of Wattman, Hidey, and Doob was a split-level in Beachwood, a Volvo with a busted muffler, and at least two hours to kill before he was once more hunkered down and watchful.

With a shiver, he realized he had again engaged thoughts about the war.

"Not a chance," he informed the desk lamp he was staring at, and straight away he endeavored to motivate himself. "Up," he suggested. And he did it. "Dress," he said, another sensible order to follow, and he began moving smartly to his bedroom.

At the Euclid Tavern in University Circle, he shook himself at the door — the storm was in full howl and a great quantity of it had fallen on him as he made his way from the UCI lot down the block — before proceeding directly to the bar, his hopes very high.

"What it was," said Floyd the bartender.

"What it is," Jonathan said, an elaborate greeting from the old regime.

Floyd met him with a bourbon: "What it shall be."

Jonathan arranged himself on a stool, took in the ambience. In old days, the Tavern had been funky, a déclassé rumpus room to while away the lonesome hours. Now it was full of chrome and mirrors, a funhouse in which to trade shooters with Count Dracula and the Three Stooges.

"Where is everybody?" Jonathan asked.

"It's Thursday," Floyd said. "No band tonight. Plus, Old Man Winter is being a real sourpuss."

Jonathan regarded the half-dozen customers, most notably a lovey-dovey couple three stools down. The girl, hair in the style of a bird's nest, looked like a witch from an amateur pro-

duction of *Macbeth*, and the guy, himself in Conan-like outerwear, could have, but for the fact he was talking passionately
about her buttocks, been her father.

"Goodness me," the man was saying, fanning himself.
"Great balls of fire."

T.T., Jonathan figured, was in the back somewhere, the
kitchen. Or he'd be along presently. T.T. wouldn't let a guy
down.

"Big change," Jonathan observed.

"New management," Floyd said sadly. "You haven't met the
owner. Straight out of *The Godfather*, spits a lot when he talks,
serenades us with old Supremes songs. I'm thinking about going back to school, get a normal job."

Floyd's real name was Martin. Away from the hurly-burly
of the Tavern, he affected to be a writer — a sonneteer, actually — but for reasons lost to Jonathan everybody called him
Floyd after the barber on the Andy of Mayberry show. It was,
Jonathan assumed, a compliment.

"Let's speak about your thighs," the Conan guy was saying,
to which the girl gulped, gave out a ha-ha-ha that Jonathan
thought surprisingly Donna-like, and for an instant he saw
himself curled in her lap.

"Full-sprung," she said. "Creamy, firm, columnar — is this
what you want?"

Floyd had come back with a club soda for himself and
leaned up close, a B-movie confidant.

"Who are these people?" Jonathan asked.

Floyd cast them a dismissive look. "He's a professor, an-
thropology maybe. That would make her his student."

"An old story," Jonathan suggested.

"The oldest," Floyd the bartender said. "I'm aghast at such
behavior. You see a thing like this, it breaks your heart. Makes
you wonder what we've come to — as a culture, I mean. I
could just vomit."

Jonathan resisted the temptation to disagree. Disagreement, however civilized, meant talking about big things, and

all he had energy for was the small. The smaller, the better. What came before *e* except after *c*, for example.

"I heard you were in rehab," Floyd was saying. "What's it been, a couple years?"

"A bad period, Floyd, I gotta tell you. Thank the Lord for comprehensive and major medical."

"You've recovered then?"

Jonathan didn't want to lie to the man. In every sense of the phrase, Floyd was an innocent bystander.

"I'm at peace with the Great Doodah," he said, another turn of phrase from the bygone era. "My mind is right. I have the rightest mind on the planet."

Floyd chuckled good-naturedly, as he was wont and employed to do. "Feeling frisky, I see."

"Like a colt," Jonathan said. "Like a teenager in springtime."

Before the fear passed, Jonathan expected that Floyd might pull out some verse to share — the man had that kind of expression. He'd perused some of Floyd's stuff, he'd told Donna once. All of it was delicate and fey, jejune meditations about flowers and bowers and happy homes, each stanza set to the oom-pah-pah of polka music. Somewhere inside Floyd the bartender, he had told Donna, lurked a third-grader with freckles and a full box of Crayola crayons. Somewhere inside Jon-boy the mouthpiece, Donna had said, was a crabby spoilsport with a heart like a prune.

"Is T.T. here?" Jonathan asked.

Floyd nodded. "You hungry?"

T.T. was the cook — a man, for those rendered ravenous by the munchies, whose hamburgers were as much metaphor as they were food.

"Tell him I'm waiting, will you?"

Now Floyd looked grievously offended. He was not unaware, Jonathan guessed, of Troy Travis Fister's chief source of unreported income — namely, medicinal quality product courtesy of a wife, June or Jane, who was an RN at University Hospitals.

"I don't want to be any part of this," Floyd said. "I'm shocked at you, sport."

Jonathan shrugged. One, he recalled, did a lot of shrugging in places like the Euclid Tavern.

"Fill me up again, Floyd. I won't be a minute."

"I'm disgusted," the man said. "I take this personally, friend."

"Don't," Jonathan told him.

Floyd gave an especially mournful shrug.

"I should throw you out of here, save your skinny ass. Hell, I should throw myself out of here."

When he got off the stool, Jonathan didn't know how he felt — slightly crazed, he thought, slightly devil-may-care — but after he heard the Macbeth girl urging her partner to speak, with pathos this time, in the specific direction of her breasts, the spring returned to his legs. Being here, he decided, was a hell of a lot better than being home.

"Globes," the man was saying, his head inclined tenderly toward the features in question. "Mounds, pertness of same."

Oddly, the kitchen caused him think of Donna again, and just inside the swinging door he paused to ponder what in the litter of his memory had brought the two — a cramped kitchen and a woman — into conjunction. Nothing substantive came to mind. The ceiling, which took concentration to look at, was grease-mottled and obviously too high to be often scrubbed. Pots and pans hung everywhere, many black and well-used, and he was loath to touch anything nearabouts. Over the griddle, the exhaust hood was on, as bothersome as a jet engine.

"Troy," he called, the name coming back at him from the grungy tile and beat-up stainless steel.

He checked his watch. Eight-ten. He made a brief calculation, imagined Merri Jane on her way from her place in Rocky River, factored in the blizzard. And then the heebie-jeebies took hold of him again, first as a thumping beneath the breast-bone that seemed disassociated from his heart. For a moment, he thought it possible that he had collapsed, or stumbled through a roaring rip in the air. A smell had come up, oily and sweet and rotten. He tasted rust, and an organ was loose inside him, anarchic and treacherous as a Tartar. With determination, he found his feet, saw they were still under him more or less, and aimed to shut out of his thoughts the screeching and wailing that assailed him from ten thousand directions. It occurred to him that he should not be here, not with his current intent, but Troy had materialized, a kind of abused-looking Pillsbury Doughboy, and there was nothing to do but talk the talk and walk the ever-loving walk.

"Jesus, Gordon, you look like crap," Troy said. "Your face is all runny."

They gave each other five in the manner of men who didn't touch much.

"Getting a cold, I think."

"Sudafed," Troy said, helpfully. "Contac."

In the back, beyond a rank of rickety-looking prep tables and between the walk-in freezer and the sinks, T.T. had fashioned himself a virtual home: a love seat, Value City end tables, a recliner and a Motorola TV, rabbit ears extended.

"Impressive," Jonathan said.

"A parlor-like atmosphere," T.T. said. "I mean, I spend ten-twelve hours a day in this dump. A man should be comfortable, right?"

Jonathan hurried to agree. Comfort was way up there on his list of conditions a man should aspire to.

"So," T.T. began, "what do you think?"

Jonathan gathered he was referring to the TV, which was on but silent. Dan Rather appeared to be in the throes of an explanation that took advantage of a goodly number of maps and charts. At this point, the war was a puzzle of blue and yellow and green, plus stars and wedges as well as miniature silhouettes of men and machines — tanks and planes and missile launchers, a high-stakes game everybody had an opinion about.

"I guess I'm opposed," he said. "Though I could be persuaded otherwise. I'm not really political."

Troy had settled himself in, legs crossed at the ankle, a king in his castle.

"It's like a mini-series," Troy was saying. "We got the good and bad guys, and a shitload of God-fearing townsfolk in between. I'm hooked till the credits roll. It's the only show in town."

So he'd been thinking about this, Jonathan said.

"Fucking-A," T.T. told him. "I'm a patriot."

Jonathan took his seat and cautioned himself to slow down. They were in it now. The penny-ante dope deal. As much protocol and ceremony attached to this enterprise as to the equally baroque business of Muny Court. In many ways, he guessed, this was preferable. You didn't have to dress up, for one thing. For another, wit had a certain do-or-die taint to it. In this trade, appeals were unheard of.

"So," Troy began, "you want a glass of milk or something? Orange juice maybe?"

Graciously, Jonathan declined. It seemed enough just to occupy a too springy love seat and watch the phosphorus and tracers and incoming over Baghdad. Moreover, he had remembered where the dog was — a kennel in the Heights. Next to the Vogue Beauty Academy.

"Getting a nose next," Troy was saying. "Two weeks, I'm gonna look like Robert Redford."

"Business must be good."

Troy contrived to appear modest, perhaps even undeserving.

"Where was I when you last saw me?" he asked.

Now it was Jonathan's turn to be coy.

"Teeth," he said. "Orthodontia. Bonding, maybe."

Unlike most dealers Jonathan had occasion to know, Troy Travis Fister invested his profits, small though they were, in himself, literally. He'd had a tummy tuck, it was rumored. The crow's-feet were gone — collagen, Jonathan guessed — and some time back there had been discussion about a chemical peel. The combined effect was chilling: looking at Troy was like looking at a Cabbage Patch Kid that could boogaloo, very tough to get the mind around.

"I'm saving for implants," he said, still focused on the TV. "You see me in a couple years, I'll have outstanding pecs, no shit."

"The wife must be knocked out," Jonathan suggested politely.

Troy made some effort at scratching his ear. A part of Baghdad was going off like a Roman candle, the night sky streaked yellow and red and white.

"The wife," he began, "thinks I ought to get a head transplant, go the whole hog."

While Troy smoked a cigarette, Jonathan took up residence in his mind's historical district. He'd scored one time from a fellow lawyer in a men's room at the Justice Center. The guy was Jeff or Jeep or Gene — something, anyway, that came out like a bark — and Jonathan remembered having to stand through a Byzantine exegesis concerning the dope under review. The word "tartarous" was used, as were the adjectives "Hebraic" and "Miltonic." The blow, it had turned out, wasn't nearly as stimulating as the vocabulary.

"I gotta admit," Troy said, "I'm kind of disappointed in you, bro. I thought you were straight now."

The subject had been changed evidently, and for a moment, trying to hold up his end of the conversation, Jonathan felt like a juggler who'd just been tossed a running chain saw to keep in the air.

"That's what Floyd said. He scolded me. He threatened to quit."

"Floyd quits twice a week," T.T. said without sarcasm. "He's a romantic, believes in the Tooth Fairy, Peter Cottontail. Me, I believe in coin of the realm."

"As do I," Jonathan said, moving for his billfold.

T.T. held up a hand, a polite signal to stop.

"Still, you're back in my neighborhood again."

That was so, Jonathan said.

"In my book, this is not straight. It ain't real crooked, but it ain't straight. Maybe bent a little."

Also true, Jonathan said.

"No offense, kemosabe. I'm just curious."

None taken, Jonathan insisted. He merely wanted the flake handy, accessible. As a test perhaps. The way ex-smokers keep a pack or two in the house. Evidence of a sort. A measure of the kind of hombre he was. The self was involved here. Plus knowledge. Plus depth, personal resources. The goods.

"You're babbling, buddy."

Here it was that Jonathan felt the blood drain out of his head in a rush.

"The war," he said. "It's making me stupid."

At the commercial, T.T. ambled into the walk-in freezer, emerging in full grin with a fistful of ground round.

"Got room for a double cheese with the works?"

Jonathan checked his watch. Eight-thirty. In a half-hour, Merri Jane would arrive on his doorstep. Some time after that, he would fall upon her, theirs an Eden of sheets and sweat and yammer from yore. That's the kind of hombre he was.

"No can do," he told Troy. "My stomach. Don't feel so good."

Troy's face, despite its gleamy artificiality, shifted through several expressions — apathy, woe, tolerance — and then, shaping the meat into a patty the size of a pie plate, he came forth with his instructions.

"Go over to Rainbow Babies and Children," he said. "Neonatal, level four. You follow the red line on the floor."

Jonathan worked assiduously at containing himself. It would be embarrassing — for both of them, he figured — to be seen hopping around like a kid on Christmas morning.

"Talk to June," T.T. was saying. "She's a floater tonight. They get a leak — somebody don't show or whatever — she springs into action. Puts her finger in the dike."

"What about security?" Jonathan asked.

Troy threw the meat on the griddle, which gave rise to sizzling and a great cloud of steam. He appeared to be relishing a joke of near prime-time proportions.

"You ever been there?" Troy said. "It's like Babylon. Security, what a hoot. Everybody wears pajamas. Just act like a dickweed, you'll be fine."

In the car, after collecting the drug from T.T.'s old lady, Jonathan spent considerable energy collecting himself: counting in the old way — "One-Mississippi, two" — and talking to his heart which was in outright revolt. Swiftly, he had entered the hospital from the Adelbert Drive lot, found the red line among its rainbow of counterparts on the floor, and, drawing himself up, he followed its trail, acquitting himself as he believed a proper dickweed ought: shoulders pulled back, knees raised high, chin up, chest out — in any event, he hoped, not as a creature likely to be mistaken for a bona fide dope fiend.

"Your left," he told himself, a cadence. "Your right."

In the elevator, he had only memories for company — each discrete and, except for Donna, each ostensibly unrelated — but when he emerged at the fourth floor, still in imitation of a card-carrying civilian, he saw he had burst upon a marvelously busy universe, one which seemed to require of its citizens both diligence and dispatch. Over the intercom, someone was reading a nearly liturgical recitation of names — Dr. Dillard wanted here, Dr. Newell there. It had been like this in detox, he recalled. At Glenbeigh. Messages from on high, and everything at breathtaking speed. Even "Wheel of Fortune" had lasted only five minutes. In detox, everybody was a coolie.

Or a coolie's keeper.

At the nurses' station, he presented himself, stated too loudly that he wanted to talk to Mrs. June Fister, and twiddled his thumbs until a woman appeared in the hall and bore down on him linebacker-style.

"What're you grinning about?" she wondered.

In the glass behind the counter, he contemplated his reflection: a face with too much wattage, his grin rictus and too wholesome to be entirely inconspicuous.

"You look lunatic," she said. "We get them all the time. They wander up from Hanna Pavilion, the crazies. Something about the children, I guess. A calming influence."

Jonathan negotiated with his organs in the order they confounded him — ears, eyes, brain.

"And I look like one of those?"

"Honey," she began, "you look like Big Bad Wolf."

She had taken his elbow and, date-like, was steering him back toward the elevator. As if read from one or another of the epic lists of ancestors in the Old Testament, more names were raining down from overhead, echoey and metallic. It was conceivable, he thought, that, given sufficient patience, he might hear, among the Joneses and Smiths being hailed, pages for the good doctors Shadrach, Meshach, and Abednego.

"So," he said, "how do we do this?"

Her hand dropped into his coat pocket, withdrew.

"It's done, sweet cheeks. You are go for liftoff."

"I paid T.T.," he said.

She released him, punched the down button.

"Whereupon he called me," she said. "I did my Sneaky Pete imitation. Script was written, ledgers erased, the wand waved. Hell's bells, I could sell the beds out of this place. Haldol, Librium 25, cafeteria trays, hairnets — what's your pleasure?"

Up close, and without an upsetting image of himself reflected over her shoulder to baffle him, she looked less formidable, less broad through the shoulders, though still a female who might use everything in a squabble, even her fists. He tried to remember if, over the course of his relationship with her husband, he'd heard any stories about her. But he got sidetracked when he patted his pocket, confirmed the presence of the vial — T.T. never used foil packets, or itty-bitty freezer bags — and felt himself besieged by what in the car he would contend was mirth as pristine and audacious and heartrending as the blow itself.

"What's the Galloping Gourmet doing?" June said when the doors opened.

"Watching TV," he said. "The war."

June's face went momentarily haywire, something weak in her revealed. That, he decided, was her story: she too had a private life earnestly out of round.

"He wants to join up," she said. "He tell you that?"

Jonathan shook his head.

"Christ, what a gomez," she said. "He's thirty-eight years old."

The doors stood open now, June having given him an encouraging push aboard.

"Gomez?" he asked.

Jerk, she said. Bozo. Buttwipe.

"I see," Jonathan said, agreeably. The doors had started to close but June's hand came forward to stop them. There was something to know, Jonathan understood. And now he would know it.

"Troy can't sign his name by himself," she said, sadly. "The man could have a stroke tying his damn shoes."

She didn't look so sneaky now. For a second, she seemed to study the ceiling, adrift in thought. Jonathan looked up as well. Over the intercom, he swore a voice was beckoning the Keebler elves.

"But what am I gonna do?" she said at last. "I love the dopey son of a bitch."

When the doors parted on the third floor and a man stepped on — a doctor perhaps, an orderly, it was impossible to tell — Jonathan had reached an interim conclusion about himself: *I am a small, fastidious man*, he thought. The sentence, like an ancient fat fish, seemed to have risen from the deepest, blackest hole in him; then, also without warning, joy overtook him anew and that picture of himself — slow-witted and cold-blooded, a true gomez — vanished, and it was time to put one foot directly in front of the other.

Happy days, he assured himself, were here again.

In the lobby, where the floor lines ended, he stood for a moment, confused by the abrupt change from institutional to domestic lighting. Headlong and immodest, thoughts were approaching him, too many of them having to do with Donna — her eyes, how she looked waking up, a walk you could sing to. Again, he felt for the vial, came away reassured. He was a penitent, he decided. A true believer. The vial was his saint's relic, inside it ash from the honest-to-goodness cross.

And then a voice was addressing him — "May I help you, sir?" — and he discovered that he'd entered the gift shop and, quick time, he enjoined himself to be more vigilant. In the future, he thought, he would need to set up watch on the perimeter of himself — setting up an acceptable watch of razor wire and Bangalore torpedoes being but one thing the E-3 in him once upon a time knew how to do.

"Flowers," he said. "My daughter. Mums. Sick."

She was beautiful, no more than half his age, hers an assemblage of parts he had no problem seeing himself bent toward to prattle about: "Alabaster" was a word that occurred to him, as did another with too many m's for ordinary lips to manage.

"Are these all right?" she said, holding a bouquet wrapped in green tissue. "It's all we have — on account of the blizzard, I guess."

He nodded, reminded himself to breathe. He felt looseygoosey, moderately dangerous. Frisky, Floyd had called it.

"Donna," he said to the girl. "We thought it was bad, Merri Jane and I, but — well, you know."

"Of course," she said, not without sympathy, and he understood completely: hers was a beleaguered and bereaved clientele, ravaged or nearly so. She was used to — even bored by — the frantic and the bedeviled, those mumble-mouthed with sleeplessness, those girding themselves against grief in public. Nevertheless, he felt impelled to explain his presence, especially how he could move his body and not fall over in a heap.

"We've had good news," he said. "A miracle, actually."

She nodded, smile on medium. The sale had been rung up and he saw that he owed her money.

"Merri Jane was completely wacko for a while," he said. "Dr. Fister's a magician. I got a million calls to make."

"Yes, sir."

Stuffed animals filled the shelves behind her — bears and giraffes, a daft-looking rhino, several monkeys in a huddle — and he aimed, with sweeping gestures, to bring them as well into the conversation. He wished Willie were here. By now, Willie would be in stitches.

"It was touch and go," he said. "I began to bite my nails."

She looked skeptical. "You're teasing, right?"

As T.T. had with him, he raised one hand. He thought of T.T.'s wife, June, upstairs, felt his blood running hard and hot in his ears. Something needed to be said, and, once the lump left his throat, he did say it.

"Can you keep a secret?"

She seemed to be looking around for help, so Jonathan raised his other hand. In many ways, she reminded him of Merri Jane. You needed to use both hands to be heard.

"I slept around," he whispered.

The girl may have said something then, but Jonathan couldn't be certain.

"I wallowed in ennui," he said. "Monsters appeared to me in the night."

It flashed in her eyes then — an edge of alarm — and Jonathan applied the brake to himself. He imagined Floyd standing nearby, wagging a finger, aghast.

"Could I have the hippo?" he asked.

He had wound down, he thought, so he brought up the bouquet to reinvigorate himself. He inhaled sharply. The smell was vegetable-like but airy as summer sunlight. Very soon, he guessed, he would be doing more purposeful inhaling.

"Your change," she said coolly, and Jonathan, now out of control, peered up from his nosegay to inquire, perchance, if she had any interest in legumes garnis. In Mardi Gras King Cake.

"Pardon me?" Her eyes had gone thoroughly out of focus. It was endearing, as were the tiny furrows between her eyebrows, and for the umpteenth time he was reminded, not unpleasantly, of Donna.

"I'm a caterer," Jonathan said. "Not here, I mean. In Los Angeles. I could set you up. You're a people person, right? I'm a good guy, really."

He was crumbling apart, he thought. His voice had gone up, a squeak, and the floor had seemed to open beneath him, the world at a parlous angle.

"Look, mister," she said, looking much put upon. "This is part-time, I'm a student, a statistics major. I'm not much on food."

Jonathan was staring into the lobby. Sometimes the heebie-jeebies took other forms, became projections, inanimate objects. He could see them now: couches, chairs, a rug, the TV, figures moving whichaway without legs.

"Just tell me to shut up, okay?" he said. "I'm really out of it. Grab me by the collar and throw me out of here."

Outside, Jonathan spread his arms wide and gasped to behold the white mess Mother Nature had piled on the ground for him. He had persuaded himself that he felt calm now and looked around to see that he had not abandoned parts of himself anywhere. Then, there on the steps, while he buttoned up his topcoat, he realized with a start, as if a howitzer round had exploded nearby, that he was crying. For a moment, he was befuddled, divided against himself. "Good God," he said, wiping at his face. He told himself to get real — "Get a fucking grip," he said — but it was too late. He was missing an essential gizmo, he thought, some contraption that kept the thing he was greased and fluid and adequately balanced. He hadn't moved, he saw, and spoke again to the limbs that had betrayed him. A second later, he had decided that his tears had to do with Donna Elaine DeWitt, and he conceived of himself wending his way to his car, a run-of-the-mill sniveler.

In their time together, she had playfully subscribed to many systems of belief — tarot, astrology, TM — and there had been especially hinky hours when she'd read to him from Carlos Castaneda and Shirley MacLaine, even the *Golden Bough*, the two of them laughing at a version of human existence that could only be comprehended if you were hepped up and wearing a boonie hat. But the week he was discharged from detox, she'd fiercely embraced the *I Ching*, seeing in its squiggly lines and artful hexagrams what Jonathan understood now were the means of escaping him. For months, she spoke seriously of yin and Top yang, of what could be divined in the images of the Wind and Rain and the Small. On the afternoon she left, she threw pennies on the kitchen floor, shrieked to observe in their arrangement at least a dozen infelicities. A minute later, she hastily made to pack her bags. Theirs, she claimed, was an Abuse of the Way — a pitiful, if pithy, excuse. They were inharmonious, she argued, as incompatible as Fish and Fly.

And now, heart thudding in his ears, encumbered by flowers and a hippo, Jonathan recalled how she'd fled from him — in an antic tempest of make-believe and wishful thinking, her car so overburdened that she resembled an Okie heading west in despair, herself not an unattractive mix of mania and misery. At the curb, she lingered, waved distractedly and put, as she might herself have described it, the pedal to the metal. Composed, he had watched her, the Mazda fish-tailing in the new snow. He was struck by the nickel-dime drama they were — characters of the VHF variety — cheaply drawn, as complicated as checkers. But when the car disappeared at the corner, too far to yell to, something thick and hard, possibly bone-like, broke free in him: he had caught sight, he supposed, of what she, night after night after night, had awakened to find camped in the easy chair of their bedroom, its face hollow and zombie-like in the milky moonlight.

The bogeyman, he thought now. Her word.

In the car, he tried to walk it back, that memory of himself.

Cocaine, he thought. Man. Woman. Then he realized he had stopped thinking, the spool of him empty and still, and it — Jonathan Gordon — was once again rising out of its chair, a common creature of murder and hunger and pride.

The bogeyman. Something real to believe in.

Across from the Sunoco on Cedar Hill, he spotted a phone booth, and, because of the snow and the slush, more drifted to it than drove. He policed himself, wound his scarf around his neck, secured the yeyo in the glove compartment. The Heights cops were notorious for their fussiness and lack of compassion, and he could well appreciate how much trouble a man could create for himself by appearing to them even marginally slack-jawed and vagrant, much less preoccupied by illicit desires.

In the booth, he referred to his Calling Card. He had an obligation and, he thought cheerfully, the wherewithal to satisfy it.

"You've reached the man," Willie's voice said, on tape. "I am indisposed. I'm making money by the pile. I have a mate with a Ph.D. in management. Still, I am depressed, blue. At the beep, I expect wonderments."

It was seven o'clock on the coast. That, itself, was a wonderment, Jonathan thought. The coast. It had, in the first place, associations — fun and frolic and tans honestly acquired — he believed himself not hostile to. In the second, it was yonder, as much as half a continent yonder.

"I'm sorry, man," Jonathan began. "It's this Iraq thing, I guess. Plus, Donna's gone. I just used your name in vain, good buddy."

With curiosity, he saw he was hewing to one side of the booth. Strangely, a picture of Willie's wife had come to mind. Nikki. She was wiry and svelte, some species of surfer princess — a woman, Willie had confessed, as daunting to confront as calculus. They had arm-wrestled once, Nikki and Jonathan, for the Championship of the Western World. She had whipped him solidly, after which she'd pranced much of

Will Rogers Beach calling for alms. "Salami," he'd said, bowing and scraping Muslim-like. "Baloney and salami."

"Listen," he said now. "Let's do Aruba this spring. That's about the only one left, right?" For a dozen springs, they'd visited the Caribbean — St. Croix, Barbados, Martinique, ten days in each, a surfeit of juvenile hijinks and college-like carryings-on.

"I want to do that parasailing," he said. "I want to — what? — gambol and cavort. I see myself suspended in air, me and the birdies."

He was yattering again, and in the midst of it he suspected that Willie was in fact not indisposed; Willie, a friend in need, was probably screening calls, in no way eager to hear again from someone who was scattering pieces of himself everywhere.

"Hold on, Willie. Something's happening here."

Jonathan watched his hand come up trembling. It wasn't war at all, he realized, that was making him crazy. This had nothing to do with war. Nothing whatsoever. He had been an indifferent soldier, his life in MR II and environs as irksome and effete in its way as lawyering was in its. His CO, a ROTC overachiever named Cletus, had called him Sergeant Bilko, his hootch The Bates Motel. When his hitch expired, he'd rotated back at twenty-three in the company of anecdotal experiences as banal as they were parochial: a marathon game of Old Maid, the misplaced Dak To commissary files, the fractured English of a moosey-maid. He had not engaged war then at a moral level and, he realized, he was not doing so now. Then and now, war belonged to those foolhardy — or fearful — enough to fight it. He was neither. War had just been a storybook adventure to have after graduation.

Now he only had cravings — for sleep, for liquid, for the means to meander and exclaim "Ooohh" over what he bumbled into, for Twinkies, for hired hands to sweep up after him, for entertainment with enough sparkle to leave him loony with laughter — for, best of all, a playmate pliant and unabashed and waiting at home.

"I'll call tomorrow," he said. "The AA book says to make amends, one of the Twelve Steps. We're to draw up a list of those we've harmed. It's the sober life, Willie. What a trip."

He'd almost hung up before it came to him, his fare-thee-well.

"Tell Nikki I'm working on my pecs," he said. "I got Rambo written all over me."

Behind the wheel, Jonathan fairly whistled. He bade the hippo a spirited "How-do" and buried his face once again in the mums. He felt shriven, almost alien to himself, as if he'd survived a long paralysis — as if, on the day Mr. and Mrs. America had given him up for good, he'd hoisted himself up from his sickbed to request, in the command voice of none other than Lt. Cletus Clodhopper, a Hostess cupcake and a rain barrel of Johnny Walker Red.

By the time he reached the Fairmount-Coventry intersection, he'd decided what to do with the dog, Blue Boy. He imagined himself in the senior partner's office, old man Wattman himself, the two of them separated by a desk big as a wrestling mat. Floyd the bartender, Jonathan would say. This was genius. Under Floyd's influence, old Blue Boy would become downright lachrymose. Floyd would read it vast amounts of undisciplined verse. Much swoon and moon and June, and Blue Boy, the yellow gone from its eyes, would become more peaceable, more poodle-like in its need to please. No more vile, snarling sort that went for the throat.

Jonathan brought the hippo to his face, went eyeball to eyeball with it.

"That's flair," he announced. "Panache."

At Lee Road, Jonathan changed his mind. He had been cruel to Floyd, and he felt soiled and unworthy. In principle, he believed himself a fair man, not a tyrant. To Blue Boy, Floyd would just be a light lunch. Donna had been right. Jonathan Wayne Gordon, Attorney-at-Law, was in Abuse of the Way. Terrible Abuse.

"Shame on you," he told himself.

At the turn on Green Road in Shaker, he pulled over, listened to the wipers click-click. Another idea had seized him, and it had become impossible to drive and whoop at the same time. If he could not deal with morality, he thought, then he would deal with justice. Smiling, Jonathan explained himself to the dashboard. His plan was a beauty. Under its rules, each of the Cliffords would tend to Blue Boy for six weeks, a month at the minimum. He was, he reminded himself, an officer of the court. He was, moreover, the de facto executor of the Ur-Clifford's estate. To get their mitts on the money and the property and the heirlooms, the Cliffords, all of them in sequence and for as long as life allowed, would first have to get their mitts on Blue Boy. Should they resist, he would visit upon them a plague of *wherefores* and *whereases*.

He would smite them, he thought. They were perfidious and profligate, and verily would he huff and puff and blow their frigging houses down.

Laughing, he turned onto his block, erect behind the wheel, alert, hands at ten and two o'clock — textbook driver's ed. The kid he'd hired to plow the driveway had not arrived yet, so Merri Jane had parked in the street, her car a hump beneath a heavy blanket of snow. She had made herself at home, he hoped. This was her first time in his place, and he pictured her, in his absence, wandering through his rooms, eyes peeled, Sam Spade in high heels. But then, as he squared himself away in the car, scooped up his presents and retrieved the toot from the glove compartment, he felt something inside unraveling — popping and snapping, one wire-like strand at a time.

Very possibly, he thought, Merri Jane had not heard him pull up, and for a second he imagined driving quietly away, seeing her in the rearview mirror as Donna must've long ago seen him: a figure in the yard, nothing visible of its fractured inner life.

"What a coward," he said.

A moment later he had hauled himself out-of-doors: He was snowbound, bent over by the wind, yet another incarnation of Sneaky Pete. Excellent, he thought. He had met the enemy and brought him to heel.

"You will reconnoiter," he said. "You will not drag ass. You, mister, will note the lay of the land."

At his living room window, he saw nothing — just furniture from which he felt thoroughly estranged, as if it belonged to the people before the people before the people he'd bought the house from. It was cold, he guessed, but it didn't matter. Nothing mattered. He was a man with a mission, a scout. Like bad vibes, cold was but an annoying affliction. Nothing at all to whatever went bump in the night.

In the lee of the house, out of the whirling winds, he took a breather, observed that his trousers were soaked to the knee. It was much after ten, he reckoned, and he trusted that the story Merri Jane had told was convincing enough to account for where the time was going. Ray-man, it had been alleged, was expert at putting two and two together. It just would not do, in these circumstances, to arouse in Ray Riley, Engineer, any suspicions.

Inevitably, suspicions led to questions. Q's implied A's. Answers, notably those derived from chicanery, were not always simple to provide.

When he shoved forward again, Jonathan glimpsed a light — the kitchen — and he went for it, slogging into a drift between his house and his neighbor's. His heart, he decided, had leapt up, and he could feel it now, banging like a fish in a tub. Everything, clearly, had conspired to render him happy and content. He had had a fray to enter, and enter it he had. He had had politenesses to exchange, parties to please; he'd demonstrated initiative, verve. Given the choice between alacrity and ordinary sour-mindedness, he'd chosen the former. His wits had been nimble, his eyes sharp. A point of view had proposed itself, and he'd cleaved to it. He had been, in fine, a wondrous work of nature. Now he would have his hank of hair, his piece of bone.

At the window, he felt flabby and loose-legged, and later — much later, in Merri Jane's arms — he thought to apply the interjection "alas" to this moment when the heebie-jeebies again laid intense waste to him.

She was washing dishes, every light in the room aglow, and on the breakfast counter behind her sat his portable TV, the war a flicker of green and white. Jonathan went slack. It was not the war which tipped him over. The war was the same as it had been for hours — talking heads replaced by bursts in the sky, its sound track thick with crackles and whistles and faint boom-boom-boom. It was, instead, Merri Jane herself.

He had forgotten that she would be in her outfit, bustier and garters, her panties red as the devil's rear end, but now, scouring a saucepan — tomorrow, he realized, the Molly Maids would have little to clean — Merri Jane looked out of place and seedy and bedraggled. In the "Kiss the Cook" apron his mother had sent from San Antonio, she seemed guileless, a child playing grown-up, and Jonathan felt his anger and fear leave him in waves, one then the other, until he had nothing inside but emotions too complicated to let go of at once. He imagined her at home with Ray Riley — like Donna and himself — and he wished to crawl up inside her and disappear. He had been wrong about Merri Jane. She was not a freak.

Jonathan felt himself sliding down the wall he'd sought shelter by. He struggled for something to say, failed. One did not bring such a woman words, he thought. One brought a toy. A wind-battered bouquet.

One brought a snowman, a man bearing snow.

When the lights went out and the TV off and he could hear the click-click of her heels heading toward the stairs, he pulled himself up, brushed himself clean. Again, he found the vial. He felt suspended — on the one side fire, on the other ice.

"I am a man in possession of a vial," he told himself.

He gazed ahead, hopefully.

"I am a man with a corner to turn," he said, and he advanced on it, hippo foremost.

"This might be love," he told himself, and before the wind slammed into him again, he presumed to believe it.

He could feel the cold now — in his shoes which were squishy, but mainly in his chest — and he checked to see that somewhere between the car and the back porch he had not shed his coat and his sweater and his shirt. At the door, teeth chattering, he produced both a key and a prayer — "Please," he whispered, "let there be no chain" — and when he had eased into the kitchen, he felt tempted to fall to the floor to utter *thank you* to whatever high above might hear him.

Music reached him from upstairs, and he understood that she'd brought her boom box. She was partial to Nine Inch Nails, Dog Rocket, groups as unambiguous in their worldview as they were angry. That was good, he decided. He had never been loud in this house. He supposed, as well, that she had brought her ditty bag in which she kept her vibrator and lubricants, her colorful scarves and lengths of rope — "Appurtenances," she'd called them.

Appurtenances were also good.

He was naked now, his clothes in a stack on the counter. The heebie-jeebies, evidently, were gone. In the dark, he waved his fingers in front of his face. A second later he'd gotten off a smile and a regulation salute. The bogeyman, however stricken and grave, did not suffer long the heebie-jeebies.

Nor did he abase himself.

"Your left," he told himself. "Your right."

He was down to his last plan, he figured. He would go upstairs, three at a time. He would burst in upon her. She might be scared, but that was okay. Fear, in matters this mysterious, was entirely acceptable. "What's that?" she would say, so he would show her — the hippo, the flowers, the flake. A moment would pass. And another, the silence going on long enough to be important. They would regard each other directly, the miles between them shrinking to a single inch.

"Egads," she might say at that point, her voice equal, and not unappealing, measures of pleasure and disquietude. "Yikes."

Such would be agreeable, he thought. This disorder, this sorrow. Then, no more than a minute later, it would be time again for ruin and for acts of the spectacular and dreadful kind.

The Human Use of Inhuman Beings

What Karen my wife calls my obsession — my angel — first appeared to me when I was eleven, one of three kids, lifelong pals virtually, who were digging a cave in the steep bank of an arroyo about a hundred yards past a cotton field behind my father's house. It was June, hot as hot gets in southern New Mexico in that month — dry as ashes, the air like brass against your teeth, the light as painful to the eye as a whine is sharp to the ear — and we had been at work since midmorning, shoveling almost nonstop, grunting with our shirts off like convicts in the hokey movies you can hoot over on late-night TV.

"A fort," Mickey had called it, but mostly our cave was to be a hideout — a refuge, really — where we would smoke the Winston cigarettes Arch Whitfield stole from his old man while we thumbed the almost greasy pages of the *Nugget* and

Gent magazines I'd found the week before under my daddy's living-room couch. We were a club, I've told Karen, and, according to our plan, we aimed to be blood brothers and camp out there so we could sneak around after dark shooting out streetlights with fence staples or spying on Mickey's big sister, Ellen (herself something, it still seems to me, out of pages private and shameless enough to hide).

Around twelve-thirty we stopped to eat the baloney sandwiches and warm Coke I'd brought. Mickey would be dead in about fifteen minutes, but, lying on my side at the mouth of the sizable entrance we'd dug, I couldn't have imagined any event like that. Instead, while Arch and Mickey talked, I was watching the distant cinder-block fence that was the back of my parents' property and thinking about how tired I felt, my scrawny arms loose as noodles and blisters already starting on my fingers.

There isn't a lot to know about this moment, nor about those, before the cave collapsed, that followed. In those days, Mickey wanted to be an astronaut (this was about the time John Glenn, so I've since heard, peed his pants in space), but this day he was talking about the Communists — reds from Cuba and China and Russia itself — and how, if they invaded in the bloodthirsty swarms Mrs. Sweem, our batty fifth-grade teacher, raved about, then we'd retreat to our cave, three pint-size Musketeers, and wreak havoc on convoys and troop movements with our BB guns and high IQs.

"We'll be guerrillas," he said. "The scourge of the land."

I tried imagining the desert all the way to the Organ Mountains, thirty miles east, filled with trucks and tanks that three chicken-chested grade-schoolers were going to disable with spit wads and bombs made from baking soda and vinegar.

"What about it, Arch?" Mickey asked. "We'll steal, pillage, forage. All we need is a uniform."

Arch said okay — a know-nothing remark from a kid who then only wanted to roam centerfield for the Dodgers, an ambition that now must seem pretty corny to the alfalfa-and-lettuce farmer he's grown up to be.

"We'll be a militia," Mickey said. "Colonels X, Y, and Z. We'll have to swear to secrecy."

For a minute, we were quiet, in the distance a cloud like a cow going left to right in the disc of sky I could see, and I went back to the thoughts I'd carried out here this morning before it seemed likely that I'd be doing battle with Fidel Castro and Nikita Khrushchev.

My parents wanted to send me to church camp in the mountains up near Santa Fe, which is about six hours by car north from the spot I was then sitting in, and of course I didn't want to go. They weren't religious people, not by a long shot — "Catlick," my daddy always said, "lapsed all the way"; they just wanted me gone for a week, so they could get down to the business (I see now) of cleaning up the disaster of their marriage without having underfoot a nosy student from the honor roll to talk around. So I was thinking about that and about the night before when I'd heard my mother say, "Professor Prescott, you're a pathetic son-of-a-bitch, you know that?" and about the thick and sour silence that followed her remark to my father. In the darkness, her voice had had an edge raw as a razor and, in my bedroom at the end of the hall opposite theirs, I felt the air around me turn cold as nights in Greenland, the thump of my heart the only noise after that to listen to.

While I didn't know exactly what was going on, I knew something profound and permanent had happened in my parents' bedroom. A statement had been made, one ugly sentence after midnight, and thereafter nothing would ever be the same — not in my house, not on the block of houses I could see from my spot on the floor of the cave; not even on the acres and acres of bleached desert I was looking to the very end of when Arch said, "Up and at 'em, you guys, let's hustle here."

I didn't want to move, and I have told Karen that nothing felt so good then as the cool earth against which I lay curled about six feet away from a mouth-like hole of sunshine.

"C'mon," Arch said. "I got to go to the pool at three. My mom will have a fit if I'm late."

"What do you say, Mick?" I asked.

His tennies behind his head for a pillow, he was beside me, his hair flopped over his forehead like wet leaves.

"I've got to go, too," I said. "We're going to the movies."

He looked peaceful, I remember, as composed and unbothered as maybe a Musketeer is supposed to look, nothing between him and happiness but the shovel Arch was pointing at him, and then he said, "Well, I'll be a monkey's uncle," an expression as full of grin and good cheer then as the night before my mother's had been poisonous and full of hiss — in any case, not the last words you or I would utter had we only six to say before place and fortune conspired to snatch us off into eternity.

I heard it then, like a bark in my ear: *Move.* It was an order whose consequence was not less than life or death — much like those I received, seven years later, from the TL I served under in Vietnam — so I scrambled to my hands and knees and stared at the entrance as though I expected my father to be out there, his face white with fear.

"Let's go, Mickey," I said and began to crawl out.

The cave hadn't started to collapse yet — that was only seconds away — but again the voice came, this time from several directions at once, not loud but urgent, not panicky but fierce, and until I scrabbled out and was picking up my own shovel, I thought I'd only heard Arch Whitfield, Junior Olympic swimmer, being bossy and clowning around and not Abaddon or Barakiel or Inias or Harbonah. Not any voice from those weightless and wanton creatures that visit from the Principalities and the Powers I eventually learned about in church camp.

Arch noticed the trouble first.

"Billy," he said to me, his voice cracking.

And then I was looking too.

At the entrance, a ragged archway tall as the big man I now am, a little dirt was falling like rain and inside, just before the ceiling itself let go and crashed down with a hollow and desolate whump, Mickey Alan Crawford was slowly sitting up to face us, his watery blue eyes not yet going from amusement to horror, his freckly arms not yet rising to cover his head.

"Guys?" Mickey said. "Guys?"

Clods came first, then slabs of earth like the concrete squares of a sidewalk, the whole thing sucking back and down on him, and for an instant — time enough anyway to wish you were as muscle-bound and honorable as Hercules — you could see him in there, through a swirling, clotted mist of sand and dirt, not making a word or a squeak, just his face baffled and eyes shiny as new paint as if, the way it must be for many, he'd been asked a question that couldn't be answered by anything less than death itself.

"Oh, no," I said, my own voice failing to hold.

But it was already over, this long-ago accident, and Arch, yelling and waving his arms, was running toward his house and I, coming apart my own self, had fallen to my knees to chop at the pile of dirt, crying and sniveling "Shit, shit, shit" until Arch was racing back — his mother, frantic and screechy with grief, trailing behind in her polkadot swim suit — and me still clawing and scratching at the dirt, finding nothing and nothing again, my fingers black with dirt, my own chest heaving as if I, too, were underground and fighting upward through the cold and the fear, the whole of the earth having landed hard on my head.

And then, as I've told Karen too often, the voice came again, as detached as those you nowadays hear from your car when the door is ajar, telling me to *stop, enough has been done, stop*, and I could see that it was coming from a man, substantial as a ditch rider, standing on the bank above me, not twinkly as angels are in Hollywood but ho-hum as a common cowboy. He was shaking his head as if, apart from this hour's mortal business, his was a job as pleasant to undertake as is the eating of cherry pie on Sunday.

"That's enough, Billy," he said. "Lie down, son. Help is coming. Rest."

They sometimes arrive in hosts, these celestials — guardian or not, patron or otherwise. Egyptians had them, as did the Irish. For the Gnostics, they were the Cosmocrators. Small birds have them, as do tame animals. There's an angel for patience, as there is one for hope and another for, yes, insomnia. Like an army, there is a chain of command, Cherubim atop Thrones, Virtues above Powers. I have no idea how they move, what conveyance they take up and down to arrive here from the gold-paved and food-filled heaven that is their usual home. That's why they're angels, I guess, because they inhabit a dimension we only have oooohhhs and aaaahhhs to describe.

Notwithstanding what Karen now says, I am not a nut about this. Honest. I've just come to know, as my daddy might have said, a thing or three. Remember, please, that seeing Mickey buried at the cemetery three days later didn't make me crazy either. I was calm, is all, even-minded as an umpire. "Shock" is what my daddy said when he took me up to St. Paul's camp the next week.

"It's a defense mechanism," he said, twice patting my knee when it probably seemed to him that I was on the verge of tears or trembling. "Time heals all wounds," he said, another cliché, and I turned to him then, barely able to hear because the top was down on his Ford Fairlane convertible.

I was thinking that I should tell him — about the voice, about the whiskery gent who had stood over me for a moment and touched my forehead, his fingers icy as well water, before, like a genie, he disappeared.

"You'll be okay," my father said, and, easing back from the brink of something terrible and sad, I sat straight ahead in my seat to see the landscape fly by.

"Dad?" I began.

I could feel him glance my way, and I think now that he was looking at me as he very likely had the night after my mother cussed him: he had come to my room and, lit from behind by the bathroom light, he'd stood in my doorway, skinny as a nail, something about his posture suggesting caution and fear and deepest regret.

"There's swimming," he was saying. "And horseback riding. Softball. Craft stuff — the works."

For a mile or so, while he told me how I'd spend my week, I watched the scrub and jagged mountains, all purples and grays and greens that don't mean anything. And I think that if I am a little like a machine, as Karen sometimes says I am, then it started here when, through one dip then another, around one turn and another, I felt the valves and gates of me close tight.

"What was it you wanted to say?" my father asked.

In those days, he was a chemistry professor at NMSU, with special interest in anisotropic crystals, so I knew — more with my heart than with any other organ that knows things, knew as my grown daughter Dede claims she knows stuff — that, as a practical man, one whose faith lay in the Periodic Table and what in his lab he could cook up in beakers and dishes, he would only be puzzled, then alarmed, if I, in his new car at sixty-five miles an hour on a road he could probably recite the exact molecular composition of, started talking about visitors and light and sound that came from above.

"It was nothing," I told him. "Never mind."

He gulped, as you would were your own unsettled self saved by silence.

"This'll be a good week," he said. "I promise."

You would think, would you not, that I should have seen an angel or two in Vietnam, where much was murdered and maimed, a place with an honest-to-goodness need for the human use of inhuman beings. After all, as Mickey Crawford had predicted, I was fighting Communists, sneaking around with a rifle and a higher cause to serve. But I did not — not once — though it did seem, during Basic Training at Ft. Bliss in El Paso, that one was present if only unrevealed.

This was in my fifth week there, me just one of thousands who were that year turned into men from the boys we'd earlier been, and perhaps fifty of us had been trucked a ways into the badlands east of the Franklin Mountains to learn how to survive a ville some gung-ho Full Bird had constructed. That morning, we sat in bleachers while below us, bobbing and weaving behind a lectern, a sergeant yelled at us about being watchful and something-something to the nth degree. Behind him stood this odd collection of buildings — mostly sticks and the like, good tinder if you had a Zippo and a punk's sense of humor — the whole of it fenced (exactly as such turned out to be way across the ocean blue). It was booby-trapped, he said. CS gas and punji stakes, not to mention pits filled with human excrement that you would fall into, sure as sunrise, if you were too damn bumble-minded to pay attention.

For an hour he went on, alerting us to trip wires and demonstrating how our adversary, the wily Mr. Charlie, could rig up an explosive — from, hell, no more than a seemingly discarded C ration can, ladies! — that would blow your leg into the next rice paddy. Or blind you. Or cause you misery for the rest of your piss-poor life. I was enthralled, I admit, eager to learn what might save my skin; and I was also semi-distracted, wondering about whatever gland or gene it was that had caused me, several days after graduation, to have presented myself at Uncle Sam's recruiting office, my only credentials a record of A minuses and sufficient leaping ability to be second off the bench for the Las Cruces High School basketball Bulldogs.

As it had been the day Mickey and Arch and I dug our cave, it was hot, the sun blazing down and the sky so blue it looked phony. We had been divided into rifle teams, Able to Foxtrot, and soon enough one team was instructed to go into that mock village to make it safe for me and mine in green. I knew a few of the boys in the first squad, all of them with nicknames having something to do with body parts or point of national origin — kids named Tex or Ears or Fats — and I was real disappointed to see each of them, one after another, not get much beyond the gate before they were "killed" or otherwise made fools of.

A minute later, another team went in, hot to trot but

stealthy as cats. Still, there were more surprises — holes out of which rose the outraged enemy, walls that were false and places for cutthroats to hide, grenades that went Boom when you flung open a door for a look-see. I was scared, I have to tell you, my heart slamming left and right — more scared, it would turn out, than I was months later when I landed in the place this wasn't the actual of, and I remember watching Swamp Thing and Doc disappear in a cloud of harmless smoke that meant, except for the months and miles they were lucky not to have lived and traveled yet, they were ruined forever. Truth to tell, I felt as I did that day our fort began to crumble, my lungs filling with air too dense with light and thorns and threads to breathe. Half of me wanted to turn and go running headlong into the desert, me shedding my pants and shirt quick as my muscles would permit. My other half, that percentage that was angry and pent up, wanted to charge up to our red-faced sergeant to tell him to stop and send us home. But I didn't. I was stuck, is all, rooted to the earth in a line, and then a voice could be heard behind me.

"Jumping Jesus," it said, amazed.

In the fake village, Tiny and Gator were inspecting a well that, according to our teed-off non-com, led to a tunnel that led to a room that was a hive of make-believe troops, and I remember turning to the voice behind me, expecting the expectable. I wanted to be out of there, and I was hoping it was an angel to make it so.

His name would turn out to be Brownie — a name no more unusual than Red or Bucky or Fender — but when I turned to him, I didn't see anything ordinary. Instead, I saw a creature aglow with blues and yellows and oranges — the effects, I think now, of too much sweat in the eyes and too much need in the chest.

"Looky there," he was saying.

Behind me, so I gathered, others of us were learning the lessons you learn when you are smashed to smithereens, but I was concentrating on Brownie, and then he had stopped staring over my shoulder, his weapon at rest in his arms, to take a peek into my eyes (which may have seemed to be spinning as wildly as those that mad scientists have).

"What's with you?" he said.

I did not know. I had seen an angel years ago, I could have told him. Maybe he was another.

"Wha — ?" he said, backing off a step, and I was wondering what had turned his face dark with confusion. Then I saw it: my hand had come up, one finger extended and moving toward him. Behind me, the sergeant was calling for Foxtrot, me and this fellow among them, but neither of us had budged. My hand was still edging forward, my index finger coming ever closer to his midmost button. I intended to see if he was real. I was going to poke him, maybe pat him down head to toe, and you could see him see that in me. You could see him, real name Brownfield Woodward, study me across the inches that separated us, his eyes narrowed and his mouth tight as the hole to paradise. Time was moving very slowly here, as it does when you can't sleep, and I remember thinking what a sparkle I myself would make when my finger passed through the twinkle he was. I expected I might burn up or be thoroughly electrified, that I might shoot up into the sky or be atomized into the dust pixies are said to sprinkle.

But I had already done it, made contact, and nothing had happened. I was touching his shirt, a patch of sweat below his breastbone, and nothing had come of our connection. Not a buzz, not any flash of fire that I had read about or thought to predict. He was human matter, like me, and I had proved it. And so, once more able to huff and puff like the Big Bad Wolf, I turned away from that trooper, thoughts settling in me like sand.

Our sergeant was beckoning, and I found myself moving, one step and another, time smooth as butter and me still a victim of it. I was sharp enough to see what imperiled me and careful enough to tiptoe around it, and then this too was over — as were the next and the next and the next I have lived to brood about.

I chose to tell it, my story about the angel, only once — to Karen the day I asked her to marry me when we were students at the University of Arizona. This was the same year my parents finally divorced and my father sold his house to move into the Town and Country Apartments up behind Apodaca Park, the baseball fields where I had played Little and Pony Leagues, and something — maybe the goo I am, or the goo I will one day be — had moved me to confess to her that the angels that had appeared to Hippolytus in the second century A.D. were so tall that, well, their feet were fourteen miles long.

"Imagine it," I was saying. "Over ten thousand came down on Mt. Sinai when Moses was given the laws. In Islam, they —"

"Billy Ray Prescott," she said, "what are you talking about?"

I took a breath, felt the links of me stiffen and clang.

Beside me, Karen was fussing with her purse, and for a moment I yearned to be small enough to fit inside it. Just me and her comb and her make-up — stuff she'd have forever.

There was a time, I told her, when I knew everything that could be known about angels. Their origin and duties. Their relationship in that hierarchy that leads to God. How they got their names. Even their personalities as such were revealed in the books and pictures I had studied in the library or, when I was eleven, in the reading room at St. Paul's.

"I'm not religious," I told her that day.

She nodded, clearly not convinced. She knew me as a Mr. Clean type (yup, I was one of those early bald fellows with a neck like a fireplug), older than the frat boys and jocks who'd chased her, plus a guy with thirteen months of in-country slaughter I had put as far behind me as memory and geography would allow.

"I'm a Libra," I told her.

She knew that, she reminded me, exasperated as she nowadays gets when cause takes a half-hour to make effect. Still, I had speech to make then, and, yes, I was going to speak it.

"I believe in justice and balance," I told her. "I'm a hard

worker, don't smoke, do my own laundry, like a clean house. Karen, I know how to fix a car. I pick up after myself."

As if I had said I was related to Little Miss Muffet — or were warning her about, say, the Communists massing to charge over the ridge behind us — she was focusing on me hard, her eyes dark as pea gravel, exactly the look I received last week when I told her about the second visit of my angel.

"Billy," she said, "are you sick? Here, let me feel your forehead."

I considered my situation then, the kids in T-shirts and shorts walking past, and for an instant I pictured me as she must've: a mostly well-mannered communications major, virtually on bended knee, yakking for all practical purposes about spacemen or plants that had mastered French.

"Mickey Crawford," I said presently. "Nineteen sixty-two."

She was leaning back a little — body language, they say. "What are you talking about?"

Something was ticking in me like a bomb, so I told her: the cave. The angel. The sky gone white as old bone. The sun like ice. The ambulance bumping across the stubbly field. That crowd of neighbors, all struck quiet and hangdog. Arch holding his mother's hand as if he expected a chasm, maybe stinky with smoke and brimstone itself, to yawn open beneath him. And my father.

"An angel?" she said, her body still doing most of the talking.

"My dad told me I could go home," I said.

She looked patient — part schoolmarm, part traffic cop.

"He picked me up," I told her. "Held me in his arms all the way back to the house. Patted me on the back. Smoothed my hair. Whispered to me all the way."

A kid was going by us now, too close on a bicycle, and until he disappeared around the faraway corner of MLB #67 — about as long as it had taken my father to lug me across the field years before — I watched, my blood pumping three ways at once in my brain.

"Billy, you're scaring me."

Whatever was ticking in me had stopped, and I had not burst into pieces or toppled over in a heap.

"Miss Needham," I said at last, "I need you desperately. Let's be man and wife, okay?"

She smiled then, in a manner that seemed to involve her shoulders and a goodly percentage of her torso, and in that first minute after she said "Yes," I understood I was obliged to put aside, like geegaws and trivia you've outgrown, all I knew about Thrones and Dominations, those swift and heedless beings who get here by magic and stay around to make us mean.

"You wait here, Billy," she said. "I'll get you a Coke."

The fall after we married, Karen and I moved to El Paso where I'd gotten a job as an associate writer for the "Live at 5:30" program at KTSM TV; and then, soon enough and fortunately, I became assistant producer, then day-of-show producer, then assignment editor for news and executive producer, rising through time, one rung then another — first the guy who does the field interview about the new tiger at the zoo, then the guy who oversees the live broadcast of what the zoo keeper can say to well-barbered talent named Doreen or Chad, then the guy who orders the guy to do all that; and finally your hero became the guy who's supervising nearly five dozen other humans whose days are spent thinking up two-minute stories about rock-'n'-roll grannies or talking lawn mowers to share with the half-million Americans with color TV in my corner of the desert.

Rising and rising, dear readers, until William Prescott, Jr., had mostly forgotten all the goofy secrets and peculiar wisdom he'd discovered in the days and years after the stringbean-like corpse of Colonel X, ravaged and limp and blue in the lips, was dragged out of its grave.

The NAB meeting was in Dallas this year, that confab where shows like "A Current Affair" or reruns of the "Mod Squad" are bought and sold, and where celebrities like Montel Williams and Regis Philbin show up to shake your hand for having rented them five evenings a week from the KingWorld syndicate.

It was the last day and I had gone up to my room off the hospitality suite the station had booked in the Westin Galleria, which is that next century of hotel from whose westward windows you can see jets climbing and falling like dragonflies from D/FW. I was tired, too full of what was being sold that day — yammer and video about a public that seemed crabbed or confused and busted in the brain, programs about pistol-packing priests or vegetables in the shape of public monuments, the whole of it served up by blabbermouths who seemed to have been concocted out of the fancy fluids and rare gases my father, before his retirement, had fussed over like a wizard. It was late, the only other person in the suite my son-in-law, Mike, who, as my assistant and a Southern Cal MBA, was along to keep track of the dollars and cents we were spending to bring to West Texas information about, oh, a cheese that caused cancer and the Arkansas moonshiner who was a new father at age seventy-six.

"Long day," Mike said. His tie loosened, collar undone, loafers kicked off, he looked like he'd reached a place in his calculations where numbers had personalities unstable enough to cause fistfights on either side of the decimal point.

"The longest," I told him.

I wasn't really paying attention. Dede, my daughter and his wife, was expecting their first child — a boy, it's turned out to be, named after yours truly — so I was preoccupied with that and with the thought, given the gut I'd seen in the mirror that morning, that I needed to lose about twenty pounds.

"Champagne, boss?" he said, pointing to the table.

The suite looked like the mess a circus leaves behind, but there were still a couple of untouched bottles and, bushwhacked by fatigue, I felt thirsty enough to drink them, plus whatever else bitter and fizzy that room service could send up in an hour.

"Don't mind if I do," I said, realizing — also with a start — that I wanted to be drunk and that, like shows about witches from Wisconsin and dogs that do long division (Corgis, I think, a snappy, prissy breed), this would be yet one more odd development I'd end up telling Karen about when I got home the next afternoon.

For an hour, we shot the breeze, Mike and me, told tales out of school — who was a crab apple, or a lazybones, or a bottom feeder nobody in management would be sad to say so long to. I told a couple of stories about my youth and Vietnam, and Mike, wistful as what the word "swain" suggests, told a really sweet version of how he'd fallen in love with my baby girl.

Once, moved by the hour and the confidences, I thought to say something about angels — their fine-spun hair, the clatter some are said to make when they land, the ghastly wail others shriek in the ears of those whose hearts tend toward evil — but Mike was telling an SC story about football, a tale that went as much backward as not (like this one you yourself are hearing), so I just treated myself to another swallow of Cold Duck and said "Uh-huh" in agreement until the punch line came to make me chuckle.

By the second bottle, we'd taken up the bigger world — Saddam and the like — all the woe-washed men and women who didn't seem to have enough virtue or good sense or ordinary compassion. I was feeling fine, clean inside and able to go back and forth in my brain without losing myself between mind and mouth. But a moment later, when Mike said he was going back to his own room, I knew I'd succeeded in getting tipsy, the physical universe a landscape of carpet and armchairs I'd have to crawl through to find my bed.

"You okay, Billy?" Mike said.

I expect I looked bleary, or partially paralyzed.

"You think anything's out there?" I asked, making a gesture meant to include all phenomena out-of-doors and wandering unattached overhead.

"You mean like UFOs?" he said.

I meant spirits, ghosts, and whatever. Trolls, maybe. Demons and devils and gnomes. The whole shebang.

"The whole shebang," he said, clearly choosing his words very carefully and comically glancing left and right to see if we were alone.

"Seems possible to me," I told him.

He was standing now, his sleeves rolled down, his belt tightened a notch or two — the actions of a normal man at the end of a normal night.

"It does?" he said.

I had eight thoughts, then eighty, several of which had to do with drinking and the truths you find doing it.

"Sure," I said, and suddenly, helpless to do otherwise, I stumbled through a spit-filled paragraph that had in it observations about little green men and hobgoblins from the nether worlds, plus wolfmen and vampires and whatever else might explain the miracles of earth and wind and fire.

"What about bleeding statues," I said. "That kind of thing?"

"I don't think about it," he said. "Honest."

I didn't think that possible and made the mistake of saying so.

"I'm not a complicated guy, boss," he said. "I just turn the mind off."

Mike looked wind-whipped, his face the color of old cardboard — just the way I'd look, I fear, if he admitted that he had a tail or scales instead of skin — so, feeling the winds whistling in me, I just chuckled to say I was kidding. I was being dumb as a doughnut, and it was time to stop.

"Sorry," I told him. "Too much Geraldo Rivera, I guess."

His was a smile not less than three-quarters full of relief, broad as a piano keyboard.

"Maybe you ought to take a vacation, boss. You and Karen go somewhere."

And so, after he'd shut the door behind him, I rolled leftward and found the floor I'd been looking for.

In bed, I didn't seem myself. The radio was going, an oldies station, and I did my best to keep the melody to "Lonely Teardrops" by Jackie Wilson and that grapevine song by Marvin Gaye, tune after tune that seemed to connect the me's I was in yesteryears to the middle-aged me I am now. Helpless as a log in a flood, I was being driven back into the past, before long finding myself sitting on my suitcase at the beginning of the bladed road leading out of St. Paul's church camp, feeling my lungs fill with simple gladness when my daddy rolled up in his Ford Fairlane to take me home.

Next, stranger memories assaulted me: my daddy hunched over the toilet bowl in his bathroom, moaning and clutching his arms — in the midst of a heart attack he would survive — and my mother standing over him, her expression sidelong and smug as a tyrant, saying, "It's just the Monday-morning blues, Billy, you go on to school." And this: one trooper from Hotel Company, a kid named Heber from the 1/26, licking a photograph at LZ Thelma in MR II. And this, too: my mother marrying a cattle rancher from the Hondo Valley, the pair of them perfect as magazine models selling wine from faraway places. I wasn't weepy, just beset, a part of me frightened as a kid in a haunted house, another part wrought up enough to have to find a way — boy, is this spooky — to make myself heard in the night.

So I sang. The shoo-bops and the do-wah-diddies that are the nonsense you make when you are, as I was, foggy-minded and utterly innocent of the real words. And then, before my angel appeared again, I was asleep, still fully dressed, in a land, as I've heard it described, of dreamy dreams, where time pools and stretches, where events come to you like clips from a thousand crummy movies; a land where you are yourself a floaty thing that can move without benefit of motors or muscle and where, before you have any other way of knowing it, it is revealed to you that in this valley of etceteras nothing is holding you up but desire and ignorance and luck.

He had not changed, my angel. Unremarkable as a shopper at a bus stop, he looked as he had that day Mickey Crawford suffocated, and for a moment, before I went down and round and the night broke into shards around me, I wondered what he'd been doing over the years between then and now.

"It's not Dede?" I said, hope and fear only two of the motivations for my question.

It was not, he said.

In the quiet, I was watching him as I believe he was watching me, creatures at the opposite ends of time. In that special voice of his, like an echo coming to your ear down a mile-long pipe, he'd arrived to warn — or prepare, or teach, or help: hell, I don't know — and for an instant, after I'd risen to sit upright and leave my bed, I feared I might still be asleep and thus doomed to turn around and so see myself lying infant-like in the middle of a king-size bed, my wrinkled suit coat up around my shoulders like a shield, but my body so brilliantly lit up that I could count the bones through my skin.

"Don't be scared, Billy," he said.

I didn't think I was, but my hands had flown up, palsied-like and grabbing at air.

"It's not Karen," he said.

Then, as if I had been conked about the ear, I knew.

Perhaps I had known the moment he had touched my toe to fetch me back to the conscious world, or maybe he had sprinkled me with dust or whatever awful powder their terrible tribe uses for the spells they cast. In any event, like a TV show — maybe like a TV show I myself was in this place to buy — I was now seeing my father in his apartment, at the stove frying the minute steaks he liked, the instant before his heart seized up and he slumped to the floor. He was smiling, my father was, his grin as fixed a feature of his face as his eye color and unlobed ears — a smile as lopsided as it had been that day, years and years ago, when he'd said goodbye to me at St. Paul's and arranged himself again behind the wheel of that spiffy Fairlane he loved. He didn't look old now, I thought. Not wizened or shrunken or ruined. Just frailer, thinner and less nimble — what I'll be when the sun goes down in 2025.

It was hitting him now, the shivers of his battered heart, and for a moment, before the floor came up to him hard and fast, he looked befuddled — like Mickey Alan Crawford the instant before the cave slammed down — as if, his eyes going flat and empty like candle wax, he was seeing death bear down on him, its approach sudden, infinite, and wrong.

"It was quick," my angel said.

They separate the sheep from the goats, I was thinking. The wheat from the tares. Our angels do not age, nor do they fall ill. They may not reproduce, neither may they marry. They become visible, so I'd once read, by choice, and to some — the daft, the hopeful, the condemned — they have appeared with wings and hands, or full of eyes and encompassed by wheels within wheels. As I've told Karen, one book claims they are the oil of joy for our mourning. They are not. That book, like so many, is lying.

"Go away," I told him.

"You'll be all right?" he asked.

It had returned, that giant's fist closing around my insides: I had heard other sentences after dark — these, like my mother's one night long ago, frightful enough to change the way the world is seen — and, air upon air upon air underneath me, I thought I had stepped off the cliff of the planet itself. All I had were the facts of me — my height, the Cadillac I drive, how clumsy I am at tennis, how loudly I can laugh when the joke is harmless and blue — those details that are the sum of you when you have but one last lesson to learn in life.

When I opened my eyes, he was gone.

It was well past midnight, my floor quiet, in the distance the wail of sirens growing fainter. Karen was up now, I knew. She had received a call from the manager of my father's apartment building — I had seen that too, one of a thousand images pulsing in my head — and she was searching in her bedstand for the number of the phone I was sitting next to. In twelve hours, I would be home. In another sixty, I would be standing graveside. But now I was here, a lamp on, the room cold as February, waiting for a bell, so that, my ears still thumping with the impossible beating of wings, I could pick up the phone and say, "I know."

How One Becomes the Other

This is the joint story Freddy Pease told me the afternoon he got ticketed up to Segregation. A classic type felon, Mister Freddy McKinley Pease. Built like Ichabod Crane, the posture of a question mark. Your basic habitual criminal, B & E style. Came from L-Block at Lucasville, Ohio's latest quote riot-torn corrections facility unquote. Interesting guy — about as predictable as flash flooding. Like a lot of dings in the cage.

Seems Freddy was in his house one day last year, listening to the Notre Dame game on his radio. Good match, he said. Much Preparation, much H. The Catholics had this running back, Bettis, now with the Steelers. "A real load," Freddy Pease said. The Miami Hurricanes fielded some ill-tempered monsters of their own, not much appreciated by the civilians in South Bend.

"The Golden Dome," I told him. "Knute Rockne, the Gipper, Touchdown Jesus —"

"Catholics versus convicts," Pease said. "Saints against sinners."

Anyway, late in the third quarter, a ruckus commences in the house next door — home of a junkie biker named Leon and his buttbuddy, Clyde. Called himself Betty. You know the kind: unaffiliated meat in need of protection, dabs on a little non-reg Revlon lip gloss, and makes an acceptable sweetie if you're so inclined. Plenty are. Said tilt in the romance department being but one method inside of time travel.

So: a disagreement develops. Domestic strife, according to Pease. That was his word, "strife." Evidently, money is missing — scrip, not street. A quarrel erupts. Freddy's word again. He was up in the Library nearly every day, a student like yours truly. "Equivocates," "parsimonious," "*ipso facto*" — he had a zillion of them, courtesy of two years of college over in Illinois. SIU maybe. The Salukis.

"So it's after lock-'n'-count," he tells me.

This was the Orient, our place in the world, us temporary roomies — him only a month up on the chain from declassification — and we were in the yard watching the population dance its usual hokey-pokey. Last summer, this story was, nothing between me then and me now but razor wire and the cheap air of high heaven.

"The ruckus?" I say.

Freddy was watching a couple of Muslims take direction from a hack named Wedge. Naked, Wedge might resemble a root system. Plus, in those days he smelled like Kitty Litter. Which, once I bid adieu, Freddy would tell him. Which — ipso calypso — would get him sent to Seg.

"It's the hooting first," he says. "High-pitched squealing. Metal on metal, I'm thinking."

"Where's the watch sergeant?" I say.

Freddy had a thing he did with his tongue, intricate as a sailing knot.

"Dentist," he says. "Man has teeth like Bucky Beaver. Only one around is this new screw, name of Nellis."

I think the thinkable vis-à-vis the scene: rookie hack, indifferent convicts, the effects of long-term incarceration. The possibilities, as my ex-wife used to say, boggle the brain.

So there's shouting, Freddy says. He's curious, takes a peek. Walkway yo-yos everywhere. Offenders he's never seen before. Lifers, ragheads, beaners, even an Indian with one of those high-maintenance Krishna hairdos. The whole tier's lined up for the showdown.

"Take your time," I tell Freddy.

Pretty soon, according to Pease, there's debris.

"Debris?"

"Leon's throwing stuff," he says.

Pease had a jaw like a hambone. Pop open his skull, I figure you find clods and spiky plants and maybe sputtering fires like at the end of the world.

"Knickknacks," Freddy is saying. "A teeny-weeny Eiffel Tower made out of matchsticks, for example. Some beads. They come flying out of there. Magazines, too. *Better Homes and Gardens*, old copies of *Silver Screen*."

"A flurry," I say, aiming to help out.

Then snack food, Freddy says. Edibles from the canteen. Vienna sausages. Hydrox cookies, Diet Pepsi, salami sticks.

I tell him then about my old lady, Ellen, what she could do in the kitchen — rack of lamb, etcetera — but he was telling a story and, as with all bad-time bad guys, you are no more advised to get between it and him than you are between hell and high water.

"The whole time," Freddy Pease says, "Betty is screaming. Motherhumper-this, motherhumper-that. Sounds like a sixteen-year-old girl."

I was watching Wedge. Like Pease himself, he could be moved to meanness by the weather, I'd heard. Plus which, according to my ex-cellmate, Fat Willie the Forger, Wedge had a wife built like Olive Oyl with the go-get-'em personality of a Doberman pinscher. God knows what Pease had outside. Maybe a Vegas showgirl, maybe an oak tree with hips.

"Seems Leon's been drinking pruno. It was an occasion."

"Raisins?" I wonder.

Freddy's got his tongue engaged again. I've counted about eight personalities so far — at the one end, Mr. Wonderful; at the other, The Prince of Darkness.

"Crushed seedless grapes," he says. "Lifer's Choice. Two pinches of pot and some Smucker's jelly."

Yummy, I tell him.

"Leon's lost control," Freddy says. "A couple times Betty comes flying out of the cell. She's wearing State-issue denim but with the zipper up the side. Flowered sneakers. Looks like a movie star."

I mention my favorite: Meryl Streep.

"Sally Field," he says.

Across the way, Wedge is writing a ticket for some Zapatista in a hairnet. Miguel or Jesus — one of those. What's true for booze on the outside is true for acquaintances on the in: never mix, never worry. You got a world in here with more rules than Chevy has trucks. Like with like, I always say.

"Anyway," Freddy goes on, "I got a ringside seat. Betty and Leon going back and forth like rats in a bag."

"You got a way with words," I tell him.

He's a poet, he says. Keats is his main man.

"Gibran," I tell him. "Kahlil Gibran."

Here it is that he talks literature, the good and bad of it. Danielle Steel, John Grisham. Most cons have a favorite. James Jones or whatever: any type of typing from the faraway — lapping waters, buxom maidens in the throes, chases like you used to get in *Mannix* and *Hawaii Five-O*. Me, I work over in Furniture. The rest of the time I'm reading, writing letters, working on what the Ohio State teacher calls my critical faculties. J. T. Yehnert, the Buckeye guy, says I should send my stuff to that magazine Issac Asimov used to own, but I'm still in the practice stage. I go for agony, ecstasy, how one becomes the other — but mainly on Mars. Got an imagination the way Kellogg's has cornflakes.

"The rest of the story," Freddy Pease says.

Beside me, he's humming, I swear. Like a radio picking up all the short-wave gossip in outer damn space.

"Leon wrecks the place. Curtains, little decorative items, pictures — the whole bit. Utterly trashed."

"Comes a moment, however," I put in.

Exactamente, Freddy tells me. Comes a moment when Betty goes asshole over elbow out the door, grabs the rail. She's enraged, teary-eyed, flushed. Got her blouse ripped. Got big nipples from being sucked on. Plus a tattoo big as a dinner plate.

"Pirate ship," I say, guessing. "Maybe a heart with a dagger through it."

Pease looks at me hard, like he's being watched by a dog that can talk English.

"You in a hurry?" he asks.

I used to run track in high school, the 880; now I just talk fast.

"Got a delivery to make," I tell him. "Over to Electrical."

He cracks a knuckle or two.

"Parrot," he says. "Gruesome — part vulture, part dinosaur."

Yonder, Wedge is doing deep knee bends, which would be comical but for the flesh going whichaway. Yesterday, he and Pease went toe to toe over a gate pass Freddy was supposed to have — bickering like Leon and Betty, I guess, but without love in the background.

"We're all jammed up," Freddy Pease is saying. "Even the new screw, Nellis, is — what? — mesmerized. Looks bug-eyed, like a frog. Betty's sporting a lump on one cheek. She's holding a bottle of Old Spice. Beautiful fingernails."

"Red," I tell him, more guesswork.

He nods. The reddest.

"Details," I tell him. "Where the devil is."

How true, he says. Whereupon he uses my nom de pen: Switchboard.

I'm the messenger inside. Take, as has been said, the chip to the dip. Make the yon hither, and vice versa. Suppose you got a confidence needs to get to, oh, West Mess or Protective Custody. I'm your guy. You get assured delivery, I get a pack of smokes or some Ho-ho's or your baked potato at dinner time. Your innermosts are safe with me: Alvie Patterson, Jr., semi-professional car thief.

"It's the quiet I remember," Freddy says, himself dreamy-like. Mr. Hyde as seen by Mr. Hallmark Card. "Silence thick as wool," he says. "Cold, too. Quiet with color, you know?"

"Ominous," I put in. I can't help myself: I'm a sucker for the who and the what. "Portentous," I tell him. "Doom-like."

Nah, he says. Climactic.

Me and Ellen, we had a couple of those climaxes ourselves — lighting like you find in Boris Karloff movies, the smells to be smelled, heart hammering in the ears, maybe smoke or fog as a special effect — what I'd rather hear about than live through again.

"Then it's over," Freddy says. "Betty's standing there, all cried out. Leon comes out of the house. He's a big fella, arms like railroad ties. Got a face you don't want to read too much into. I figure Betty's going over the rail. Swan dive or full gainer. Make a splat on the floor."

Pease has me in his gaze again, eyes about as life-affirming as lug nuts. Apparently, it's my turn to talk.

"Holy moly," I say.

The holiest, he says. The moliest. Leon takes a step, then another. "Ponderous" is a word that springs to mind. He's got scratches across his cheek, a little blood trickling from the ear — a bite, maybe. You can hear Betty breathing, gasping like she's been underwater. "*You cold?*" Leon asks. "*Why you want to know?*" Betty says, still on guard. Leon shrugs, bashful per-haps. "*You're shaking, baby,*" he says. Betty brushes her cheeks, tries to huff up a little. She's got her pride, sure, but something's obviously been settled. "*You sorry, Leon?*" she says.

"The scrip?" I ask Freddy Pease.

He's nodding. Birthday cake for Leon. Betty had scored a pint of sour cream icing from the cook in East Mess. Plus a hand-tooled leather belt from some fish upcountry.

I wonder about Nellis, the new hack.

"About does a back flip," Pease says. "Beaucoup applause. He nearly craps his pants."

I'm standing now, casual-like. The 4:30 whistle has gone off, so it's time for me to chop-chop.

"Happy ending," I tell him. "That's sweet."

For a moment, we watch Wedge. He'd been looking our way like we were stuff to step on. Out in the world, so we'd heard, Wedge yodeled country-western. Had the voice of Tom Turkey himself, we'd heard. Wore the outfits, too. Chaps, high-heel boots, shirts with pearl buttons. Looked like a riff-raff Roy Rogers.

"So they kiss and make up, Leon and Betty," Freddy says. "Ozzie and Harriet all over again."

J. T. Yehnert, the OSU guy, says stories have to offer insight. So here it is: we're sentimentalists and proud of it. Patriotism, the handshake that seals the deal, what you can say about somebody's mother — we take it all seriously. Hell, I've seen your average armed robber go mano a mano over the Fifth, Eighth, and Fourteenth Amendments. Aside from law-breaking, only difference between us and the Boy Scouts of America is maybe bad table manners, plus certain disputes pertaining to other couth commandments.

"Look at that grease-dripping pig-sucker," Freddy says.

Wedge is on the move now — another climax I aim to avoid. Like seeing the worst bad habit come your way. Besides, I got a piece to write — all about freezing ourselves and then waking up in a future run by octopus-like bureaucrats we're the fatty food for. Not to mention my aforementioned delivery. After that is dinner (shepherd's pie and orange Jell-O: it was Wednesday), maybe a half-hour of pinochle with Fat Willie, then a call to make up in rec. Had to find out how my boy Alvie Two is doing. I got only one more question.

"So who won?" I say. "The football game."

Freddy Pease, humming anew, is eyeballing Wedge.

You take a personal life made of spit and rust, not to mention every comic-book hero from the DC syndicate, and dress it up in a pea-green uniform, and — Whoa, Nellie — you got mayhem itself on the hoof.

"Convicts," Freddy says. "In a walk."

As Fate Would Have It

When you meet, she should be mightily charmed by the gestures you practiced in the mirror an hour before — your bon vivant's smile, for starters, or the Eastwood-like tilt of your head. She has to adore your hair, your cologne, the Italian loafers you paid too much for on the PCH in Long Beach. All day long, from the instant you rolled out of the rack, you should have felt yourself moving toward a possibly providential discovery, something as momentous to you as was the apple to Adam. It should be a party in the hills, Halloween on Devonshire Court, the crowd a throng of geeks and witches and gremlins, but it should not be too noisy at first — a celebration subdued, in this case, by the news, revealed only minutes before you tossed your keys to the kid from valet parking, that your host has a mistress.

His wife, lipstick smeared red on her teeth, ought to be moderately drunk — frantic and edgy, a woman who kisses hello too hard, then jams a breast in your arm. Dressed like Marie Antoinette, she should be sloppy, outrageous as a voodoo queen, her hug almost fierce enough to crack your back. "Ooooh-la-la," she should squeal to the air beyond your ear, evidently tickled to see you — tickled to see, in fact, Kong and Nero and Sweet Betsy from Pike, all of whom followed you up the walk.

Immediately, a beverage must be spilled, Marie a sudden whirlwind of parasol and petticoats to clean it up, so this then will be the instant you see her — your new sweetheart. She might be standing next to a gray-haired guy who seems overwhelmed by his cape, the Count of Monte Cristo. In any event, you should feel your ribs cracking open, an astounding amount of light pouring in on your quivering, oily organs. You are about to gasp, you should think. In her eyes, she will have a glint that suggests that, like your own eager self, she has come to this party with no more to lose than time and terror.

"A tart," Marie should be saying to the room at large. "At forty-six, Mr. Big Shot's got himself a floozie."

She — your dreamgirl, your angel, nothing whatsoever like your ex-wife — should be close-pored and deep-socketed, her skin like mayonnaise. With a handshake implying, even in costume, that she could bench press you to the ceiling, she should have beautiful hands — you've always liked women with nails too long to be practical in the real world. Without the tee-hee-hee and the annoying trail of dreamdust, she should be Tinkerbell, her outfit the choice of her girlfriend Roxanne, who will turn out to be the tall redhead in the gold lamé swimsuit with the banner reading "Miss Congeniality" across the bosom. They're starlets, Roxanne and your true love, Sandi. They've been in commercials, industrial videos, even a feature at Paramount — which is good to hear because, as fate would have it, you're in the business, too.

"A musician," you should say. "A drummer."

A half-hour, spent in splendid conversation, should go by. Eventually, you must be introduced to Roxanne. They have a duplex down Eagle Rock Boulevard from Occidental College, you will learn. Roxanne has a Siamese, Mr. Mister. It came with her from Oklahoma.

Loud as a tuba, she will be the kind of woman that's always scared you a little — too chatty, too brash, too many parts to keep track of, a woman with too much past — so you should concentrate instead on Sandi: slow, quiet, steady, perfect Sandi.

You've worked with Kenny Loggins, you will say. Toured with Glenn Frey. Jackson — Browne, not Michael — is an acquaintance of yours.

"I want a drink," Roxanne should be saying. "Miss Congeniality wants a whole lake of drinks."

At some point well before you catch yourself crashing through the landscaping, before your fancy shirt is torn at the elbow, before you fumble with your keys so you can start the car and get the hell out of here, you will stand on the balcony with Freddy Krueger, your host. He should've known you nearly five years — "A friendship of long standing in these parts," he will remark.

You're buddies, he is to remind you. You Tonto, him the Lone fucking Ranger.

You should wonder about Sandi. She had gone to the powder room and then you thought you saw her talking to one of the Munsters.

Impatiently, Freddy should ask you if you're listening.

You have to be gazing at the lights in the valley, a sea of flickers and winks you still remain awed by, and it should not surprise you that you're thinking about your future — about being out there, in a car, going somewhere special, the horizon lit up like highest heaven.

"Roxanne," Freddy will be telling you, "she's the girlfriend."

You like Freddy, you should tell yourself. He's a facilitator, you will have heard many times. He puts deals together —

"like nitro and glycerine," he should've said once. "Watch for the flash and see what's left when the dust clears."

They met at the Red and the Black, Freddy should be saying. Roxanne was having a cocktail with her agent, an ogre from ICM. The wife doesn't know the particulars, at least not that he's been laying pipe two afternoons a week above the Main Bar at the old Beverly Wilshire.

"Right," you will say, trying to keep up your share of the discussion.

Torrid should be a word used a lot. *Passionate.* You will be asked, more than once, how you feel about passion.

You favor it, you should think. Really, you do.

"The whomp of it," Freddy must keep saying. "It's like hitting a goddam wall in a bus."

Freddy will have a joint — one whose name you've never heard before: Crunch or Crud — eighteen percent THC, it should be said. "The marihoonie," he will call it. "Rhymes with mooney." Stoned, Freddy should hold forth on a number of subjects — the points he almost had in "Aladdin," plus a crisis with ASCAP and getting old — but he should keep returning to passion. With a capital P.

"Roxanne," he will confide to you, "is an animal. A lynx. A tiger."

"Terrific," you are to remark. "Honest."

Here Freddy should be working his lips as if his teeth hurt.

They're breaking up, he should say at last. Complications. Tumult. It's tough shit, but there it is. Roxanne doesn't know yet.

Now, Freddy should seem soured, divided into fifteen, or fifty parts — no flash anywhere. In a brotherly fashion, you might clap him on the shoulder, concerned. Besides having found you the most ruthless divorce lawyer in California, he's thrown significant studio work your way over the years. He's an independent, he will have reminded you often, indebted to no man. With connections to everybody but the Ace of fucking Spades.

Did he mention how invigorated he feels with Roxanne, he

should be saying to you. "A new man," he should insist over and over. "The corpuscles fairly hum. Honest to goodness, it's like the Vienna Boys Choir set up shop in the belly."

You like the idea of that, you should tell him, but days and days and days from now, even a month after you've sent candy and flowers to apologize for the ruckus, passion will seem as wanton to you as weather, as much a matter of fear as of beauty, a frenzy as much to flee from as to wallow in.

When the silence sets in, a few seconds after Freddy has explained his views concerning God and the blessings that are steadfastness and tough genes, you will make to excuse yourself. You've spotted Sandi, you should think, in animated conversation with Jesus of Nazareth.

"What's she doing now?" Freddy should ask you.

"Roxanne?" you will guess.

Freddy's reaction — part shrug, part wince — has to be semi-painful to behold.

"No, man," he should sigh. "Marie Antoinette."

You mustn't know how to answer. Before you came out here, Marie will have been in the den, scissors in hand, snipping methodically at the seams in one of Freddy's jackets, her audience — two of the Stooges and nearly half of the Ten Little Indians — as enthralled as cavemen at a science fair. "It's a Vestimenta," she should have been saying. "Four figures from Sami Dinar."

"She gets crazed," Freddy should inform you. "Always takes it out on the clothes."

You ought not to know many other people at the party — they're suits mostly, management hustlers or A & R types on the prowl — though the fellow dressed like a pumpkin seems familiar. At the bar, shoulder to shoulder with Cabeza de Vaca and one of the Four Horsemen of the Apocalypse — Pestilence, you think — you must keep an eye out for Sandi, and try to stay out of the path of the more serious hoopla. Freddy's wife, her massive powdered wig slipping over her eyes, will be yelling into the telephone in the kitchen. In spite of her fury — or perhaps because of it — she should appear unspeakably gorgeous, much of her chest exposed, her breastbone so milky white you can't help the lowlife ideas that assault you five and six at a time.

"She weeps," Freddy will have said to you. "She yowls. Swear on a stack, she gnashes. It's like being married to Minnie Mouse."

The CD will have come on again, a whole house system it probably took a month to install, and when Popeye has begun demonstrating something frug-like to a creature that could be Pocahontas, you should think of your ex-wife, Darla — to dancing, you have to note, what bullets are to gunplay.

She should be in Texas, a suburb of Dallas, with your son and namesake, Jimmy, the boy — what? — fifteen or sixteen. That you are uncertain will embarrass you. Drink in hand, you should remember his hair, surfer blonde like his mother's, and his eyes, which are yours, blue as a kind of ice. Although you send the child support yourself, you should try to recall when you yourself actually talked to him, or Darla. It could have been Easter. Or Memorial Day. Very probably, you should guess, you were on the road. St. Louis, maybe. Or Kansas City.

At this moment, Little Bo Peep will be advancing on you, behind her a man in gauzy robes and a scary quantity of white, windswept hair. She should ask what you are, your costume. Her companion, his fake beard frosted white and crooked underneath his nose, has to be wild-eyed, a snow-covered cannibal fresh from a rampage.

Old Man Winter, he should tell you. That's what he is.

You will try to clear your head, but your thoughts, usually ordered as infantry, have to be competing for space with the wails the Breeders, at 110 dbs, are blasting into your brain. Not for the last time will you wonder where Sandi is, your long-lost true love. Like a weapon, Bo Peep should be carrying a staff, large and hooked at one end.

You've forgotten, you should tell them. You've been out of town. You aren't dressed as anything.

Puzzled, they must consult with each other, Bo Peep and Old Man Winter. "We're surprised. We thought you were a cowboy. A young Bat Masterson, for example. Or a younger Lee Van Cleef."

A week from now, when you are nearly asleep and when you feel like a sickly child who's seen a bad shape skulking in the trees, you should remember that time, at this point in your adventure, passed in a disturbing way, as broken and ill-fitting as space was in the aggressively silly art Darla once dragged you around Brentwood to gawk at. Freddy's place will have become more crowded. Attended by a Nubian slave, Nefertiti should arrive. The crew of the Starship Enterprise, Mr. Spock on crutches, must materialize.

You're a cowboy, you will tell George and Martha Washington. You've just mislaid your *pistoles.*

You'll have another drink — and another — and when you hear the name Harrison Ford, you should wonder if he's here as well, or just his Han Solo lookalike. Sandi will have said she'd had a part — itsy-bitsy, albeit — in *The Fugitive,* but while you dread for the ten-thousandth time that she's run off with Colonel Sanders or the Michelin Tire Man, you should glimpse Roxanne trapped on the couch at the far end of Freddy's lobby-like living room, her expression completely stricken, absolutely helpless, while a woman heaves and sobs in her lap. It will be Marie Antoinette, her hoop skirt fanned up over her shoulders like a turkey's tail, while behind them Frankenstein is doing a handstand for Heckyl and Jeckyl.

Here it must occur to you, in the frighteningly corny way all insight has occurred in your middle years, that you are ravaged. Thoroughly trashed.

Near the door to the bathroom, you should lean against the wall, an effort to take stock of yourself. Something is missing, you have to feel. Your wallet. Or that interior tissue, the result of many centuries of natural selection, that's meant to keep humankind from slobbering all over itself. Your hands, normally light and strong, should feel clumsy as crates and too heavy to carry around for the next hour, but in them you should find, not one, but two drinks. Yours and — whose? You should endeavor to reconstruct the last five minutes of your life, an exercise that proves as futile as trying to swim to Siam. The marihoonie, you decide. The Crud.

You will imagine yourself elsewhere — at the beach, or the gym on Pasedena Boulevard. Christ Almighty, you should be in bed. You have a session in the morning, Julio Iglesias or the like. The producer — an inconceivably hairy guy, a virtual Wolfman, another of Freddy's connections — will expect you to be sharp. Really, you ought to leave now, but between you and your car stand several munchkins and famous murderers, all of them amused by your ability to keep the wall from crashing down over your head.

And then the bathroom door has to open. It will be Sandi, the only person in the world able to renew you with a single wave of her wand.

"There's a problem," she has to tell you.

You should repeat the word, startled to find what could only be tears at the bottom of it.

"The ex-boyfriend," she will say.

A bone creaking inside, you should remember what you learned about Sandi before the Aga Khan, on the claw of a Maine lobster, interrupted you earlier. The ex-boyfriend should be named Jake — or Slate: a name as contrived as are hats on hyenas — and he should be an actor notorious for off-screen escapades involving sports cars and semi-automatic pistols. Like a billboard for tanning butter, he should be handsome, and mean as a hammer. Sandi is afraid of him. Really. Before rehab, he ran with the Brat Pack — Judd Nelson, Emilio, that bunch. A certifiable brute.

"This was totally unpredictable," she should be saying now. "Typical Slate. The story of my life."

You should groan, more truth bearing down on you.

"What about a rain check?" she should ask. There's a place in Burbank. The Palace of Mystery. Maybe you could meet her there?

Like someone shown the modern world with the lid yanked loose and the gears inside spitting off grease and flame, you should understand that, among the arachnids and yammering vegetables, among the living dead and the various extraterrestrials, Slate has just appeared, the latest of Freddy's guests.

"Burbank," you have to say. "The Palace."

Events will unfold very swiftly now. You may find yourself dancing, your partner a vigorous blonde you believe you rooted for on *Baywatch*. Wobbly on her high heels, Roxanne should break in with news about Freddy and Marie. In one of the bedrooms, so it's to be reported, they are sitting calmly on a settee, sharing a joint Freddy has speared on one of the gleaming knife blades that are his fingers; apparently reconciled, they are said to be singing a verse of "Some Enchanted Evening." Without question, this image should move you. You are not insensitive, no matter Darla's opinion on the issue. You do have a sentimental side, and for a moment, while Roxanne struggles to tear her banner off, you should imagine having slept with Sandi, the different things you could have learned — about her body, sure, or her habits in bed, but also about your own self at its best. She will have told you that, as a triple Virgo, she is trustworthy, but, apart from behavior to read about in the Calendar section of the *Times*, you have to wonder, as a Scorpio, if that ever boded well for you.

Meanwhile, Roxanne, at war with her outfit, will have attracted a crowd. Dracula, Porky Pig, Jimmy Carter, Thelma and Louise—even the caterer, his hat a miniature mushroom cloud. Nearby should stand the fellow in the pumpkin outfit, his expression composed and abstract, as if he's chanced upon a problem he could solve with his calculator and graph paper. At last, you should recognize him — the Virgin exec you worked overdubs for at Groove Masters in Santa Monica — Fenton, or Felton. He wanted to be called Finn, you should remember. He desired more boom-boom, or comparable effects. More hi-hat. More chuffa-chuffa. More of what you didn't have that day.

The bottom is out of you now, you ought to realize. Lordy,

you're litter inside, a wretched wind howling through the center of you.

"Help," Roxanne should be yelping, slapping and swatting at the glittery script of her banner. She wants this thing off. Right fucking now.

"Calm down," you should tell her. But at the instant you prepare to wade in to assist her, which is also the instant Sandi appears with Slate, you should realize you are about to do something both stupid and violent. Your heart suddenly frozen, you pause, dumbstruck by your own goofiness. You won't believe it. You're the peaceable kind, you should think. Once upon a time, ages ago, you marched.

Nevertheless, as dazzled by your own lunacy as you might be were a Martian to land on the stage of the Dorothy Chandler Pavilion on Oscar night, you should turn away from Roxanne: you are now, against all odds, a man with one last good office to perform. You are the nitro, you should think. And the glycerine.

"Mister Drummer," Roxanne will be saying, tears in her voice. "Where the hell are you going?"

Near the foyer, Slate and Sandi will have appeared. Notwithstanding what you've heard from Sandi's own luscious lips, they should present themselves as sufficiently arm-in-arm to convince you that the world has rules as twisted and bassackwards as are its ruled. It's the Crud, you should believe, that's making you think this way. It is not, you feel certain, a permanent but heretofore unacknowledged feature of your character. Nor is it a condition, like a pimple on your ass, you can ignore or forget about.

As if seeing this episode from the rafters, or on Freddy's big-screen TV in his media room, you should be amazed. Utterly bamboozled. You are, clearly, a man in need of some help yourself. If Roxanne — or anybody — is hollering at you, they ought to be doing so now. In a kind of stupor, you should look about. If there's someone to save you — Attila the Hun, maybe, or the June Taylor Dancers — they should be doing so now, before the ground opens beneath you, before the lights start flashing and the banshees break into song.

"Hey, pal," someone should be saying. "Long time, no see."

Distracted, Slate has to be looking elsewhere, but Sandi — beautiful, tasty, faithless Tinkerbell — should be trying to warn you off with her eyes. Bravely, you are to attempt to ignore her. A principle is involved here, you will be telling yourself. Something big — bigger than the two of you, more monstrous than happiness itself — is at stake, and if you could summon them up, you should like to say a few words about it.

Still, halfway to Slate — which, to you, is halfway between one life and another, halfway between fate and circumstance — you have to discover that you are, remarkably, only half-hearted about what's befallen you. You are, God help you, re-signed. You are motion, not movement; activity, not action. Your blood running cold in your throat, your fist should be cocked, but you should feel powerless, dutiful, obliged. Once again, you should wait for your brain to catch up to your feet. The world, you have to decide, is almost rotten, and there's only one thing you, alas, can do about it: you — Noley James Gilmore, formerly of Star Route 2, Luna County, New Mexico, Western Hemisphere, Planet Earth — are about to throw a punch.

You should be face to face now with Slate. Sandi should have been only partly right: he is a Nazi, yes, but with a smile from a toothpaste ad.

"Is this the guy?" he should be asking Sandi. "This can't be the guy. Say this ain't the guy."

With a shudder, you should understand now that the punch, the first you've thrown in anger since the Mayfield Junior High School lunchroom, has no chance of connecting — for a thick-legged mesomorph, Slade will be fast as a flyweight — and that, slack-minded and off-balance, you will tumble past St. Francis of Assisi and crack your head against the tile-covered stairs.

Your punch still unthrown, you should see yourself moaning like an infant on the floor, your universe muffled and swirly and murky, colors running gooey at the margins of your vision. You should see yourself crawling, slowly at first, then with greater determination. Briefly, you should imagine something sharp attacking your ankles and knees, a mob going after your kidneys and thighs. Then, your flung fist flying feebly in the air to nowhere and the focus coming back to your eyes, you should envision being later assailed from on high.

It will be the Pumpkin man, bent over you like an orange Florence Nightingale. Whispering over and over, "Hey, pal," he will be trying to help you up, and, like a bullet into your forehead, knowledge will be reaching you that, a knot throbbing over your eye and your shoulder bruised, you are leaving here with a tiger.

Roxanne.

In the car, she will have something to tell you. A secret.

Behind the wheel, you should be taking an inventory of yourself. The stinging in your wrist. The faint ringing you should hope, however stupidly, is coming from an ice-cream truck lost way after dark. Amazingly, you should be in good spirits. Pumped and jittery — wasted, sure, but somehow clean — as athletes are said to feel on the verge of victory. But then you should recall your shameful exit from Freddy's house, in particular that pathetic attempt from the floor to explain yourself, the sneers of contempt given you by Little Red Riding Hood and the Big Bad Wolf beside her, and you will feel your heart give an unpleasant lurch sideways, the steering wheel about the only thing in free America to hang on to.

Her real name is Alma, she should tell you. After the city in Oklahoma, her parents' idea of cute. "Near Muskogee," she should add. "Where Merle Haggard comes from."

Here it is you should yearn for other things to happen tonight. A drive-by, say. Or a flash fire roaring in the canyons leading out of here. A catastrophe equal to the hour and atmosphere. An earthquake.

"*Roxanne* is so much more evocative," she will say. "I could just strangle my mother."

You are in this together, you must realize, two fools in fantasyland. So you should ask her what she'd like to do now. You know a dozen clubs you could get to in twenty minutes — Sparky's Melon Patch, for example, the Frog and the Peach, the Crest Cafe on Sunset — but you should assume she'd be embarrassed to show up in a swimsuit and see-through raincoat. You could shoot pool, you will think. Maybe sneak down to the beach. It will be past midnight, the sky cloudless all the way to Jupiter, the ocean somewhere dark and forever in front of you, the desert over the scrub-covered mountains behind, and you will say *Okay*, a part of you cold and brittle, when she says, in a tone both mischievous and business-like, that you should surprise her.

"Freddy Krueger," she should say. "What a dipshit."

At your place — the bungalow on Valencia Street in La Canada, the house Darla will have left in a huff one spring so long ago you can't remember your reaction — Roxanne will be thrilled that you're so tidy.

"A neatnik," she should call you. "Not like you-know-who."

Here events should become roiled, disordered as war itself. One minute, Roxanne might be inspecting your drumset, maybe timidly trying her hand at banging the floor tom; the next, she is drinking Cuervo, sniffling over how crooked life has turned out. One minute you might be kissing her — she will almost be too tall for you, the kiss curiously without current and heat — and the next she is chattering about calligraphy, hers a language about nibs and strokes you struggle to make sense of. It will be morning late and morning early. A streaky dawn and deepest darkness. Tumbledown and upright. The air smelling clean as Clorox. You will find yourself ahead of her and behind, both smarter and dumber — maybe, you have to concede, as you've been with all women — and then a moment will arrive, unexpected as lightning, when you find yourself in your hot tub beneath the gazebo in the backyard, only hundreds and hundreds of gallons of bubbling, frothy water separating you from a sodden woman who, as Miss Oklahoma Rodeo of 1986, once barrel-raced astride a quarterhorse named Hardhat.

"Poor Julio," you will say. It should be obvious to you now that you're in no condition to go anywhere.

"Yes," she will hasten to agree. "Poor Señor Iglesias."

The crud should have seemed to wear off, but there will be a vast space between your ears you fear was once filled with memories and plans.

Roxanne will ask about your eye.

"It's sore," you have to admit.

"Here's to that," she will say, and from somewhere previously out of sight a bottle of Dos Equis will rise in salute.

On the outside speakers, your only album, *Wet Places at Noon*, has to be playing. John Hiatt, himself a wild man in those days, should've helped you with chord changes and horn arrangements. This should've been your drug years — Percodan, Xanax, the exports of Mexico and Peru. Back then, it might seem to you, you had no trouble with words.

"Who's Finn?" Roxanne will want to know.

"The pumpkin," you should answer. "Another music mogul."

She has to look at once bedraggled and revivified, her red hair slicked back like a seal's, and then you should realize that you, your brow still thumping, probably don't look so swell either.

Finn gave her his card, she will announce. Tucked it in the top of her suit when he was leading you out the door. She's to call his service next week. Tuesday.

You should study the evidence, soggy in her fingers.

"Poor Señor Finn," you will say, and, taking the card from her, you have to drop it over the edge of the steamy tub, where it should lie for a nearly a week until the maid, Mrs. Dominguez, picks it up and asks Señorita Roxanne, the last lady in your life, if it is *importante*.

Deliberately, you are approaching the end of something,

you should conclude. Not an era, certainly. Merely a phase. A confusing but not unimpressive period of warp and woof, of riot and silence, of ruin and rain.

"Noley," she will say. "What kind of name is that?"

"It's a ranch name," you should answer, and several images will spring to mind of you and your father discussing T-posts and salt rubs and spavin in the cattle you have grown up tending.

With the awful clarity of a clairvoyant, you should foresee what's to happen next. An hour from now, Roxanne will have asked you if you want to make love, a prospect that will have struck you as inevitable and necessary and sad. You should say *Yes*, but at the moment the two of you rise from the tub — Roxanne still hasn't gotten her banner off and it should droop from her shoulder, water dripping as you walk toward the house — she will say she has a story to tell.

You like stories, you should remind her. Hell, you've told a few in your own life.

She was in an auto accident, she should begin. On the Ventura freeway, near the Laurel Canyon turnoff. Last August. A pretty nasty affair. A three-car pileup. Somebody died, the idiot who caused it.

You should be in your bedroom now, both of you looking at your bed, a car alarm woo-wooing nearabouts.

It's afterwards she will need to tell you about. When the ambulance arrived.

You should have your soggy pants off at last, your shirt somewhere you will laugh to discover when you awake ten hours hence.

It's the paramedic, she should continue. He was so gentle, so careful. He talked to her like a lover. Held her head, went through her hair slowly, searching for glass. For the cut that would account for the blood beside her ear.

The alarm should be gone now, but another noise will have become clear to you — a clanking, rattling sound that could be an engine, something infernal and wrong.

His name was Ric, Roxanne should tell you. With a c, not a k. She'll remember that forever. His tenderness.

It is your heart, you will decide. At the moment the two of you climb into your bed from opposite sides, still wet, still slow and cautious, that noise, thunderous and leaden, is your heart.

"His touch," she should say. "I wanted Ric Martin Pettibone to take me home. I almost asked."

The whomp of it, you should think. It's like hitting a brick wall.

But this scene shouldn't have happened yet. Time a fluid as likely to travel one way as another, you will still be back in the tub, the future an hour away from history, and you should be telling Roxanne about Darla. On the stereo your most famous song should be playing, "All Things, All at Once," a ballad, complicated as any poem you studied in college, that peaked at 84 on *Billboard*. The advent of a Santa Ana, a breeze should have arisen, hot and dry as air from a grave, and you must be telling a story about your mother, how you once saw her slug a horse. Another story should occur to you, this about backing up Jeff Beck years ago at the Coliseum outside Cleveland, and you should describe how it felt, eerie and exhilarating, like being able to fly, when the crowd applauded and you couldn't get the shouting out of your ears.

Water burbling under your armpits and between your legs, you should speculate aloud about Sandi, even about Slate. You're planning a vacation, you should say. Aruba, the Azores. Australia, maybe. You should fetch Roxanne another drink — Ron Rico now, you're out of tequila — and, on the way back, you should notice how doughy you look, how you didn't have a gut even a month ago.

You don't swear, you should tell her. Generally, you're law-abiding, considerate. You owned a dog once, a collie, and would again were you home regular hours. You vote, mainly Democrat. You've given money to United Way, to the AIDS people. For a couple of days, you were a Boy Scout. You tried college, Arizona State, but you were — are — a musician. A drummer. You've played with Jackson Browne. With Ray Davies, from the Kinks. Bonnie Raitt, God bless her, is a pal of yours.

"You're shaking," Roxanne should say to you.

With effort, you ought to be able to bring yourself under control. You should have experienced the first of many flashbacks, this one the moment that you lay crumpled more or less at Slate's feet while Little Bo Peep, urged on by the squeaky cheers of Old Man Winter himself, whacked at your knees with her terrible staff.

"What happened?" Roxanne will be saying to you. "To the horse your momma socked."

"Nothing," you have to say. "She busted two knuckles."

It will happen now. Or not at all. Head back, looking at the stars, Roxanne will say the magic words, those few unique to all matters of love and loss.

"I'm lonely," she should admit. "Flat-out pissed off."

Awkwardly, you should reach across the tub to her. Something, you should feel, hangs in the balance between you. A compact having more to do with the soul than with the flesh. Her skin should be water-wrinkled, like your own. She will be Miss Congeniality, you a young cowboy after all. Your mind, which you have always thought of as a cluttered storage attic, should be clear, nothing between the first and the next thing to do but water and air and time. You have to feel fortified, stalwart even.

"Please," she will say to you. "Put it on again. That song."

And you should.

You will.

You have to.

· ·

A Creature out of Palestine

I n those days, this was how you got to my place: down
from Ruidoso and Ski Apache, you took US 70 (yes, the
very route that Billy the Kid, notorious bandito and
youngster, hightailed it horse-style to freedom in olden
times) through Tularosa, past Ray's Tire and Lube and the
C & C Restaurant and Lounge, into Alamogordo ("Sunbird
Capital of the World!") to the 54 cutoff where Wal-Mart Dis-
count City meets ShowBizz Video and Big Jack's RV. Coming
from the west — say, for argument's sake, you were over in
Las Cruces, shaking your booty at El Patio or goofing on the
cholos creeping their low-riders up Solano Street — you zoom
through the Missile Range, past White Sands (the National
Monument, bro!) and Holloman Air Force Base. Keep an eye
peeled for the Taiwan Kitchen and Guy's Transmission. You
spot Lester's Satellite Inn, you've gone too far.

From El Paso, which is how I got to where the going went,

· · · · · · · · · · · · ·

it's a whole other story: up 54, straight through the heart of the Ft. Bliss Military Reservation (remember, sweet pea, don't get off the road: Uncle Sam has posted signs — Danger! Peligro! Unexploded Shells, etc. — death and destruction for the lost and lamebrain among us). About halfway up — it's eighty-three miles of scrub and chamisa and creosote and snakeweed and gnarled-up yuccas and, like set decoration from the cruel genius of Rod Serling himself, ugly mountains left and right of you across a desert flat and depressing and trackless as a nightmare — you wheeze into Oro Grande. Take a breather, compadres. Stop in at Dyson's Auction Barn, holler howdy or the like. If it's summer — shitfire, it's almost always summer thereabouts — pray to whatever beasts and gods you fear. Make an offering, neighbor. Write a last will and testament. Check your hoses and belts, your tire pressure, your capacity for self-denial. Call your blood relations. Reconcile yourself to woebegone within you, slap on a sombrero, some sunscreen, then vamoose. Look for the Oro Grande National Forest on the west side of the road. It's a single tree — a Chinese elm, maybe — as angry-looking as you would be were you lonely and windbeaten and ill-tended and bug-ravaged and laughed at for a lifetime.

An hour passes, you're almost at my place. You see O'Brien's Dog Ranch (imagine the hellhound they breed out there — bald, probably, plus drooly and big as a ninth-grader). Next is Alamo Transit Mix. You'll see Southend Road — this section of US highway, two miles of blacktop and beer cans, is brought to you by the Hyper Hub Club — then Sunrise Doughnuts and the Golden Spur. Go as far as the Hi-D-Ho Drive Inn — no way am I making this up; we're talking corny here, not to mention trite, grim, imprecise, and dopey. You run in, say *buenas dias* to the chiquita of the month, then oblige her to turn your ass around, amigo, because in your excitement and relief, in your fever and frenzy, you done missed my estate. Mi rancherito. Mi casa grande. Me, R. C. Hidey, late of this and that, white boy extraordinaire, master of disaster, former third-team All Ohio defenseman for the Cleveland Heights Tigers hockey squad — you raced right by, podner. Didn't honk. Didn't wave. Didn't flip me the bird. And now here I wait, a half-mile south of you, standing on the two or three blades of Bermuda I tend, wearing dress sandals and my go-to-meeting Hanes T-shirt, the prime of my youth, brown as a creature out of Palestine, and utterly, unspeakably, inconceivably sore-hearted because once again, in a manner mysterious as the twentieth century itself, I have been overlooked. Ignored. S-n-u-double fucking b-e-d.

How I came to be there in 1981 is, like the scorched geography itself, another circumstance worth a boo-hoo or two, so let's stipulate the following: pretend you're a student — an *estudiante*, as it is habloed in Nueva Mexico — no magna come louder to be sure, but a fifth quarter junior Lambda Chi, eye-balling veterinary medicine, the USMC or rock-'n'-roll star as career options. Say, according to the minor characters your life needs in order to be the 3-D adventure it is, that you're a "poop-head" (your last girlfriend, a double-jointed knockout named Nancy), a "slugabed" (your mother, Beverly, the Mighty Mouse of domestic engineering), or a "rounder" (your dad, Martin Hidey, Esq., attorney-at-law). Say you got all your fingers and toes, can snort Budweiser through your beezer, and recognize — so you think — the vast whatnot our to and fro has made of modern times. Suppose, moreover, that you're a standard-issue ectomorph who more or less believes in life after death and the one-shooter theory vis-à-vis JFK. Suppose Moby, suppose Dick, suppose the whole damn Great Chain of Being, and when you're done with that — when a lanky, blond lefty with a birthmark like a tophat on his hairless heinie has come vividly to mind — then suppose this inexplicable Blah-Blah-Blah from the Wide World of Yadda-Yadda: comes a day, lo and verily, in the middle of English 563, Recent American Fiction (about page 68 of whatever helpful hogwash one talented typist has let spill from the yap of a dippy protagonist you've been told to root for), when you announce, in a voice like hail on a tin roof, "Christ Almighty, what am I doing here?" After that, Mister and Mrs. America, it's a stroll in high cotton.

You rise, imperious as Caesar himself, leave the books behind, bid adieu to aghast Buckeyes near and far, clean out your cave at the frat house, stow the bong, and take up residence in the basement room of your old man's pile of bricks on Stratford Street. Don't move for five months, fatten up like a swamp frog. Grow the beard you'd find on sixty percent of Pegleg's swabbies. Attend to the Grateful Dead. Learn the learnable via Marvel Comics and Phil Donahue. Piss into the wind. Look a gift horse in the yarbles. Wish upon a star. And then — drum roll, Ringo — say "yup" when Papa Bear, steamed as The Lord Humongous, suggests you might be better off were you, golly, elsewhere. With your Uncle Hal, for example. In the Mountain time zone, in point of fact. The Great Southwest, in particular. The Land o' Enchantment.

Which is how this sorry specimen came to be as he was where he was when he met C-Dog Simpson and thereafter came to know, as surely as Hardy follows Laurel, shit from Shinola.

C-Dog looked like a man with three things on his mind, two of them involving money or disease. That's what I was thinking that day he rumbled into my yard. I'd been watching the Flintstones, lusting unkindly for Betty Rubble, and keeping an icepack on an eye that had turned black subsequent to a disagreement the night before at the Bear Trap, a bar I frequented Mondays and Thursdays. This must've been a Friday, I'm guessing. Late afternoon. The day like an oven on broil — more hours from the less gladsome verses of the Old Testament. And me with a visitor in a vintage Chrysler Imperial. That's when I had my insight. Little did I, and so forth.

"Hey in there," he called, and I, thus beckoned and always intrigued by the foolish among us, moseyed forth.

He had red hair — rusty, actually. About the same rubbed-out, sunfaded color as the beat-up Triumph sports car he was pointing to.

"This yours?" he asked, his second instance of snappy dialogue.

"Nope," I said, reasonable-like in spite of a hangover that Guinness might have wanted to hear about.

What with his posture and such, I had him made as a senior flyboy out at Holloman. Maybe that selfsame sumbitch who, by dawn's early light, buzzed my acreage in his F-16. That, or a Texas-style horse owner from the Downs up at Ruidoso.

"What about this?" he said, indicating what lay around and about.

I studied what I was the sulky caretaker of: pallets of slump block, stock tanks, ATVs and brush hogs, a backhoe with a safety cage, a gooseneck hay trailer, PVC in quantity, John Deere's idea of a home-style tractor mower, a couple of generators — well, you get the picture: pre-abused manufactured items, all of which, given enough grease and greenbacks and cusswords, might in fact one day work.

"Hal's," I told him.

He nodded, doing something Dracula-like with his lips.

"My Uncle," I said. "He's the broker," I added, using the word I'd been told to. "I'm the help."

He was sitting in the Triumph now. Flyboy, definitely. Had that sassy cockpit manner about him. Made you want to scare up a claw hammer, mash it on his trigger finger.

"So where can I find Hal?" he asked.

In town, I told him. Did he know the Si Senor restaurant?

"On Tenth?" he said.

It was my turn to nod now. Next to the Happy Booker, I told him. Couldn't miss it. I had a girlfriend worked there. Mona. Mona Elena Fernandez. Ummmm-doggy.

"Got the trots there once," he was saying, heaving himself out of the Triumph. "The combo plate, I believe."

He seemed to be expecting an apology, but I, nephew and dingleberry, wasn't about to deliver it.

"He's not my uncle, actually," I said. "My mother's cousin, more like it. I call him Uncle as a courtesy. He's Arab, we think. He's got a green card —"

Like a farmer in a field, he was walking in and among Uncle Hal's holdings — cast concrete cesspools (looked like teacups from one of Disney's bad dreams), some lawn jockeys (many absent a hand or an arm), about fifty oil drums, and related debris. It was my duty, so I'd been informed my first hour on site a month before, to accompany the customer wherever. To the moon, if need be. "Guy says pole," Hal had told me, "you vault." So there we wandered, me and Captain Courageous.

"How's the eye?" he said.

I was tiptoeing through a spread of Delco, Mopar, and FoMoCo leftovers.

"Listen, mister," I started, "can we do this another time? I got places to be."

In addition to being snotty, this was true: my running buddies — Shorty, Slim, and Whitey, none of whom were — aimed to drop by in, oh, six or seven hours. We planned to make the rounds, from Boot Town to Blake's Lotaburger, hunting for the side-winding Mescalero who'd waylaid me the evening before.

"You're a friendly fellow, ain't you?"

"Say what?" I said. That was me at my smartest back then. Amiable as a Klingon. Courteous as a cobra.

"All's I'm saying is, you catch more flies with honey than with vinegar. Get my drift?"

I looked around, innocent as the Gerber baby himself.

"I mean, snarling and back-sassing is no way to get along in this world. You see what I'm saying?"

Sixty miles thataway from my back stoop rose the Organ Mountains, good for throwing beer bottles at when you're otherwise inexpressive. Thisaway, across more miles of rock, not to mention reptiles big as your leg, stood the Sacramentos, all purples and grays and jagged as a villain's teeth. Another thing for tourists to gawk at. But now there was nothing to point at. Just me and the jet jockey. One of us at a crossroads.

"Mister," I said, "blow it out your ass."

That's when he popped me.

Point of the chin. My head snapped back. Stars burst. Between my ears it was Independence Day — sparklers and sputtering pinwheels and cherry bombs — and from the outer darkness a chorus was heard, voices thick as maple syrup and thoroughly cheerless. I went down. Not felled like a tree, but more or less melted.

Became, I admit, a fair-sized puddle next to his boots.

Inside, I came to, on my sofa. C-Dog, my assailant, had himself arranged right next to me, his a chair I'd once upon a time slept twenty hours in.

"How you feeling, boy?"

I took a second, inspecting my more tender tissues. Munchkins, single-minded as savages, were inside my head with air drills, ventilating. I could be a wise ass, I thought. Or something entirely else. Plus which, I was still seeing two of everything, including a manila file folder balanced on his knees.

"What's that?" I asked.

For an instant, he seemed as surprised as I to find paperwork near at hand and relevant.

"Randall Charles Hidey," he began, "this is your no-account life."

I pointed to the folder, about an inch thick.

"That all?"

"I see you've recovered your good humor," he said. "I like that in a subject."

He was wearing those reading glasses you see a la Ted Kennedy, half-lenses at the tip of his nose, a dandy prop for the clucking and head-shaking and tsk-tsking that TV likes to give the earnest to do. Vice-principals, for instance. Or loved ones you've busted the very hearts of.

"Bad news?" I asked. Feeling had returned to my extremities. I put one of them, a leg, on the floor.

He held up a well-manicured finger. Wiggled it slyly in my direction.

"Not so fast, son," he said. "Give it a while. You've had a C-Dog respect tap, is all."

Maybe an hour passed that way — me in coffin-like repose, Rocky Marciano licking his thumb and turning the pages before him — the outdoors ignorant of me and my predicament. I had, of course, the customary questions. For example: Who the dickens is this guy? And: Cripes, what a time to be unarmed in a democracy. This was, as my father used to say, a Sit-you-HAY-shun, but, owing to an ache in the jaw and gray matter gone suddenly soft as cooked cauliflower, I was unable to find my way out of it.

"Is it twilight," I asked once, "or just me?"

It was the aftereffect, he said. The physics of the knuckle sandwich as demonstrated by an aficionado of the sweet science.

"Middleweight," I guessed.

"Strictly amateur," he said. "Golden Gloves, Uncle Sam, AAU. I'm a sportsman."

More time went by then, as only time can when you're being held hostage in your own castle, so before he told me about my father and Uncle Hal and the tanning he'd been sent to administer, I filled part of it by thinking about Mona, my Si Senor sweet cheeks. I had it bad for that woman, I swear. Badder than bad. She was to me as carnage is to war-mongers. Hell, some evenings I used to park across the street (in that well-dinged Bel Aire Uncle Hal had loaned me) and just watch her through the windows, the six-pack on my lap my steadfast companion. Which is not to say, sad to say, that she returned my affections. To her, I was as I was to too many in yesteryear: a sourpuss wiseacre, one hundred eighty-five pounds of attitude as foul as the Führer's.

"You got a soda somewheres?"

C-Dog had wandered back to the kitchen, a good time for me to sit upright.

"What do you eat, boy?" he asked, coming in to join me anew. "You got nothing but beer and Ritz crackers."

"Vegetarian," I said, as large a lie as I could muster at the moment. "Buddhist. Full prajna."

He looked like he'd just found a hundred bucks in his pocket.

"I'm a religious man, too," he said. "Powerhouse Tabernacle of God in Christ. Odessa chapter."

I tell everybody nowadays — the white collars I work for at Fab 7, the duffers I play golf with at Painted Dunes — that C-Dog, once you got him to take off the aviator shades, was a forty-percent-handsome man. Had eyes blue as marbles you play keepsies for — the best description I could come up with in the quarter-hour we considered each other almost knee to knee in my living room way back when.

"This is how it's gonna be," he said at last.

I'd wondered about that.

"You're getting a spanking," he said.

Imagine you're relaxing on your porch glider one splendid spring sunset, a jug of lemonade at your elbow, Wilson Pickett on the stereo, the wisteria and lilac in glorious bloom. Your wife — her name is Mona, by the by — is whipping up such edibles as are worshipped by the fatsos at Good Housekeeping, and your God-fearing children, Mary Beth and Randy, Jr., are in their rooms doing homework of the straight-A ilk. You got your health, Savings Bonds from work, and an automobile with thirty months left on the warranty. This is Shangri-la, folks. Home of the brave as fetched up for you by Metro, Goldwyn, and Mayer in cahoots with the poets at Burma Shave.

Then imagine an eerie sound — part whoosh, part whine — the trees here and there twisting sideways under an enormous wind, your picket fence flung plumb out of sight. Fierce light follows, whirling spots and glares from every corner of Kingdom Come. The ground quakes, geysers erupt hither and yon, and three of your neighbors' houses go blammo in a column of flame. It's a spaceship, big as a suburb, and it's landing atop your hydrangea. That's how I felt for an instant — as if R. C. Hidey had risen from idleness and was now doing the hand jive with a frog-eyed, earless Venutian midget who might vaporize North Dakota for amusement.

"Dumbfounded, ain't you?" C-Dog remarked. "Most usually are."

"No shit," I said, still my own clever self.

Whereupon he laid it out for me, the scenario. One supercilious ingrate, me. One hired gun, him. Ten solid whacks on my hindmost with a belt and, praise Jesus, maybe a change in the common catastrophe that was my character.

"A belt?" I said.

He indicated his own, a hand-tooled specimen with artful gothic lettering.

"What's it say?" I asked.

He stood, bade me read him from loop to loop.

"'Encouragement is oxygen to the soul,'" I read, a muscle in me beginning to quiver. "Oh, boy."

"Saw it over in Jal," he began. "An insurance company on the Hobbs highway. Impressed me. Hope you don't think it's too corny."

I know what you're thinking: head for the hills, tenderfoot! But something peculiar had come over me, possibly a sense of righteousness as spontaneous as are visions to the crazed or eurekas to the eggheaded, so instead of bolting for the screen door, I leaned back into the couch, crossed my legs like a banker looking at his strongbox. At long last, I thought, mysteries were being revealed. Me, R. C. Hidey, was going to know stuff.

"My daddy and Uncle Hal, huh?"

He tapped the folder solicitously.

"Plus your mother," he said. "Your sister, your frat brothers, couple of teachers, even Mona Fernandez. It's all in black and white."

"What teachers?"

He told me, names that went down me like stones in a well.

"Anyone else?"

He shrugged, abashed. "Well, there's Shorty, Slim, and Whitey —"

"Geez," I remarked.

He seemed saddened, too. "How true."

Funny what the mind turns to in moments dire or potent or providential. Mine turned to C-Dog's shirt — a western affair, naturally, with pearl snaps, line drawings of buzzards and barbed wire, plus a pattern of gold and ruby and soupy green that made you dizzy to focus upon. Just about the most ill-considered outerwear ever seen on the unaddled adult.

"C-Dog," I said. "That's a nickname, right?"

"Navy," he told me. "Got it in the Philippines. On account of my enthusiasm."

That made sense. Given the givens, there didn't seem to be anything about this encounter that couldn't, in this vale or its counterparts, make sense. So I asked him what his real name was.

"Marion," he said. "After my mother. Middle name Gilroy, from my father."

We shared a moment then, solemn as a night in church. I could hear cars on 54 going by lickety-split, occasionally a tractor-trailer bleeping something nasty through its air horn. Outside it was all sunlight and dry heat rising in waves; inside it was cold as the bottom of a trench, a room in a haunted house, me breathing deeply but pleased my foot had stopped trembling. The last time I'd been whipped was after I'd fist-fought Phil Trafton following orchestra practice in the fifth grade — laid that puley mama's boy out so he'd be useless for the cello for a week. My daddy swatted me, his hand swelling up afterward like a ping-pong paddle. The next night, unaffected as a felon and as merry a soul as Old King Cole, I was peeping in Marci Hightower's window and slicing the garden hoses of my neighbors. Incorrigible is what I was. Delinquent as the crinkly-eyed celebrities you see in the pictures in the post office. R. C. Hidey had been heedless, so the written record put it, mindful of little but satisfying his basest appetites.

"Ready?" C-Dog asked.

He had gloves on now — "for the grip," he'd say later, "I'm a professional" — and I remember staring at them with fascination. They seemed at once delicate and demonic, tender and terrifying, rare as angel's wings.

"Ready," I said.

You got one question, I bet: Did it hurt much?

Well, do this: go outside to your car (me, I'm hoping you're driving a land yacht — a DeVille or Crown Victoria), open the trunk, place your index finger near the lid latch, then slam that devil hard. Don't pussyfoot. Get your weight behind it. Leap up if you have to. That's how it hurt, for in spite of his girth, C-Dog Simpson was part Hercules, part Charles Atlas — as gifted with leather-lashing as Gabriel had been with horn-honking.

"You can cry if you want," he said.

I was across his lap, boy-like, butt in the air, the only thing between me and "encouragement" a much-washed pair of BVDs. I could smell him now, Jade East or the like, a fragrance I still associate with singleness of purpose.

"Don't think so," I told him. My heart already thumping wildly, blood rushing to my lowered head, I was concentrating on his Tony Lamas, boots with sufficient sheen to see my gritted teeth in. "Get on with it."

I heard his arm draw back.

"Suit yourself," he said.

By blow three, I was in full bawl, sucking air and sniveling. Teardrops — genuine teardrops, big as boulders — were running through my eyebrows and into my hair. He let fly, belt whistling overhead, and I braced for contact, a noise which is spelled in cartoons as "thwap!" It burned. Like sitting on a cigar the size of a Louisville Slugger. Then came a spell when I felt nothing — an "interregnum," C-Dog would say later — before pain, ferocious as prairie fire, spread down my thighs. I tried thinking elsewise — of snow-skiing, which I was fair at, and of ice cream, which I could eat in industrial-size quantities — but my brain, the loaf of it, was filled with words like "welt" and "blister" and "flayed."

"Nineteen sixty-seven," C-Dog said after swat five. "Did this to a youngster up in Raton."

I couldn't respond with anything but syllables with h's and f's throughout.

"Feisty boy," C-Dog was saying. "Took a half-hour to settle his hash."

I'd found a spot on the floor to concentrate on, something that had no opinion about me or the immediate drama.

"Turned out okay," C-Dog said. "That boy is now Lieutenant Governor of Texas."

Then my fanny caught fire again. And again. And again.

"Did me a pachuco in Silver City once. He's an astronaut. You should see my scrapbook. Got me a police chief in Denver, a college dean, a couple of California movie actors. Females, too. You ever hear of Miss New Hampshire Universe 1968? Mother of five now. An eye doctor."

At this point I was overcome by a vision: C-Dog at the wheel of his Imperial, on the highways and byways. A man, clearly, with more than a line of work. He had a calling. Wrongs to right. Justice to dispense. Half Zorro, half King Arthur. In his trunk probably a full suit of armor. A shield. A lance. A terrible, swift sword.

At numero ocho, he seemed to shift, his own breath raspy and short.

"Out," he said, huffing. "Of." Puffing. "Shape."

Me, I was feeling giddy, as oddly good-humored as a drunk. I was still sobbing, it appeared, but, wrong end up, mine was a world gone blue and orange, a noteworthy glow around most of my furnishings. Happily, there was less pain now. I figured my flesh was hanging off in strips, like fresh beef jerky, and that C-Dog was merely exercising himself against the thin, nerveless bones of my behind. Speech hadn't yet returned, but I was suffering fewer thoughts with gibberish at the core.

Then we were done, and I had evidently moved into the last chapter of my story, the part wherein I am face down on my couch and Marion Gilroy Simpson, flush-faced as Porky Pig, is standing over me, his special gloves out of sight, his belt once again around his oh-so-enthusiastic midriff.

"Here," he said.

Near as I could make out, he was offering me a bargain-size can of Crisco.

"It's vitamin E," he said. "Takes the sting out. Promotes healing."

I nodded. I may have even smiled.

"You mean I ain't dead?" I said.

He grinned himself, ten thousand of the most perfect teeth in the Northern Hemisphere.

"Slop that stuff on as needed," he said. "You'll be shipshape in no time."

That was nice to hear, and I said so, now in complete control of both the mind and meat of me.

"You hungry?" he asked.

I considered it. Lordy, I was.

"Me," he was saying, "I always work up a hunger on a mission. Got supplies in the car."

That was nice, too. Hell, everything was suddenly nice — the weather, my situation on earth, all the peoples of the planet, even the dinner C-Dog fixed (melted cheese, olives, tomato soup, store-bought eclairs for dessert), which, like a nurse or a friend from heaven, he served me bite-size. Anything seemed possible. Silk ties on herd bulls. Circus seals from the sky. Tin-pot despots opening their jails. I had been, as my kids nowadays say, morphed — changed from the inside out. Though woolly-minded and agog, I felt I'd emerged from a virtually sleep-like state and now, weird as a night on Neptune, awfully strange sentiments were coming — yes, trippingly — from my tongue.

"Thought I might clean up around here," I distinctly heard my chastened self say. "Paint that sign by the highway."

A good idea, C-Dog told me. Damn good.

Then it happened again — more parlez-vous from some-body who sounded a whole lot like me.

"Got to get a haircut, though. Maybe shave a bit more often, too."

That was the spirit, he said, then started gathering up the dishes, the proper washing of which he gave me elaborate instruction about for the next five minutes. Presently, he was back in front of me, hitching up his trousers, and for an instant I feared the bell had rung for Round Two, more whomping and wailing — more of me upended and praying for deliverance. But he only shook my hand and said it was high time he hit the road, which gave me to imagine myself stranded on a wayside, thumb out, shabby as a hobo looking for help to go yonder.

"You take care, Randall Hidey," he said.

I would, I told him, and watched him head for the door. In front of me was his — now my — folder, pages sobering to ruminate upon.

"You're not a pilot, are you?" I asked.

It was a dumb question, the answer obvious as the Pope's faith of choice, but C-Dog was sufficiently civil to address it anyhow. Not a chance, he said. He'd been a lot of things — farmer, a sewer contractor out of Big Spring, a wholesaler of Mexican artifacts, a diesel mechanic for an OTR outfit called Handy Haulers — but never a flyboy.

"Scared of heights," he said.

"What about the Triumph?" I asked. "A trick, eh?"

He shrugged: What could he say, he said. In his business, you needed to be sly. Catch the subject off-guard.

So that's when I put it to him. About the shirt.

For a moment he looked mystified, like a grown-up watching an infant cha-cha-cha.

"I wonder if I might buy it," I said.

To be sure, this was a seriously sappy exchange, but, as I told Mona the next day, this is how life is among the kind we are — sappiness, goo, every icky thing else pooh-poohed by know-it-alls.

"Buy it," he repeated, words clearly new to his vocabulary.

"A keepsake," I told him. "A memento. Like a postcard. Or a curio. Say you been to the Grand Canyon, or the Empire State Building, naturally you want —"

"Hell," he said, "I should give it to you. No charge."

Which he did. Unbuttoned that eye-popping item and made me a present of it.

"Got ten more of them anyway," he said. "Buy in bulk, son. That's my motto."

Briefly, I considered rising to watch him leave, but my butt would have no part of that plan. I lay where I was, belly down, chin on a pillow C-Dog had brought me once the athletics had ended. I lay there, I say, heard him open and close the door to his Imperial, a thwunk as good to hear as are the squeaks of delight your offspring make when they see you striding up the walk after work.

He didn't start her immediately, and for an instant I wondered if he'd forgotten something or had changed his mind about the shirt. Then that car turned over, chugga-chugga, and you could hear the crunch of gravel as he pulled around toward the highway. It was late evening now, many stars to bask beneath, and no snot-nosed smartypants out there to disturb the peace of it. He honked adios and for a time I listened to him go south, his a motor with rumble enough to make you smile, until there was only silence and me alone at my place.

The Talk Talked between Worms

ONE

According to the tapes, my father, then about as run-of-the-mill a man as Joe Blow himself, didn't want to see the thing. *Not a damn bit,* he says. But there it came anyhow, roaring in hard and tumbly from the west with a comet's fiery tail, and then ka-BOOM — enough bang to rock Chaves County left and right like a quake.

This was summer 1947, almost nothing to see but weeds and hummocks and desert all the way to the red clay of Texas in the east, and my father, Totenham Gregory Hamsey, gentleman cowboy, was out there. Riding his pickup bouncylike on the fence line, he was hunting for the gaps in the barbed wire that several yearlings had escaped through, when it — the UFO — went *whump* to the east of him. Maybe like your own self — certainly like me in a similarly serious moment —

he was dumbstruck. His blood ran rank and grainy in his chest, his mouth opening and closing on thinnest air. Something from the clouds had tumbled earthward, and nobody had seen it but a twenty-nine-year-old red-haired rancher with thirty dollars in his pocket and the current issue of the *Saturday Evening Post* on the seat beside him.

His truck had stalled, another mystery he lived to tell about, so presently he gave up on it and hopped onto the hood to study the scattered fires and the long, raggedy trench the Martians — or whatever the hell they were — had made when they quit their element for ours. First he thought it was a plane, a top-secret jet out of Roswell Army Air Field, or a V-2 rocket gone haywire from White Sands, which gave him, naturally, to expect company — more planes maybe, or soldiers with rifles to shoo him out of there. These were the days of Communists, he says on the tapes: sour-minded hordes from Korea and the Soviet Union that even Governor Whitman had warned you to expect on the doorstep of city hall itself. One hour went by that way — Tot Hamsey, rich man's youngest son, saying to himself what he'd say to others if they, in pairs or in a mob, were to rumble over, say, that hill yonder and want their busted contraption back. But none did. Not for that hour anyway. Nor for the several that followed. Nothing arrived but a turkey buzzard, wings glossy and black as crude oil, which gave everything the once-over — the smoking debris, the perplexed human being, the prickly flora all about — before, screeching in disappointment, it wheeled west for better pickings.

That's when Tot Hamsey, my father, gave his Ford a second chance. Climbed back in the cab, spoke angrily in the direction of the starter button, and breathed deeply with relief when its six cylinders clattered to life — under those circumstances as welcome a noise to hear as is conversation from the lady you love. He could go back to town, he figured. Thirty-five miles. Find Sheriff Johnny Freel. Maybe Cheek Watson, the dumbbell deputy. Tell them the whole story — the sky a menace of streaky orange and yellow, the howl coming at him over his shoulder, the boom, and afterward soil and rock pitched up everywhere. Be done with it then. Bring the bigwigs back here, sure. Possibly hang around to gab with whatever colonel or general showed up to get his property back. Still get home in time for supper.

But Tot Hamsey was a curious man — a habit of character, my mother once said, you like to see in those you're to spend a lifetime with — and he was curious now, more curious than hungry or tired or wary-witted, and so he put himself in gear to drive slowly down a sandy draw and up an easy rise until he had nowhere to turn but into the raw and burned up acreage this part of New Mexico would ever after be famous for.

Everywhere was space-age junk, various foils and joints and milled metals as peculiar to him as maybe we are to critters. All the way to more sizable hills a half-mile east, the landscape had been split and gouged — the handiwork, it appeared, of a giant from Homer or the Holy Bible racing toward sunrise and dragging a plow behind. Fires flickered near and far, and Tot Hamsey, father of one, could imagine that these were the cooking fires of an army heedless enough to make war against God. The sky had gone mostly dark, several stars twinkling, but no moon to make out specifics by. Just dark upon dark, and sky upon sky, and one innocent bystander in a Stetson from the El Paso Hat Company tying a bandanna over his mouth and nose to keep from breathing so much vile smoke.

The silence was likewise peculiar, somehow cold and leaden, another thing to spook you in the night. He thought he'd hear wildlife, certainly. Coyotes in a pack. The sheep from Albert Tulk's place. But nothing, not even a dry wind to sweep noises here from civilization, which gave him suddenly to believe that all he'd known had vanished from the empire of man. His daddy's banks. His mother Vanetta and his two brothers. Mac Brazeall, his own hired hand. His wife, who was my mother Corrine, and me as well, only a toddler. Even the town of Roswell and all others he'd suffered the bother to visit.

He turned himself on his heels, eyes fixed on the collapsed horizon, a full circle. Panic had begun to rise in Mister Hamsey, him a Christian reared to believe in peril and the calamitous end of everything. It did seem possible, he thought. All of modern life, now gone. Streets he knew. The Liberty Bar, Brother Bill Toomey's radio station, his grammar school on Hardesty Road and the crotchety marms that taught there. Every bit of it, great and small. The President of the United States, not to mention those muckety-mucks who ruled the world beyond. Maybe even the vast world itself. Which was probably all rubble and flame and smoke and which, as he thought about it, meant, Lord Almighty, that maybe Tot Hamsey was the last of whatever was — the last man in the last place on the last day with the last mind to think of the last things on Planet Earth.

You can go out there your own self, if you wish. Just visit the UFO Museum. Not the classy outfit across from the courthouse near Denny's, but the low-rent enterprise way south on Main Street, past the Levi's plant and Mrs. Blake's House of Christmas. The man there is Boyd Pickett, to matters of heaven and earth what, say, the Devil is to truth and fruit from a tree. For ten dollars a head, he'll drive you out there in his Crown Victoria — it's private property, he'll tell you, him with a sweetheart lease arrangement — and show you the sights such as they currently are. For five more dollars, he'll dangle a Tyco model flying saucer on #10 fishing filament behind you and snap you a full-color Polaroid suitable for framing, which means — ha-ha-ha — you with a moron's grin and hovering over your shoulder physical evidence of a superior intelligence, which you are encouraged to show to your faithless friends and neighbors in, oh, Outer Mongolia or wherever it is you tote your own heavy bale.

For $8.50 you can have the as-told-to story between covers: how in July of 1947, one Mac Brazeall, ramrod for the Bar H spread out of Corona, heard a boom bigger than thunder and, as dutiful a Democrat as Harry Truman himself, went out to investigate; how he found what he found, which was wreckage and scalded rock and scorched grama grass, and how he took a piece of the former to Sheriff Johnny Freel who viewed the affair with skepticism until Mac Brazeall, patriot and full-time redneck, crumpled a square of metal in his hands and put it on the table, whereupon, like an instance of infernal hocus-pocus, it sprung back into its original shape; and how Sheriff Freel, heart plugged in his throat, got on the phone to his Army counterpart at the air base; and how, in the hours that passed, much ordnance was mobilized and dispatched, and heads were scratched and oaths sworn; and how by, quote, dawn's early light, you could look at the front page of the *Daily Record* and see there a picture of jug-eared Mac Brazeall, smug as a gambler atop a pyramid of loot, taking credit for a historical fact that had begun when my father, Tot Hamsey, heard the air whip and crack and, as if in a nightmare, witnessed his paid-for real estate turn to fire and ruin in front of him.

I've been out there a few times, the first with Cece Phillips (now my ex-wife) when we were hot for each other and stupid with youth. This was summer 1964, me only fresh out of high school and not yet in possession of the tapes my father, once a doctor-certified crazy man, would one day oblige me to listen to. Ignorant is what I'm trying to say, just a boy, like his long-gone daddy, unaware that what lay before him was a land of miracles terrifying but necessary to behold; just a boy fumbling at his girlfriend's underclothes while everywhere, invisible above, eyes might have been looking down.

That night the moon was up, golden as a supper plate from the table of King Midas himself. In the backseat of my mother's Chevrolet we had gone round and round for a time, Cece Phillips and me, breathless and eager-beaver, nothing there or there or there outdoors but sagebrush and the shapely shadows hills make. We must've seemed like wrestlers, I'm thinking now. Clinch, paw, and part. Look this way and that, not much coming out of our mouths but breath and syllables a whole lot like "eeeff" and "ooohh." Cece said she couldn't — not now anyways, not in this creepy place. And I, an hour of lukewarm Coors beer my inspiration, said she could. Which gave us, for a little while, something else to talk about before it became clear she would.

Not much to report here. Nothing oooey-gooey, anyway, from romance books or love songs. Just how time seemed to me to pass. One second and then another, like links on a chain that one day has to end. This is who we were: Reilly Hamsey, beefy enough to be of parttime use to the Coyotes' coach for football; and Cece Phillips, hair in the suave beehive style of the stewardess she intended to be. We had music from KOMA out of Oklahoma City, and no school tomorrow or anytime until fall when we were to take up college life at New Mexico State University in Las Cruces. This was us: bone and heat and movement, as we had been at the drive-in or in my mother's rec room when she was away at work. Just us, youngsters who knew how to say "sir" and "ma'am" and "thank you" and be the seen-not-heard types adults are tickled silly to brag about.

Then this was over, and I was out of doors.

Was anything wrong, Cece wanted to know, and for a second I believed there wasn't.

"I'm gonna take a leak," I told her and moseyed away to find a bush to stand behind.

A pall had fallen over me, I think now. A curtain had come down, or a wall gone up. Something that, as I stood with my back to the car and Cece, I could feel as plainly as I only moments before had felt the buckles and bows of Miss Phillips herself.

Behind me, Cece was singing with the Rolling Stones, hers a voice vigorous enough to be admired by Baptists, and I, for the first time, was doing some serious thinking about her. About the muscles she had, and the dances she was unashamed to do at the Pit Stop or in the gym. She could stick-shift fast as I and knew as much as many about engines, those farm-related and not. She was tall, which appealed, and loose in the legs, swift as a sprinter.

"Don't go too far," she was saying. "We got to go pretty soon."

Thinking about her. Then me. Then, oddly, my dog Red and how the fur bristled on his rump when the unexpected rapped at our front door on Missouri Street. Then my still pretty mother and the colonel from the New Mexico Military Institute she was dating, him with a posture rigid as plank flooring. Then, inevitably, my father, Tot Hamsey.

"Darn you, Reilly Jay," she hollered out. "You tore my skirt."

I imagined my father exactly as my mother had once described him: in front of the TV in the dayroom of his ward, his long face empty of everything but shock and sadness, his eyes glassy as marbles, the sense that in his head were only sparks and such thoughts as are thought by birds.

"You all right?" Cece called. "Reilly, you hear me?"

I was done with thinking then. I had reached a conclusion about Cece and me, one I was surer and surer of the closer I came to the car.

"Reilly," she said, "what's wrong with your face?"

We were doomed, I was thinking, the fact of it suddenly no more surprising than is the news that it's hot in hell. We would go to college, that was clear. Cece, I guessed, would become pregnant. Yours truly would graduate and work for, say, Sinclair Oil in Midland and Odessa or thereabouts. More years would then roll over us, a tidal wave washing through our lives as one had smashed through my parents' own. Eventually, I would find myself back here in Roswell — exactly, friends, as it has come to pass — and very likely I would be alone. As alone, according to the story, as my father had been the night he, years and years before, learned what he learned when the sun was down in this weird place and there was nothing else to do but heave himself into madness.

"I'm fine," I told her. "Put your clothes on."

Tot Hamsey finds the body in this part. The extraterrestrial. Finds it, listens to it, watches it expire. Then, having wandered a considerable distance away, he leans himself against the crumbling bank of an arroyo and, sprocket by spool by spring, feels his own simple self come plumb apart. *The very him of him disassembled,* which are his own words on one cassette. His boyhood, which was largely carefree and conducted out of doors. His school years, which go as they came, autumn by autumn. His playing basketball. He had popped an eardrum by diving in the wrong place at the Bottomless Lakes, and that went, as did the courtship of several town girls, including Corrine Rains, who became his wife and my mother, as well as his years at the Nazarene college in Idaho. He put aside — "*very carefully,*" he says on the tapes, likening himself to a whirlygig of cogs and levers and wheels — all he'd done and thought about doing. About being for two whole days the property of Uncle Sam, and the tubby doctor who discovered that Tot Hamsey was one inch shorter on the left side. About working carpentry with his brother Ben at the German POW camp south of town. About being another man's boss, and knowledge to have through the hands. About me even, the tiny look-alike of him. For almost an hour, until he heard the sputter of Mac Brazeall's flatbed well east of him, he sat there. He was only mass and weight, one more creature to take up space in the world, more or less the man I visited in 1981, the year after I came back to this corner of America — a man who regarded you as though he expected you to reach behind your head to yank off your face and thus reveal yourself as a monster, too.

For a time, so he says on one tape, he didn't do much of anything that July night in 1947. Sound had returned to the world, it seemed. He could hear the cows he'd been searching for bawling in the hard darkness south of him. He was in and out of the debris field now — back and forth, back and forth — the smell of char and ravaged earth sometimes strong enough to gag him, so he kept the Ford moving. Every now and then, slowing to roll down the window, he hollered into the blackness. If it was a plane from the Army base, then, shoot, maybe somebody had bailed out before or otherwise survived the crash. He might even know the pilot or those the pilot knew. But no answer ever came back. Not at point X or the other points, near and far, he found interesting. So for a while he didn't stop at all, fearing that if he did leave his truck he might find only a torn-off part of somebody — a leg, maybe, or a familiar head rolled up into some creosote bush — and that was nothing at all Tot Hamsey cared to find by himself. You could be scared, yes. But you didn't have to be foolish. Instead, you would just stay in the cab of your nearly new Ford pickup and if, courtesy of your headlights, something should appear, well, you would just have to see that, wouldn't you, and thereafter make up your own mind about what smart thing to do next.

He's hearing the voice now, he says on the cassette. He's been hearing it for a while, he thinks. Not a voice exactly, but chatter akin to static — like communication you might imagine from Shangri-la or a risen and busy Atlantis. Bursts of it. Ancient as Eden or new as tomorrow. The language of fish, maybe. Or what the trees confide in each other.

"*Trees*," he says, his own voice a whisper you would not want to hear more than once after sundown. "*Vipers. And bugs. And rocks. The talk talked between worms.*"

He's stopped the truck now. But he's not jumpy anymore — not at all. This could be a dream, he thinks, him still at home with Corrine and nothing but work in the sunshine to look forward to. He thinks about his friends, Straightleg Harry Peterson and Sonny Fitzpatrick, and the pheasant they'll hunt come winter. He thinks about his daddy's deacon, Martin Willis, whose porch he's promised to fix on Saturday.

It's a dream, he tells himself, feeling himself move left and right in it, nothing to keep him from falling over the edge. It's a dream, water a medium to stand upon and wings everywhere to wear. It's a dream, yes, time a rope to hang from and you on a root in the clouds.

"*It's a dream,*" Tot Hamsey says on the tape, but then it is not — never has been — and there he is at last, staring into the face of one sign and terrible wonder.

The books describe it as tiny, like a fourth-grader, with a head like a bowling ball on a stick. *The Roswell Incident* by

Charles Berlitz and Bill Moore. *UFO Crash at Roswell* by those smart alecks from England. They all say that it — the spaceman my father found — was hairless, skin gray as ash, its eyes big as a prizefighter's fists. Something you could lug for a mile or two, easy. They're wrong. The thing had skin pink as a newborn's with hands like claws. You could see into it, my father says on the tapes. See its fluids pumping, an ooze that could be blood or sparkly liquids or goo there aren't yet names for. And probably it could see into you. At least that's the way it seemed to him — it with a Chinaman's eyes that didn't close and no ears and nothing but sloppy, wet holes the size of peach pits to breathe through.

"Touch," the thing said. The static was gone, English in its place — more phenomena we're told that Uncle Sam has an interest in keeping hush-hush. "Don't be afraid."

My father looked around, no help on the horizon. He'd been given an order, it seemed, and there appeared to be no good reason not to obey it. So his hand went out, as if they knew each other and had been summoned hereabouts to do common business.

It was like touching a snake, he says. *Or the deepest thing from the deepest blue sea.*

"Help them," the thing said — another sentence you probably find silly to believe — and only a moment passed before my father noticed the three others nearby.

They were dead. That was easy to tell. Like oversize dolls that have lost their air — a sight downright sad to see but one Tot Hamsey told himself he could forget provided he now had nothing else awful to know and thereafter nothing more to remember.

"Wait," the thing told him. "Sit."

Ten paces away the pickup was still running at idle, headlights on but aimed elsewhere, and my father imagined himself able enough to walk toward it.

In an hour he could be home. He would eat supper, play with his boy, listen to the radio. Corrine was making apricot jam, so he would sample it. He would take a bath, hot as he could tolerate. And then shave, using the razor his father had given him for Christmas. He could shine his lace-up shoes, read a true story in the *Reader's Digest*, or tell Reilly more about Huck and Tom and Nigger Jim.

Sonny Fitzpatrick wanted him to help put the plumbing in a bungalow being built by the road to Artesia, so he could puzzle over that — the supplies he'd need and what to charge Sonny's father for the hours involved. He'd been good at math. At geometry and angles to draw. He'd been better at literature, the go-getters and backsliders that books told about. He was only twenty-nine. A husband and a father. Much remained to be done in life.

But this, he thought. This was like dying. Like watching a horrible storm bear down on you from heaven. Nowhere at all to hide from the ordained end of you.

"Listen," the thing said, and Tot Hamsey was powerless not to.

My mother has told me that he came home around sunrise. He'd been gone overnight before, so that hadn't worried her. Sometimes he had a two-man project to do — a new windmill to get up or a stock tank that needed to be mucked out — so she had slept that night, me in my crib in the other bedroom, imagining him holed up in a rickety outbuilding in the badlands, eating biscuits hard as stones and listening to that blowhard Mac Brazeall say how it was in moldy-oldy times. She was not surprised when she heard the truck, nor when she looked out the window to see him standing at the gate to the yard. He would do that on occasion, she thought. Collect himself for a minute. Slap the dust from his jeans or shake out his slicker and scrape his boots clean if it had rained. Then he'd come in, say howdy to Reilly, maybe swing him around a time or two, and over breakfast thereafter tell what could be told about doings in the hardscrabble way west of them.

But for a long time, too long to be unimportant, he didn't

move. He had a finger on the gatepost and it seemed he was taking its pulse. Behind the curtain, my mother watched, her own self as still as he. He'd lost his hat, evidently, and half of his face, like a clown's, seemed red as war paint. She wasn't scared, she said to me more than once. Not yet. This was her husband, a decent man top to bottom, and she had known him since the third grade. She'd seen him dance and, drunk on whiskey, play the piano with his elbows. He could sit a horse well and had a concern for the small gestures of courtesy that are now and then necessary to use between folks. So there was nothing to be frightened of, not even when he came in the front door and she could see that his eyes had turned small and hard, like nail heads.

Whatever wound in him was wound too tight, she thought. Whatever spun, now spinning too fast.

After that, she says, events happened very quickly. He gathered up several tablets and disappeared into his workshop, a pole barn he'd built himself back behind the clothesline. She put his breakfast out — bacon from Milt Morris's slaughterhouse and eggs she'd put a little Tabasco in — but in an hour it was still outside the door. She could hear him in there, a man with a hammer and saw, something being built. Or something coming apart. She took me to the Hawkins house so I could play with their boy Michael. At noon he was still in the shop, the door shut.

"Tot," she said. "You hungry for lunch?"

She could hear him, she thought. Like the fevered scraping and scratching of a rodent in a wall.

Later, the afternoon worn white with sunlight, she told him Sonny Fitzpatrick was on the phone.

"He wants you there first thing in the morning, okay?"

She tried the door then, but something was blocking it, and she could only see a little through the space: Tot Hamsey's back bent to a task on the table in front of him.

"Tot?" she said.

He turned then, eyes hooded, nothing in his expression to

suggest that he knew her from anybody else who'd once upon a time crossed his narrow path — a look, she said later, that froze the innermost part of her. The vein or the nerve that was like wire at her very center.

"I'll tell him you'll be there," she said.

After she picked me up at the Hawkins house, she tried the door again. This time it didn't move, so she went to the window. He was still at the bench, a leather apron on, passing a piece of metal back and forth in his big hands. She could see now that the door had been blocked by his table saw, a machine that had taken both him and her to move four months before. Exasperated, she rapped on the window.

"Supper in an hour," she said.

But he didn't come out for that. Nor for the serial on the radio. Nor for my bath, or for the story time that was supposed to follow. At the back door, she stood to watch the workshop. The lights were on, but he'd put a cover over the window. A sheet possibly.

This time she knocked harder. His supper dishes were still on the step. Untouched. "You've got to eat something," she called. "Tot Hamsey?"

A moment later, she'd said his name again. And again. She thought he was just on the other side of the door, maybe his face, like her own, against the wood, the two of them — except for the pine boards — cheek to cheek. He was huffing, she thought. As if he'd raced a mile to be there. As if he had more miles to go.

"Oh, honey," she sighed.

It was the same the next day, she has said. And the day after that. No evidence that he'd come out of the workshop. Only the slightest sign that he'd eaten. Once she thought to call his father, Milt Hamsey, but he was the meddlesome type, quick to condemn, slow to forgive. A holier-than-thou sort with a walleye and hair in his ears and no patience whatsoever with the ordinary back and forth of lived life. Too much anger in him. Like a spike in the heart.

No, she thought. Tot was only fretful about something. Or working an idea to a point. Besides, it was nobody's business what went on in Tot and Corrine Hamsey's house.

On the fourth day, she got the newspaper from the box by the fence line near the road. Whiskered Mac Brazeall was in it, a picture of his idiotic self on the front page, with his cockamamie story about the flying saucer parts he'd found off the Elko trail leading into the Jornada. Other articles about bogeymen in the skies above Canada and Kansas and all over the West. The base was involved, she read. Soldiers and officials from the government everywhere. Maybe spies. Just about the most far-fetched thing she'd ever heard of.

At the step to the workshop, she asked Tot if he knew anything about this. "You were out there," she said. "That's where you were, right?"

Tot Hamsey came toward the door then. She heard the table saw being shoved aside. He would look like a hermit, she believed. Ravaged and blighted. Then he was in front of her, not a giant step away, and she thought briefly that he'd had his heart ripped right out of him.

"What's it say?" he asked, his first words in nearly one hundred hours.

"You coming out?" she wondered.

He had that look still. Murder in him maybe. Or fear. "Give it here," he said.

Now she was scared, a part of her already edging back toward the house. The room behind him, though ordered as her own kitchen, was cold as an icebox, the smell of it stale, like what you might find if you opened a trunk from another century. She told herself not to gasp.

"This has to stop," she said.

"It will," he told her. He was reading the paper now, his lips moving as if he were chewing up the words.

"When?" she said, but the door was already closing.

They had reached an understanding, she decided. She was not to trouble him anymore. She had her own self and me to tend to. If anybody called — Sonny again, for example, or nosy Norris Proctor or Tommy Tyree from the Elks Club, anybody wanting anything from citizen Hamsey — she was to make up an excuse. A broken leg, maybe. The summer flu. A lie, anyway, that he and she would one day laugh about. In turn, she was to get about her own business. She would have to call her dad for money, but that was okay. He owned two hardware stores and was rich enough for three families.

She was to wait, she thought. A hole had opened in her life, hers now the job to see what creature crawled free from it.

He possessed treasure, he says on the tapes. Not the pirate kind. Not wealth, but secrets. "My name is Totenham Gregory Hamsey," he scribbled on the first page of the tablet I would one day find. "I was born in 1918, on March the 13th. My mother says I was a sweet child." For page after page, he goes on that way, his handwriting like a million spiders seen from above. He'd seen a human die, he wrote, and had watched another, me, being birthed. He knew a U.S. senator and had shaken the hand of Roy Rogers. In Española, he'd ridden a Brahman bull and had taken a trolley in Juárez, Mexico. "I look good in swim trunks," he says on one page, "and have a membership at the Roswell Country Club. I am no golfer, though." He knows bridge and canasta and can juggle five apples. Jazz music he doesn't like, but he'll listen once to whatever you put on the record player.

"I have knowledge," he writes, and by page 26 he has started to give it. Pictures of how it is where they live. Their tribe names and what they do in space. The beliefs of them, their many conquests. They are us, he says, but for the accidents of where and when we are.

On the fifth day, according to the tapes in his file cabinets, he goes into the house. He doesn't know where his wife and child are. Nor does he much care. They could be strangers, people at a wayside: they're going one way, he another.

Beside the couch in the living room, he finds the stack of

newspapers — the Army everywhere and Sheriff Johnny Freel looking boneheaded. It's a weather balloon, my father reads. A Rawin Sonde, a new design, a balloon big as a building in New York City. A colonel from Ft. Worth has confirmed this to all who thought the opposite. The intelligence officer from the base, Jesse Marcel himself, has put minds at rest. Mac Brazeall, cow puncher, was mistaken, wrong as wrong could be. Not spacemen after all. Not Communists either. Just Uncle Sam measuring winds aloft. All is well again.

He feels sorry for them, my father says. They have small minds. They are insects.

For the next hour, he busies himself with practical matters. He gets out his good suit. For the journey. He showers, shaves, brushes his teeth. He eats, for fuel only. He settles his affairs. "I am not coming back," he writes to my mother in a note he'll put on the dining-room table. "You are young. You can be good to someone else."

Outside, the landscape fascinates. Dry and cracked and endless. Storm clouds boiling up in the distance. They are there. His friends.

"Reilly," he writes to me in the same note, "study. Know your sentences and your sums. Do not give offense to your elders. Keep yourself clean. We move. We ascend. We vanish."

Carefully, he dresses. It is important, he thinks, that he look presentable. He wears cufflinks, stuffs a handkerchief in his coat pocket. In the mirror, he sees a man of virtuous aspect — hair nicely combed, shoulders squared, tie in a handsome Windsor knot. He hears himself breathing, amused that he still needs our air.

On the phone, he asks for Charlie Spiller personally. "I need a taxi," he says. "In one hour."

He imagines Charlie Spiller on the other end of the line. A man with a fake leg. A lodge brother. Another creepy-crawly thing from a vulgar kingdom.

"One hour," he says. "Exactly."

He's at the end of something, clearly. All that can be done

has been done. He is not here. Not really. The past has closed behind him. He's gone through a door, a seam. There is no point in looking back.

On the dresser in the bedroom, he leaves his wallet and his Longines wristwatch. For a little while, sadly, he will need money. To pay Charlie. To pay for the Greyhound bus. To eat a sandwich along the way. He will not need his driver's license. Nor other papers. He is not anybody to know. None of us is. We are wind and dirt and ash. We are weight that falls, flesh that burns. We are oil and mud. We are slow and cannot run. We are blind and do not see. We are echo and shadow and mist.

At the workshop, he checks the padlock. Inside, beneath the floorboards, in a pit he has dug, are his secrets. His papers wrapped in oilcloth. In the box are the metals. The meshlike panels. The tiny I-beams. Dials and switches and wires. His keepsakes from the future.

He turns once to look at the house. He imagines his thoughts like laundry on a line. All is well.

This is not lunacy, he says on the tapes I would find. *I'm a man who's died and come back, is all.*

At the dirt road by the fence line is the place he needs to be in a minute. Charlie Spiller drives a Dodge, a big car to go places in. Charlie Spiller cackles like a crone and can take direction. He can tell a joke and crack his knuckles, tricks to perform in the places he goes. Charlie Spiller: another human to forget about.

From his pocket, my father takes his keys and throws them as far as he can into the desert. He straightens his tie, shoots his cuffs, buttons his suit coat.

If it is sunny, he does not know. If raining, he cannot feel it. Instead, he has a place to be and a passel of desire to be there. He speaks to his feet, to his legs and hips, to the obedient muscles in each.

The voices. They've returned. The stones have messages for him. The cactus. The furniture he's leaving behind. Much is being revealed. Of sovereigns and viceroys. Of sand and of rocks. Listen. You can hear them. Like water. Like lava a mile beneath your feet.

"*I had knowledge,*" he says. "*My name was Tot Hamsey. All was well.*"

TWO

In 1980, for all the reasons unique to modern times (boredom, mainly, plus anger and some sickness at the pickiness of us), Cece Phillips and I went bust. She got the house in Odessa, not to mention custody of Nora Jane (like her mother, a specimen of womanhood sharp-tongued and fast to laugh at tomfoolery), and I came back here, to Roswell. The city liked well enough what it read on paper and so put me to work in the engineering department, where I compute the numbers relevant to curbs and gutters and how you get streets to drain. Besides the physical, you should know, much had changed about me. I'd sworn off anything stronger than Pepsi and did not use a credit card and had learned to play handball at the YMCA on Washington Avenue. In the mayor's office next door, I met a Clerical II, Sharon Sweeny, and spent enough agreeable hours with her at the movies and the like to think, in boy-girl matters of moon and June at least, that two and two equaled more than the four you'd expect. I ate square meals, cleaned up my apartment regularly, and kept my p's and q's in the order they're notorious for.

Then, in 1981, the curious son of a curious man, I went to visit my father.

"You're Reilly," he said, his first words to me in decades.

"I am," I said, mine to him.

He was living in, quote, a residential facility, meaning that if you've got enough money, you can break bread in what looks like a combination hospital and resort motel with a bunch of harmless drunks and narcotics addicts and taxpayers who need to scrub their hands thirty times before they can dress in the morning. He'd been there since early in 1954, after my grandfather — who is himself dead now — found him up at the New Mexico State Hospital in Las Vegas and drew up papers that said, as papers from rich men can, that T. G. Hamsey could live at the Sunset Manor here until the day arrived to put him in the family plot in the cemetery on Pennsylvania Street.

I didn't recognize him. Umpteen-umpteens had gone by, and I was looking for the stringbean adult in the snapshots my mother had given me. He was collapsed, if you must know. Time had come down cruel on him, the way it will on all of us. Plus he was over sixty years old.

"Do you have a cigarette?" he said.

We were standing in a lobbylike affair, couches and end tables with lamps on them, the windows beyond us giving onto a view of K-Mart and Dairy Queen and all else crummy the block had become.

I'd quit, I told him.

"Perhaps next time," he said.

He was a stranger, as unknown to me as I am to the Queen of England. He was just a man, I was telling myself, one I shared no more than cell matter with.

"Are you scared, Reilly?"

That wasn't the word, I told him. Not scared.

"What is the word then, Son?"

I didn't know. Honest.

"I'm something you've heard of, right? I'm a river to visit. A monument somebody wrote about. Maybe a city to go to."

We had sat, him in an armchair that seemed too small, me catty-corner on a leather couch so slick you could slide off. I wanted to leave, I'll admit. It was my lunch hour, and I thought of myself at El Popo's, eating Mexican food with my friends, little more to fret about than what paper needed to be pushed in the afternoon and which shoot-'em-up Sharon Sweeny and I could munch popcorn in front of that night at the Fiesta.

"I knew you'd come," he said.

It was hot outside, the heat shimmering up in waves from the asphalt parking lot, but I yearned to be out there in it, striding toward my car.

"Just didn't know when," he said. "You're a Hamsey."

True enough, I thought. Cece Phillips had once told me that I was about as predictable as time itself.

"How is she?" he asked. "Your mother."

She was in Albuquerque now, I said. She'd married again — not the colonel from NMMI when I was in high school, but the man after the man after the man after him.

"That's good," he said. "She used to come by, you know."

"A long time ago," I said.

That was right, he said. A long time ago, she used to visit with him, in this very room, tell him how it was with his parents and his brothers. With herself. With even their growing-up son.

"You didn't say much," I told him. "That's what Mother says."

He cast me a look then — equal parts disappointment and confusion. "That's not how I remember it."

He seemed fragile and delicate, not a man who once upon a time could heft a hay bale or hogtie a calf. He was neither the snapshots I'd seen nor the stories I'd heard. He was just a human being the government counts every ten years.

"I'm tired," he said.

He was dismissing me, so I stood.

"Shall we shake hands?" he asked.

I had no reason not to, so we did, his the full and firm squeeze of a candidate for Congress.

"You'll come back?" he said.

I had been raised to be polite, I was thinking. Plus this had only cost me minutes, of which I had a zillion.

"Next Friday," I said.

Nodding, he let my hand go then, and I turned. This was my father, crackpot. Loony-bird. This was Totenham Gregory Hamsey. And I, suddenly thick-jointed and lightheaded and not breathing very well, was his son.

"Reilly," he called.

I had reached the door, only a few feet between his life and my own.

"Don't forget those smokes, okay?"

He was a man who'd survived a disaster, I thought. A fall from a ship or a tumble down the side of a mountain. He'd walked through a jungle or maybe had himself washed miles and miles away by a flash flood. Buried alive or lost on Antarctica, sucked up in a tornado or raised by wolves — he was as much a figure out of a fairy tale as he was a man whose scribblings on the subjects of time and space and visitors I would eventually read often enough to memorize whole sections. Yes, he had horror in his head, events and visions and dreams like layers of sediment, but that day he only wanted cigarettes. So, the next week, I brought them.

"Luckies," he said, smelling the carton. "A good choice."

"A guess," I said. "I didn't know you smoked."

"I have seniority," he told me. "I do what I like."

This time we didn't sit in the lobby. We went to his room, and walking down the corridor he pointed at various doors. "Estelle Barnes," he said at one. "A dingbat. Nice woman, but thinks she's a ballet dancer. Sad." At another, he said, "Marcus Stillwell. Barks a lot. Sounds like a fox terrier." It was like that all the way: people said to weep or babble or to seek instruction and wisdom from their house pets — our own selves, I told Sharon Sweeny that night, except for chance and dread and bubbles in the brain.

At his own door, he jiggled the knob. "Locks," he said. "I'm the king of the hill here."

It was like an apartment — a class-A kitchen, a sitting room, a sizable bath, a bedroom — the fussed-over living quarters of a tenant whose only bad habit is watching the clock.

"You like?" he asked.

I'd thought it would be different, I told him. Smaller.

He looked around then, as if this were the first time that he himself had seen the place. "Yeah," he said. "Me, too."

The Talk Talked between Worms 175

I almost asked him then. I really did. I almost asked what you would, which is *Why* and *What* and *Why* again. But, owing to what I guess is the *me* of me — which has nothing to do with the pounds and inches of you nor the face you're born with — I didn't. I was only a visitor; he, just an old fellow with a dozen file cabinets and maybe a thousand books to call his pals.

"You turned out okay," he said.

I had, I thought. I really had.

"You know," he began, "I've seen you a couple of times before." He was sitting across from me, his head tilted, a cigarette held to his lips. "Come here," he said, rising and beckoning me to his window. "Over there."

Outside, nearly a hundred yards away, stood the back of a Seven-Eleven. Beyond that ran the highway to Clovis — the Cactus Motel and the Wilson Brothers' Feed and Seed. The sight wasn't much to whoop over, just buildings and dirt and three roads I had once calculated the code-meeting dimensions of.

"You had a city car," he said, gazing afar as though I were out there now. "You wore a tie. And cowboy boots."

He was right. Eight months earlier I'd been with a survey crew — storm drains and new concrete guttering — and now I was standing here, seeing what he'd seen.

"You have your mother's walk," he said.

Cars were going up that street, and I remembered being out there, once or twice turning to look at where I stood now, once or twice one wet winter day thinking I knew somebody in that building. My father.

"You're a boss, I take it."

Sort of, I told him. There was a wisenheimer, Phelps Boykin, I reported to.

He was still staring straight ahead, and as if by magic I imagined I was inside his head, feeling time snag and ravel up, the present overwhelmed by the past. He was at my shoulder, me close enough to smell him, and he was leaning forward, nose almost to the glass. His hand had come up, small and speckled with liver spots, my own hand in twenty or thirty more years, and it seemed, having recognized something out there, he was going to wave hello.

"You know what I'd like?" he said.

That hand, unmoving and open and pale, was still up; and, my own hand twitching at my side, I had no idea what he'd like.

"An ice cream," he said. "I'd like a dish of vanilla ice cream."

The tapes don't say a lot about the State Hospital in Las Vegas, a ragtag collection of brick buildings — one of them, maximum security, surrounded by barbed wire atop chain link high enough to fence out giraffes, and each with a view of the boring flatlands you have to traipse across to get out of the Land of Enchantment. All I came to know is that Charlie Spiller drove Totenham G. Hamsey to the Greyhound bus station, where the latter bought his ticket and got aboard with nothing in his hands but air and heat, him in a seat all to himself. He says he stood at the State's door until they took him in. Says he marched up to the receptionist's desk and told that wig-wearing woman that he knew exactly where he belonged, that he could see into the knobs and fissures of her soul, that she was like we all are, which is puny and whiny and weak — just spines with blabbing meat at the top.

She was goggle-eyed, he says, and looked up and down for the joke. Says he stripped to his undershorts and shoes then, to show her that he meant business, and uttered not another peep until a director, a fussbudget with an eyebrow like a caterpillar and hair like a thatched roof, escorted him into an office for a man-to-man chat, whereupon time — "Of which," he says, "there is too goddam much" — went zoom, zoom, zoom, and the past snapped away from him like a kite from a string in a hurricane.

I'm not sure I believe any of this, though I like the idea of a Hamsey semi-naked in a public place. Still, given what I know — from the tapes, from the papers in the boxes and files in his apartment, from two visits to his hidey-hole at the farm — all he said seems as straightforward as breakfast. Given the givens, especially how I turn out in this story, I sometimes see him chalk-faced, his teeth gritted, outerwear at his feet, no light or noise in his world except that rising up in him from memory, nothing but gravity to keep him earthbound, only ordinary years between him and eternity.

When he was alive — when I was visiting on Fridays and taking him to the Sonic for a chili-cheeseburger or out with Sharon Sweeny and me to the Bottomless Lakes for a cookout — he didn't talk much about such matters. Talked instead about the Texas Rangers, whose games he listened to on KBIM, and about the mayor's father, Hob Lucero, a man he'd busted broncos with, and what it's like to tango and box waltz with someone named Flo, and how to tell if your cantaloupe is ripe or which nail to use when you're pounding up wallboard.

He was a Republican, he said one week. Which meant to him gold bullion and gushing smokestacks and cars you hired a wetback to polish twice a month.

Then, a week later, he asked me about NORAD — what I knew of it.

"What?" I said. I was preoccupied by a loud difference of opinion I'd had with Phelps Boykin earlier that morning.

"The Marine Corps has a metallurgy lab in Hagerstown, Maryland," he said.

He was mainly talking to himself, I thought. Didn't make a whit of difference who sat in the seat beside him.

They were liars, he said. Lowdown pencil-pushers who wouldn't know the truth if it bit them on the fanny.

Here it was I left off thinking about crabby Phelps Boykin, supervisor, and took up the subject of cracked Totenham Hamsey, father. It was a moment, I think now, as dramatic in its circumstances as maybe gunfire might be to you in yours.

"Del Rio, Texas," he announced. "December 1950. A colonel — one Robert Willingham — reports an object flying at high speed. Crashes. He finds a piece of metal, honeycombed.

Had a lot of carbon in it. Cutting torch wouldn't melt the damn thing."

He put a Lucky to his lips, took a puff, held it for seven beats of my crosswise heart. "There's more," he said. "A whole lot more."

We were parked off McGaffey Road, southwest of town, the two of us eating burritos in a city car. Across the prairie the humps of the Capitan Mountains were the nearest geography between us and another time zone. We'd been doing this for nearly two years, going to Cahoon Park or down to Dexter or up to Six-Mile Hill. Father and son — an hour or two of this or that.

"There's hoaxes," he said, still gazing afar. "Spitsbergen Island off Norway, September 1952. Aztec, New Mexico. March 1948. A yahoo named Silas Newton says there were one thousand seven hundred scientists out there. You can't imagine some of the goofballs running around."

I was looking at the ground, specifically at a slumped area a few yards ahead of us. For a moment it seemed that something grotesque might charge out of it, and me with only a greasy paper bag and a new driver's license to defend myself.

"You don't believe this, do you?"

I could see clouds in this distance, shapes that ought to be meaningful to someone like me. "Not really," I said.

"It's like God, isn't it?" he said. "Maybe necromancy. Or fortune-telling."

Sharon Sweeny believed in God, I told him. Which was all right. And Cece Phillips had recently said that our daughter, Nora Jane, believed in ghosts and astrology. But me, I didn't blow much one way or the other.

"That's too bad," he said.

It was about as useful, I told him, as pretending you could fly or see through walls.

"There's a lot like you," he said.

I had started the car, the air conditioning throwing a fine cold blast on my hot face. "I gotta get back," I said. "There's a man I gotta see."

He was sitting up straight now, his the expression teachers get when you mess up, and I realized that two conversations had been taking place, but me with only ears enough for one.

"I could tell you everything," he said at last.

I revved the engine — more cold air, more words in it to worry about.

"I could do that right now, Reilly. All you have to do is give me the go-ahead."

I was thinking furiously. Me with a brain like a Looney Tunes engine, all its clever gears whirling and grinding off sparks. He could tell me. About the 3rd of July in 1947 and all since. About his leaving. About my mother and me, left behind.

"What do you say, son?"

We stood at a crossroads, I believed. In one direction lay the past; in the other, tomorrow and the tomorrows after that. One was mystery and sore hearts and done deeds you couldn't undo; the other, me and a girlfriend and a GMC truck to make payments on.

"No, sir," I told him. "I don't need to know any of that."

Which is how we left it for that month, August, and the next, and those others that passed before he showed up at my office late in May, him in a suit-coat and white shirt and handsome string tie. As fashionable as a State Farm agent.

"I walked," he said. He looked flushed, maybe thirsty for an ocean of water, so I asked him if he wanted a fruit juice or an RC from the machine in Drafting.

"You're a messy one, aren't you?" he said, waving at my desk and my table and my cabinets, charts and state-issue reference works piled haphazardly atop each. "Hamseys, so far as I can tell, are not a cluttering people."

"Yes, sir," I said. Clearly, he had something in mind. A surprise to spring on his only child.

"Your mother kept a clean house."

He was right about that, too. So spotless and tidied that one Friday near Easter I'd come home from school after track practice (I put the shot) and, my house as still as a tomb, I'd thought that my mother, like her husband before her, had also vanished.

"Tell me about her," he said. "The man she married." He was smoking now, flicking his ashes in his cuff, his movements deliberate and precise, as if he had to explain to his shoulder and his elbow and his fingers what to do.

"His name is Barnett," I said. "Mother calls him Hub. He's something at Sandia Labs. Management of some sort."

He took another drag — not much air in here to push the smoke around. "Military?" he asked.

I didn't think so, I said. He was about to retire.

"A big man, I'm guessing. Your mother liked big men."

I hadn't thought about it, I admitted. Hub was about average size, maybe a bit overweight. Had a big laugh, though. Like Santa Claus.

"A man of substance, I take it."

Tot Hamsey was like an adding machine, I thought. This information, then more, eventually the sum he was adding for.

"Is he kind?" my father said.

I guessed so, I told him. Didn't exactly know.

"Corrine never went for coarse types," he said. "Ask Norris Proctor."

It was a name, like many others, I could not attach to a face. Tommy Murphy, Pug Thigpen, Mutt Mantle, Judge Willy Freedlander — these were people I'd only heard of, names no more than jibber-jabber to go in one ear and out the other. Folks either old or gone or dead.

"I don't have any regrets, Reilly. Not a one."

He was gazing at the most impressive of my wall maps, the city's zoning laid out in a patchwork of pink and blue and red and yellow, section after section after section of *do*s and *don't*s — where you could manufacture and peddle, where you could only sleep and mow your lawn — a world I probably took too much satisfaction in being a little bit responsible for.

"Project Mogul, they called it," he was saying. "Radar targets — foil, so the story goes — being strung from a balloon."

"Yes, sir," I said. This was his surprise: the there and then that had become the here and now.

"The 509th," he said, "right here in Roswell. Only air group trained to handle and drop atomic bombs."

I felt as I had that Friday afternoon near Easter. With my heart like a fist in my throat, I started to tell him again that I didn't want to know any of that talk.

"Sit down, Reilly," he said. He was speaking to me as he'd once himself been spoken to; so, looking at him as I guess he'd looked at it, I did. "Pay attention, boy. I don't have all day."

I was to wait. To sit here as I had there. I was to be quiet. Above all, I was to concentrate on something — that color photograph, say — and not look away from it until the floor was the floor again, and I would not be falling toward it.

"Project Sign," he was saying, "ATIC in Dayton. Hell, Barry Goldwater's in this. You still with me?"

I was. Me. And the photo. And the floor. And one man of substance.

CUFOS, Erv Dill, Ubatuba in Brazil, 1957, 1968, Nellis Air Force base in Nevada, magnesium, strontium, the Dew Line, *True* magazine, radio intercepts, MUFON, the sky, the Vega Galaxy, the suits they wear, the vapors we are helpless without, the bodies in the desert, the sorry-ass home our rock is, the swoop and swell, the various holes in heaven — all this and more he said, me and the walls his respectful audience. And then, loopy as time to a toad, a half-hour had gone by, and he was through looking at the map.

"I'm not crazy, Reilly."

I told Sharon Sweeny later that I was playing a game in my head — *A* is for apple, *B* for ball — me not capable of offering aloud anything neutral yet. I was at *F* — for fog — when he spoke again.

"There's no power, son, no glory. There's nothing — just them and us and the things we walk on. I have proof." Wiping his forehead with a tissue he'd drawn from his trousers, he seemed finished, the back a little straighter, no spit at the corners of the mouth. "Here," he said, another item from his pocket.

I took it. A key ring. Maybe ten keys attached.

"My files," he said.

G, I was thinking. What was *G* for?

Sharon Sweeny — my sweetie then, my Mrs. now — says the call that Thursday came at about the exact minute Peter Jennings was demonstrating how soggy it was in rain-soaked West Table, Missouri. I have no memory of this; nor have I any recollection of going to the phone and barking "Hello" in a manner meant to mean "No" to those interrupting my dinner hour to sell me something.

Sharon Sweeny — as right a wife for me as white is right for rice — reports I said "Yes" two times, the latter less loud and certainly with too much "s" in it.

Next, I've heard, I sat. In the chair by the table I usually pay my bills from. I eased the phone away from my ear, I am told, and regarded it as naked primitives are said to stare at mirrors. I appeared frazzled, my foot tapping as it will when I have eight somethings to say but only one something to say it with. I am told — by Sharon Sweeny, who was between bites and only a few steps away — that I mumbled only one sentence before I hung up, which was "I see," words she thinks must've taken all I had of strength and will to get loose. When I stood, she tells me, it seemed also an act with maximum effort in it.

"Where're you going?" she says she said.

On a hook by the front door hung my jacket, and Sharon Sweeny claims I approached it as though I expected the sleeves to choke me.

"Quik-Mart," I evidently told her. "I'd like a cigarette."

She was frightened, hers truly on the brink of teetering or breaking into a full run. "Who was on the phone?" she asked.

"I haven't smoked in years," it's said I said. "But tonight, just now, I'd like a pack. It's a foul habit, you know. Hard as the dickens to break. I wouldn't wish it on anyone. Not a blessed soul. You believe me, right?"

She had come toward me, I understand, a woman now close enough to see the focus flashing in and out of her man's eyes, him with his chin lifted as though listening for a sound not to be heard twice in a lifetime.

"Reilly?"

So, his own strange news to deliver, Reilly told her: Totenham Hamsey, middle initial G., was dead.

Congestive heart failure, it was, that old man going down at the feet of his dance partner Estelle Barnes, would-be ballerina, still eight or nine bars left of "Woodchoppers' Ball." But, as I say, I remember not an iota of how I came to share this knowledge with my beloved big-boned Clerical II. I do not remember the next day either, nor the day that replaced it. About the funeral, at the gravesite his father had paid for years and years earlier, I recall only a single incident — me and my mother and her husband Hub and a preacher named Wyatt who looked like he was trying out for a community-theater musical, plus a handful of residents from the Sunset Manor, accompanied by a nurse who stood as though she had wood screws in her heels, and sunlight pouring down on us like molten metal but me not melted in the middle, and then Sharon Sweeny, my hand held in hers, leaning to my ear to whisper, "Stop humming, sweetheart. I can't hear what the man's saying."

The day after that, I recovered myself, came to — in my father's apartment, me appointed to move his stuff out to somewhere else. His colognes, I think, hastened me back. Frenchy fragrances of vanilla and briar and oily smoke — odd for a fellow never known, so my mother has since said, for other than Vicks or Old Spice. "Sweet smellies," he'd called them that first day he'd showed me around. So there I was, with several packing boxes from city hall, me too big in a bathroom too brightly lit to flatter, feeling myself return, as if to earth itself, inch by inch by inch, until I had no one to lead me about except the familiar blockhead in the mirror and him in need of both a haircut and a professional shave. Mother wanted none of this — not out of meanness, I hold — so Sharon Sweeny had made arrangements with the Salvation Army to take all it had a use for; I was the labor, a job I'd apparently said "Yes" to when, after the casket was lowered, that nurse with the sore feet had waddled over to remind me of the workaday consequences of death.

I packed his clothes next, only two sacks of mostly white dress shirts and slacks you apparently are urged to buy in lots of ten, plus lace-up shoes — all black — that you could wear for another half century. For reasons owing to sentimentality and the like, or so Sharon Sweeny later insisted, I kept the string tie for myself, it being his neckwear the last time we'd visited. Then, the kitchen having only food and drink to throw away and not much of either, I went to the living room and, my innards clotted and pebbly and heaped up hard beneath my ribs, stood in front of the steel cabinets I had the keys for.

"My treasure," he'd said four days earlier. "Yours now."

Out the window I noticed the spot where, years before, he'd seen me at work in boots and my own starched white shirt. I imagined him watching me then, as abstract and fixed as my mother had been the morning, years and years before that, when she stood behind her curtains to study him at their gate, nothing in him — I would soon enough learn — but ice and wind and heavy silence.

"You take care, Reilly," he had said in my office, and now, no other chore to distract me, I was.

For company, I had turned the TV on — *General Hospital*, I recall, in which attractive inhabitants from a made-up metropolis were falling in love or scheming diligently against one another. They were named Scorpio and Monica and Laura and Bobbi, and for a moment, it as long as one in war, I desired to be at the center of them: Reilly Jay Hamsey in a fancy Italian suit, his teeth as white as Chiclets, him with lines to orate and a well-groomed crowd happy to hear them.

"In the shop," he had said. "At the farm. That's where."

I was fingering the keys, each no bigger than my thumb. One fit one cabinet, another another, and all I had to do was turn locks clockwise, no real work whatsoever for the hand and wrist of me.

"Under the floorboards, Son."

T. G. Hamsey, I was thinking. Son of Milton Hamsey, banker, and Vanetta Fountain Hamsey, homemaker. Brother of Winston Lee, oil man, and Benjamin Wright, bankrupt cattle baron. All deceased. Nothing now but these cabinets and me. In one, only papers and tape recordings; in the other, bone and flesh and blood.

Music had come up from next door, a foot-tappy ditty that for a minute I endeavored to keep the steady beat of.

In the desert that night years ago, Cece Phillips had declared that we — you, me, all the king's men — had been put here on earth for a purpose: "We're meant to be the things we are," she said. It was an idea fine to have, I told her, if you're sitting atop a pile of us and have nothing at all but more whoop-de-do to look forward to. "Fine to have," I'd said, "if you don't have to get up when the alarm says to."

That's what I was thinking when I slipped the key in the lock of the leftmost cabinet. What if you're one Reilly Hamsey, a middle-aged municipal employee with only a remote control to boss around and tomorrow already coming up over England? What if, no matter the wishes you've wished, you've nothing above your shoulders but mush and nothing in your wallet but five dollars and nothing in your pants pockets but Juicy Fruit gum? What if, when your hand turns and the lock clicks open and that first drawer slides out, you're always going to be the you you are, and this will always be the air you breathe, and that will always be the ragged rim of the world you see?

"I hate them," my father had said, teary-eyed. "Look what they've done to me."

On the TV a wedding was taking place, Lance to Marissa, their friends and relations elbow to elbow and beaming, squabbles and woes set for the occasion aside. They were gowned and sequined and fit, no illnesses to afflict, no worries that wouldn't — in one episode or another — disappear, theirs the tragedies you only need a wand to wave away.

"Hey," I said, addressing those Americans from the American Broadcasting Company. "Look what I'm doing here."

THREE

They had crammed it all in his head, he'd said on the tapes. What conveyances to take, the packs of them, their minerals and gases, the councils they sit at, their rectitude in matters moral, their currencies, their contempt for us. They have prisons for their villains, schools for their youngsters. They have nationalities, chancellors and princes, blood allegiances to fight for. Leaders have risen up among them. They are disappointed, spite-filled. "They have been to the end of it," he'd said. "Where the days run out. The minutes. Where the fires are."

The fires — one image to have between the ears the day Sharon Sweeny and I parked at the road leading to the farm. The place wasn't much to look at, the city having crept up to the nearby cotton fields, the irrigation canals mostly intact but the fence line in need of expensive repair.

"You still own it?" Sharon asked.

My grandfather had sold it, I told her, maybe five years after. Part of the proceeds had put me through college. The rest my mother had given me for the house in Odessa.

We'd stopped for a Coke on the way out, and she was drinking the last of it now, looking at the tumbledown buildings, while I, like a clerk, was scrambling to sort out my thoughts big to little. "Seems tiny, doesn't it?" I said at last.

"When I visit my parents in Socorro," she began, "I can't believe I ever lived there. I mean, it's like a dollhouse."

The day was bright, the sun as fierce this morning as it would be this afternoon, nothing between it and us but seconds, and I was glad I'd brought a hat.

"You ready?" she asked.

Briefly, before the roof of my stomach caved in, I thought I was. "Give me a moment, okay?"

I'd dreamed about this last night. I'd read his documents, page after page that seemed less scribbled on than shouted at. I'd listened to his tapes, hours and hours of them, and then, Saturday already faint in the east, I'd dreamed. Me. And treasure to find. And strong Sharon Sweeny to help.

"You think she'll like me?" she was saying.

My eye was focused on a tumbleweed snagged on the barbed wire at the gate, my mind on the single reason for not backing out of there. "Who?"

Nora, she said. Nora Jane.

I had forgotten. My daughter, a sophomore at Sul Ross, was coming over for summer break — a chance to meet Sharon Sweeny and maybe later tell her mother, Cece Phillips Hamsey, what good fortune her old man had finally stumbled into — and, Christ, I had forgotten.

"Cece says she likes golf," I said. "Maybe you can take her over to Spring River for a round."

I felt tottery, I tell you, as different from myself as tea is from tin. And before I gave in to the coward in me, I imagined myself standing down the way a bit toward town, me a shit-kicker with nothing to do but stroll past that unremarkable couple sitting in the city car at the end of a rutted road leading to one ramshackle house.

"We could leave," I told Sharon Sweeny, which prompted her to lift her eyebrows and take my closest hand.

"No, we couldn't, Reilly."

She was right, but I would require several more moments, thoughts surfacing twelve at a time, to realize that.

"There's money," I said. "Seems he had a lot of it. I found a Norwest bankbook."

That was dandy, she said. And I believed she meant it.

"We could get a house," I told her. "I always wanted a swimming pool."

That was also dandy, vocabulary I now couldn't hear too much of.

"Nora could have her own room. Maybe spend more time with us. A real family."

Her hand tightened on mine, and something sharp and whole and nearly perfect passed between us.

"Reilly," she said. "Start the car."

Like my father, I guess now, I too am excellent at following orders, so I did as told, pleased both by how I kept my hands on the wheel as we rolled up closer and closer and closer, and by the fact that I could look left and right if I wanted to.

"How long's it been abandoned?" she asked.

Didn't know, I told her. Tax records described it as a lease farm, the land owned by a conglomerate out of Lubbock. Mostly silage was being grown. Cotton every now and then.

"It was pretty, I bet."

The night before, yes, I had dreamed about this. One tape, then another. Tot Hamsey's voice raspy and thick and slow, as though it was oozing up through his legs out of the ground itself. Then, my bed ten sizes too small and ten times too lumpy, dreams. Of spacemen. Of smoke. Of one sky rent clean in half.

"It won't be there," she was saying. "The box."

I had braked to a stop beneath a Chinese elm more dead than alive, the uprights for the adjacent wood fence windbent in a way not comforting to contemplate.

"You'll see," she said. "It's a delusion. A fantasy."

Half of me wanted her to be right, and it said so.

"He was a nice man," she said. "Just — well, you know."

I did, and said as much — not the worst sentiment, even if wrong, that can go back and forth between beings.

"Let's eat afterwards," she said. "I'm starved." She had her sunglasses on now, her feet on the dash, a paperback mystery in her lap. Her toenails were painted and, time creaking backwards inside of me, I believed pink the finest, smartest color ever invented by the finest and smartest of our kind.

"Sweetheart," she said. "Put your hat on."

Which I did. And soon I was out and the trunk was open and shut, and there I was, Sharon Sweeny's garden shovel in hand, already halfway to the square building on the right, nothing but dust to raise with every step, nothing to hear but a fistlike muscle in me going thump-thump-thump.

The padlock was gone, as he'd figured it would be, so I had little trouble tugging that door open, its hinges flaky with rust. This was five months ago now — before I went back a second time for the box — but I still see myself plainly, me smelling the musty smell of it and going in, the darkness striped by sunlight slicing through many seams in the wall, and the scratching of mice or lizards finding holes to hide in. The room was not as he recalled. No jig or bandsaw. No hammers or clamps or drills hanging in their places on the walls. No work apron on a peg. Just dirt and cobwebs and broken lengths of wood, plus a bench toppled on its side and a huge spool of baling wire and a short-block V-6 engine and a far corner stacked with cardboard high as the ceiling.

I felt juvenile, I tell you, this too much like a scavenger hunt for an adult to be doing, and for an instant it seemed likely that I would leave, me suddenly with an appetite, too. In ten minutes, Sharon and I could be at the Kountry Kitchen, only a table and two cups of coffee between us. But then something hooked and serious seemed to twist in me — a gland perhaps, or a not-much-talked-about organ, or whatever in us an obligation looks like — and, the air in that room dense and hot as bath water, I found myself knocking on the floorboards with the shovel — whack, whack, whack — listening for one hollow whump, me the next Hamsey man to hunt for something in the dark.

Three times I traveled the length of that room — shoving junk out of my path, twice banging my shins, once almost smacking myself in the forehead on a two-by-four hanging from a rafter — before I heard it, and heard it again. Which means you are free to imagine me as I was: unmoving for two or twenty heartbeats, in me not much from the neck up —

exactly, years and years before, as my father must've felt in the desert when he rode over that hill and saw what he saw. Then sense began coming back, thread by thread, and I crouched, knees cracking. Sound was again plain from the outside world — a tractor's diesel motor and the corrugated metal roof squeaking and groaning in the wind — but that shovel now weighed at least one thousand ugly pounds, and cold upon cold upon cold was falling through the core of me, light raining down like needles, with darkness here and there in spouts and columns, and no terrors to know but those you can't yet see.

"Oh," I think I said. And thereafter, nothing more to exclaim, I was on my fanny, prying up the first of four boards.

I was thirty-seven years old and thinking of those years placed end to end, which gave me to wonder where they had led and how many more I had, and at last those floorboards were loose and flung aside and at least the easiest of those questions had been answered.

It was like a root cellar, roomy enough for you to lie at the bottom of and throw open your arms.

"Okay," I said, my last sensible remark that hour.

I'd had a vision years before — me and Cece Phillips and the desert at night and how the future would turn out between me and her. This time, on the way to a different car and a different woman, I had none. I had lifted the box, skimmed the bundle of papers wrapped in oilcloth, put it back, and now — well, I didn't know. Thousands and thousands of days ago, a terrible thing had crashed in my father's life. Today, something equally impossible had landed in mine.

"It wasn't there, was it?" Sharon Sweeny said.

I had put the shovel in the trunk and, brushing the dust off my pants next to her door, I thought of worms. Their wriggly, soft bodies. The talk they talk. "Just a lot of trash," I said.

She was relieved, I could tell, me once again as simple a character as any between the covers of the book in her lap. "What took you so long?"

My father had died, so Estelle Barnes had said, with his face composed, maybe even peaceful, and to my mind came a picture of him curled on the floor at her feet — his eyes blank, his thin lips parted, his hair thick and wild. The end of him, the beginning of me.

"What do you think I'd look like with a moustache?" I asked Sharon Sweeny.

"I don't like them droopy," she said. "Makes a fellow appear sinister."

I needed another minute here, I was thinking — time that had to pass before anything else could commence.

"You still hungry?" I asked.

She nodded, a gesture as good to see as are presents under the tree at Christmas, so I started around the car to the driver's seat. I was counting the parts of me — the head I had, the heart — and for the next few steps I had nothing at all to be scared of.